PRETTY DEAD

ALSO BY ANNE FRASIER

The Elise Sandburg series
Play Dead
Stay Dead

Hush
Sleep Tight
Before I Wake
Pale Immortal
Garden of Darkness

Short stories
"Made of Stars"
"Max Under the Stars"

Anthologies
Deadly Treats
Once Upon a Crime
From the Indie Side
Discount Noir
Writes of Spring
The Lineup: Poems on Crime
Zero Plus Seven

Nonfiction (Theresa Weir)
The Orchard, a Memoir
The Man Who Left

PRETTY DEAD

Anne Frasier

Published by Thomas & Mercer, Seattle

www.apub.com

Amazon, the Amazon logo, and Thomas & Mercer are trademarks of Amazon.com, Inc., or its affiliates.

ISBN-13: 9781503944183
ISBN-10: 1503944182

Cover design by Cyanotype Book Architects

Printed in the United States of America

CHAPTER 1

He was hooked on death. No shame in that, Jeffrey Nightingale always told himself. At this point the body count was so high and his appetite for murder so strong that he'd lost track of how many lives he'd ended. One thing he did know—the more he killed, the more he wanted to kill.

Profilers called it escalation; Nightingale called it addiction to the quest for pleasure. Some people did crack or meth or heroin. He killed.

They made it so easy—the cops. Early on, Nightingale had learned to shift and change his MO. He wasn't an idiot who adhered to the ritual and the pattern. Sure, he'd prefer it that way, but he took his drugs any way he could get them. If that meant switching things up to maintain his high, so what? The high was what counted. And another thing. When you'd been killing for so damn long, it got boring if you didn't add some variety, if you didn't experiment—because where was the buzz in doing the same kill over and over? He'd never understood that.

He kept ahead of investigators with false clues and by moving from city to city. Hell, they thought his kills were committed by several different guys. That cracked him up. But now winter had hit with a vengeance. He was sick of snow, and he'd decided to head south. Winter made everything harder, including murder.

The city he'd chosen as his next home wasn't big, not by Philadelphia standards, anyway. It didn't have a huge police force, had no substantial FBI presence. It would suit him for a while. Maybe a year, maybe two.

How many kills could he get in before they figured out the murders were connected? He was betting five or six. How many before they started getting the least bit close to catching him? That would never happen. He was too smart and had been in the business too long.

A pro didn't approach this stuff blindly. He didn't just pack up the car and head out. It took careful planning. It took fake IDs. It took a new persona. It took an in-depth study of the other team.

From his spot in the Philadelphia coffee shop, Nightingale clicked his laptop keys and pulled up an article he'd already read several times. A piece about a woman named Elise Sandburg who'd been made head detective of the Savannah Police Department. The article included a photo of her, taken in a cemetery that was apparently located right behind the police station. How cool was that? She was attractive, with straight dark hair that fell to her shoulders, and a direct, no-shit gaze, her arms across her chest, white shirt, black slacks, badge on her belt. Standing a little off to one side was a guy in a dark suit.

David Gould.

Since Nightingale was in a public place, he allowed himself only a slight smile. The detective's name was one he recognized. He remembered every agent and cop who'd pursued him and failed. And it didn't hurt that Gould was so handsome Nightingale got hard just looking at him.

The photo of the two detectives was like some movie poster or a promo for one of those stupid TV shows that was so popular.

But this wasn't fiction.

In real life, what came first? The killer or the kill? Were people born to it? Or was it like a drug? One taste and, if you had an addictive personality, you were hooked? He'd read about that kind of instant addiction. And he'd damn well read about other killers. Everything he could get his hands on. He devoured profiler books, and he knew how to avoid the stereotypes. So with each move, he became a different person. A different profile for each city.

He didn't discriminate. That helped. Sure, he had favorite victims. Who didn't? His taste was for twenty-something, dark-haired males—younger versions of David Gould—but Nightingale was also what profilers liked to call an opportunistic killer. Those were harder to catch. And in order to play against type, he sometimes went for females. They weren't his drug of choice—females were a little like smoking pot or drinking when you really wanted to mainline something awesome—but that was okay. He was all about keeping things positive.

And the great thing about his addiction? Other than basic expenses like rope and duct tape and plastic and whatever his chosen persona needed, it cost nothing.

Free. Not many addictions were free.

He closed his laptop, stuck it in his bag, and zipped the case. His chair scraped the wooden floor as he got to his feet.

He'd been coming to the hippie café for almost a year, working remotely at a job he could do from anywhere. Handy when it came to his true calling.

He'd miss this place.

"Meet your deadline?" the barista asked when he saw Nightingale heading out.

"Yep. Hit 'Send' a few minutes ago."

Feeling sentimental, Nightingale dug into the back pocket of his jeans and pulled out his worn black billfold, opened it, and extracted a five-dollar bill. He tapped it into the tip jar and smiled at the young guy behind the counter.

God, how Nightingale would love to do him.

And by "do" him, he meant tie him up and make sweet love to him for a week or so before finally killing him and dumping his body.

But he wouldn't.

The guy smiled. "Thanks, man."

Thanks for not raping and murdering me, you generous bastard.

"You're welcome." Nightingale smiled back, and the smile was heavy with the unshared humor of the moment. "You're *very* welcome," he told the barista. *I saved your life today and you don't even know it.*

Sometimes doing nothing was the biggest gift of all.

From a table behind him came the kind of conversation he loved, conversation that was in many ways the payoff, or at least part of the payoff. Kind of like the afterparty that followed a great show.

"Did you hear about the latest murder?" a woman was saying. And then, "I want to move. I want to get out of this town. We could have a serial killer living right next door, for all we know."

Nightingale turned to see a middle-aged couple seated at a table, hugging their lattes, a newspaper with the dead-body headline between them, an incomplete crossword puzzle to one side. He was near enough to see that twelve down was still blank. Had the puzzle been too tough? Or were they just too dumb?

"Awful, isn't it?" he asked. He knew how to play this. Years of watching sappy movies, then practicing facial expressions in front of the mirror, had made him a master of the perfect response.

The woman's eyes locked on him. The horror of what she'd just read could be followed all the way to her marrow. He never got tired of that.

She shook her head. "Terrible."

"I'm blowing this place," he announced. This was another thing about him. He loved conversation. He loved engaging people. "Today," he elaborated.

Her face opened up in a shared understanding of the seriousness of having such awful things going on so close to home—a situation her husband seemed unconcerned about. Right now he had his nose back in the crossword puzzle, a frown on his face, as the woman continued to stare at Nightingale, confusion replacing their brief bit of bonding. "But you aren't the killer's demographic," she pointed out.

"Right," he said. "But a crazy like that? Maybe he'll change his demographic. And anyway, how many murders now? Six?" He shrugged. "I just don't want to live in a town where this kind of thing has become commonplace. I've had enough."

"Good for you." She glanced at the man across the table. He was still ignoring them. Then she looked back at Nightingale—her partner in distress. "Good for you."

Yeah, good for me.

He hitched his messenger bag over his shoulder and gave the woman a nod. At the door, he paused. "Twelve down is exsanguination."

The guy finally reacted. He stared at the folded paper in his hand, then raised his pencil in a gesture of excitement. "You're right! That was a tough one."

Nightingale left the café. There was a whole big world out there. Like Savannah, Georgia.

CHAPTER 2

Four months later . . .

Fifteen minutes after arriving at her office on the third floor of the Savannah Police Department, her coffee yet unsipped, breakfast just a pipe dream, head homicide detective Elise Sandburg received an alert about a dead body. She immediately put in a call to her partner.

"I'm five minutes out," David Gould said. Through the phone, she could hear the sound of traffic. "Meet me in the parking lot." He disconnected with no attempt at conversation.

Elise let out a sigh and headed down the hall to the elevator.

Six months had passed since they'd bonded over injuries suffered at the hands of the monster the press called "the Organ Thief." For a brief time it seemed their relationship had smoothed and fallen into an easy camaraderie. Pals, friends, albeit cautious friends. Yes, there'd been that time, that one time . . . Like two teenagers, they'd almost gone all the way. Almost. But that was in the past. This new thing—and she was beginning to think that, with David, there would always be a new thing—had zero to do with "almost."

David wasn't happy unless he was stirring something up. Unless he was trying to get under her skin. Typically just annoying stuff or kind of funny stuff she might even admit she secretly enjoyed. But this new thing could only be considered betrayal.

Blatant, in-your-face betrayal. Of course *he* didn't see it that way. And of course he thought she was making something out of nothing. But it was a lot more than *nothing* when your partner befriended the very person who'd ruined your life. The very person she'd taught herself to hate with the hatred of a thousand burning suns.

Her father, Jackson Sweet.

David had helped him find a place to stay. And now he was trying to help him find work. They'd even gone fishing together. Fishing!

Elise could have dealt with the job hunting and the housing. She might have begrudgingly done those things herself if David hadn't stepped in first. But the fishing. Fishing was something you did with buddies, with good friends.

And not only that. It had also altered the relationship between Elise and David. It meant there was no more dropping by David's apartment—not with the chance her father might be there. Not if it meant she might be sitting in the same seat her father had vacated minutes or hours earlier. That kind of presence lingered after a person was gone. Sometimes days, sometimes weeks. And sometimes it never went away. Why couldn't David see that? Why didn't he understand the level of his betrayal?

Caught up in this preoccupation with her homicide partner, Elise was hardly aware of taking the elevator to street level, hardly aware of pushing open the police department's double doors, hardly aware of stepping outside.

A man shot off a bench and lunged at her.

All reaction and no thought, Elise slammed him against the trunk of a tree, her forearm to his throat as she pulled her gun and pressed it to his temple.

His hands shot up and he stammered, "I'm Jay Thomas Paul from the *New York Times! New York Times!*"

She stared at him a moment, gauging his fear—the dilated pupils behind hip glasses, the perspiration on his forehead.

She released him and slipped her Glock back into her shoulder holster, as he nervously watched her and rubbed his throat.

"Bad idea to startle a cop," she said.

"I was excited to finally meet you. I've read about you. Heard about you. Sorry."

That kind of comment raised the question: *What* had he heard? That she'd been left on a grave as an infant? That her dad had returned from the dead decades too late, after she no longer gave a damn?

Behind her, people who'd stopped to watch her initial overreaction moved on, toward the police station. The ones who worked there would probably report the incident to Major Hoffman, who would then feel inclined to ask if Elise needed to schedule an extra appointment with the department psychologist, along with a few days' leave. And all the while Hoffman would wonder if it had been a mistake to give Elise the job of head homicide detective.

And all the while Elise would wonder the same thing.

Because, hell yeah, she was jumpy. It wasn't this Jay Thomas Paul person's fault. Her reaction simply underscored a problem she hadn't yet gotten a handle on. Her psych evaluation, which she'd never seen, although she'd love to, probably said something about the psychological ramifications of being taken captive and tortured by a madman.

She'd done okay at first, after it was all over. But now she suspected post-traumatic stress disorder was kicking in. She hoped it would eventually kick its way back out. If not, she might have to step down as head of homicide.

"Sorry," she told the man named Jay Thomas Paul.

He gave her an almost shy smile and pulled out a business card. "That might be the most unusual meet I've ever had in this job."

He was in his early forties, with curly dark hair a bit on the long side, a clean-shaven jaw, and a manner that felt casual and friendly—now that she was no longer trying to kill him. His overall vibe, combined with his multipocketed khaki vest, his jeans, and his sneakers, shouted "reporter"—a type she made a point of avoiding.

She slipped his card into her pocket. "Your name isn't familiar," she said. "Why are you here again?"

"From the *New York Times*. We're doing a piece on you and your partner. I was told you'd been informed and had given your okay. I'm supposed to shadow you."

She took note of the photo ID clipped to his breast pocket. Curly-haired guy smiling at the camera.

She had a vague recollection of Major Hoffman pulling her aside and giving her a pep talk about an interview. "Good for the department. Good for the city." Something like that. Problem was, cops and reporters didn't mix. Elise was sure there were ethical reporters out there—the kind who weren't so obsessed with their own careers that they would risk blowing a case—but the ones cops tended to run into were barely a step above the paparazzi. And now, to have to play big sister to this guy . . . It didn't sit well with her.

"I'm too busy today." She turned and walked away.

He dogged her with all the determination of his occupation, matching her stride with a bouncy step that could only be described as boyish and enthused. It wasn't hard for him to keep up since she was still in physical therapy for the injuries she'd sustained at the hands of the Organ Thief. At least she no longer needed a cane.

In the parking lot, Elise hit the fob on the key ring she'd been given at the checkout desk upon her arrival. An unmarked car answered, and she shot for it, Jay Thomas still glued to her side while she tried to think of ways to shake him. The easiest would be to simply get in the car and drive off. Yeah, that would work.

"I'm supposed to come along," he insisted. "That's what shadowing is. Spend the whole day with you. Well, actually weeks."

"Weeks?" Cripes. She had to put an end to this right now.

Elise pulled out her phone and poked at the touch pad. While waiting for Major Hoffman to answer, she crossed her arms and leaned against the car, eyes on the man in front of her. Hard to believe an hour ago she'd been enjoying the beauty of the May morning—admiring the flowers that were the glorious harbinger of summer, colorful blossoms everywhere, brightening up even the darkest of streets. Now she had to deal with a dead body and an overenthusiastic reporter.

He smiled at her.

She stared back.

He was actually rather attractive. God, she couldn't believe the thought had even popped into her mind. Where had it come from? But he was. Not handsome like Gould, who was the kind of perfection that turned heads. This guy was familiar and safe. He wouldn't notice or care about her scars. More to the point, she wouldn't care if he saw them.

"I've got somebody here who looks like he's going on safari and says he's supposed to shadow me," she said as soon as her boss picked up. "Curly hair. Hipster glasses. Vest with a hundred pockets. Please tell me he's lying."

"Jay Thomas Paul. He was just in my office," Hoffman said.

Elise imagined Hoffman sitting at her desk, a bag of her current choice of snack food in front of her, red nails, red lipstick. Always immaculately groomed.

"I told him to wait outside," Hoffman said. "Glad he found you."

At that moment a black Honda Civic squealed into the parking lot. The engine cut, the door opened, and Elise's partner, David Gould, tumbled out, an insulated coffee mug in his hand. He strode toward her, looking all movie star, coattails flapping, a question on his face as he took in the new guy.

Elise shrugged as Major Hoffman went into a spiel about how they needed to be more transparent, needed to seem more like real people, needed to boost the department's image; how Elise especially needed to come across as professional, as well as personable. "We've already talked about shedding that chilly persona," Hoffman reminded her.

"I don't think it's a bad thing for me to keep my distance, especially now that I'm head of homicide." A weak argument, Elise realized.

"I'm not saying you need to kiss babies, but just be a bit more approachable, that's all. And this article they want to run could help you achieve that. Try to be more like Detective Gould. Not *that* casual, but you know what I mean."

Elise turned her back to the two men and walked away, ducking into a shaded corner of the lot and whispering into her phone. "He's going to go for the conjurer's daughter angle. No matter what they told you, that's the story. You know that's the story."

"It won't be the story, because the piece has to be approved by you and the department before the paper runs it. He signed an agreement. Like it or not, we're locked into this."

A contract. Elise had lost the argument before she'd even started. All the things she'd planned to say were kicked to the curb. "I want you to know I think it's a bad idea."

"I would have been surprised if you'd said otherwise."

Elise laughed, disconnected, slipped her phone into her jacket pocket, and turned to see the two men watching her with guarded eyes. One guy afraid she might kick his ass again, the other . . . Well, who knew what David was *really* thinking?

Over the past couple of months he'd made advances that she'd either ignored or fended off until he'd finally stopped. And once he stopped, she'd found she missed the flirty part of their interactions. How ridiculous was that? But his giving up was for the best. She'd even heard he was dating somebody now. Who, she didn't know. And she didn't know if it was serious or just something he did for release. For sex.

"Don't we have a body to visit?" David finally asked.

She dumped her thoughts while hitting the car's "Unlock" button once again. They all piled in—Elise behind the wheel, David in the passenger seat, and her new friend directly behind her. One cozy family.

"Details?" David asked as he clicked his seat belt.

"Female and dead." Elise maneuvered the car out of the parking lot and made a left onto Drayton. "That's all I got."

David took a sip of coffee. "Who's your buddy?"

"Somebody from the *New York Times*. He has *three* first names. Jay Thomas Paul."

"And he's going to be with us how long?"

"Could be weeks."

"That sucks."

"Truly."

This was what they did. Elise considered it a mental exercise. A type of relaxation. Light conversation to prep themselves for what was ahead.

"Do the crossword today?" David asked.

"Didn't have a chance."

She was fast suspecting the whole crossword thing was David's way of trying to retain some form of relationship. Every morning he arrived at headquarters with the puzzle partially done. They'd share their answers and, with luck, complete it together by grabbing a few minutes here and there throughout the day. It had been going on for two months now, and the crossword device was becoming another thing that irritated her, even though she knew her reaction was extreme. Maybe because it wasn't really about the crossword puzzle at all. Why didn't he just come right out and admit he'd butted in where he shouldn't have? Why didn't he just apologize?

"I would have had it done in fifteen minutes, but I got hung up on one word," David said. "The clue is 'the Cornish Wonder.' Four letters. What the hell does that mean? Cornish Wonder? Is that anything like a Cornish hen?"

"No idea." Traffic. The tedious pattern of going around the one-way squares, stopping for horse-drawn carriage tours and tourists clutching maps.

From the backseat came one word: "Opie."

Gould turned so he could eyeball the reporter. "Opie?"

"John Opie. Known as the Cornish Wonder."

"That's obscure."

"Very," Jay Thomas agreed.

"You do the crossword puzzle?" David asked, with sudden interest in their new friend. *The* crossword puzzle.

The crossword puzzle used to be the one in the *New York Times*, but there was a new kid in town, a new puzzle designer who was said to be as mysterious and reclusive as J. D. Salinger. Maybe Jay Thomas and David could bond over crosswords, Elise thought. Maybe she could step aside.

It didn't surprise her that Jay Thomas was a fanatic. The whole country seemed to be humming about the new puzzles. The first one had run a year and a half ago in a few city papers. Other presses quickly followed, and now a new puzzle was a weekday feature in the *Savannah Morning News*. The popularity of the puzzles had elevated interest in physical paper sales throughout the country—a true phenomenon in this digital age. It seemed most people still preferred to fold the paper and hold it in their hands, filling in the squares the old-fashioned way, with a pencil or pen.

The popularity of the puzzles was a bit of a mystery, but some thought it was because the clues were often clever, sarcastic, and funny, and as toughness went, they ranked in that sweet spot somewhere between those in *USA Today* and the *New York Times*. Adding to the appeal was the mysterious nature of the designer. Nobody knew his or her identity, although many people took stabs at guessing, one of the most popular theories being that it was the president of the United States, due to his well-known love of word puzzles. But you couldn't have a president supplying clues for words like "manwhore." Plus he had a job to do. A big job.

"I consider myself an aficionado," Jay Thomas said.

Elise glanced in the rearview mirror and spotted a small silver device in his hand. "Is that a recorder? Are you recording us?" She turned her attention back to the road in time to see the stoplight ahead of them turn red. She slammed on the brakes, and every object that was unattached hit the floor. "Sorry," she mumbled.

"You okay?" David asked. "You seem a bit more . . . wound up than usual."

"Forgot my coffee on my desk." True, but an excuse all the same. Her next choice would be PMS, but PMS got a bad rap. Her theory about PMS was that it simply lifted the veil. It wasn't always pleasant to see the world so clearly, so it only happened once a month.

The light turned green, and Elise drove through the intersection. At the same time, David unlatched his seat belt and dove at the backseat, swiping the recorder from Jay Thomas's hand.

"What the—?" Jay Thomas protested as David plopped back down.

"You're not recording anything." David examined the device and hit some buttons, presumably erasing files. "Especially not our lame private conversations. Pull that again and I'll open the door and toss you out in the street."

"That's how I work," Jay Thomas mumbled. "It's the only way to be a good journalist."

"Find another way."

At a stop sign, David lowered his window and stuck out his head. "Hey," he said to a kid straddling a bike. "Catch." David tossed the recorder, and the kid caught it while Jay Thomas made a sputtering sound of outraged protest.

"It's okay," David shouted to the kid as Elise pulled through the intersection. "I'm a cop." As if that would explain his actions.

"Is everybody here either hyperreactive or an asshole?" Jay Thomas asked.

David hit the "Power Window" button, once again sealing them off from the rest of Savannah. "Pretty much."

CHAPTER 3

Elise saw the beauty that was Savannah every single day. She lived in the heart of that beauty. She drove down the city's tree-lined streets, passing under shadows of Spanish moss, sheltering and mysterious. She walked past blooming azaleas and magnolia blossoms.

Born here.

Abandoned here.

But time and familiarity hadn't bred desensitization. Daily, the city took her breath away. Different times, different views, different lighting. But always an appreciation of the brick sidewalks edged with wrought iron and draped in pink blooms. The steeples and palm trees against the bluest sky and the whitest clouds. Fountains and street musicians and ships docked in the harbor. All of those things filled her heart and made her glad she hadn't left—something she used to swear she'd do. But not so much anymore. Not so much since she'd made a conscious decision to embrace her heritage, regardless of how she felt about Jackson Sweet. Yes, she was the daughter of a root doctor. Daughter of a conjurer.

And maybe a bit of that decision not to leave had to do with David.

As they walked across the grass toward a gathering mob that indicated their target spot, she let out a sigh. "One of my favorite parks. Why in one of my favorite parks?"

The scene was familiar. Police cars, white coroner van, yellow crime-scene tape. Waiting in the wings was a threat of rain hinted at by a darkening sky.

Beside her, David matched her stride. "Beneath beauty lie many dark deeds."

"I'm not familiar with that quote." Jay Thomas trailed behind them, forgotten until he spoke. "Who said it?"

Without giving him a glance, David replied, "Me."

The reporter's pen scratched in his little notebook.

Elise felt bad about the recorder. Bad for Jay Thomas and bad for herself, because she was sure David's behavior would mean a call to Hoffman's office, where she'd be reprimanded. Funny how Elise had thought being head detective might put an end to those visits.

"Stay back," David told the reporter once they reached the barrier.

Elise and David ducked under the yellow tape and were quickly spotted and recognized by a female officer who briefed them on the situation. "Body was found by a homeless man," the officer said. "We've already taken his statement."

"Anybody else see anything or hear anything?" Elise asked.

"Right now we only have the one person. Officers are canvassing nearby houses to see if we can find anything to add to the picture. And now"—she glanced up at the sky—"looks like rain. Sent someone for plastic tarps, and the crime-scene team is trying to collect as much evidence as possible before the storm hits."

Elise and David did a cursory visual of the body. A young woman with long dark hair. Nude. Ankles bound with silver duct tape. Fingerprint bruises on her throat, arms, and thighs. Discolored and swollen face. Blue lips.

John Casper, coroner and medical examiner, straightened away from the body and gave them a nod of greeting, eyes silently communicating something none of them would talk about here.

Even in the darkest of circumstances, John could be counted on to lighten the mood. There was no sign of that happening now, his face pale and looking older than his thirty-some years.

A body left on display in the heart of one of the most beautiful and loved parks in Savannah was especially heinous. This was blatant. This was someone who wanted attention. This was a nose-thumbing at the police department and the city itself.

The young woman had been placed faceup, her arms bent on each side of her head in what Elise would describe as the goalpost position—just like the last body. And again like the last body, this one had what appeared to be a single word, written over and over, covering every visible piece of flesh.

Undeniably ritualistic.

"Damn."

That one syllable from David said it all. It said everything they were both thinking.

The first body had been put on display, but they hadn't wanted to think the worst. Sometimes family members or friends or boyfriends or sick kids did such things. It hadn't meant there would be more—even though the profiler in David had worried that the unsolved crime might be the beginning of something bigger.

They wouldn't know for sure until the autopsy, but a visual told Elise this was the same killer, same MO. Two didn't mean serial killer, but it looked like they might be on their way.

"Damn," David said again.

Someone jostled Elise. She looked over her shoulder to see Jay Thomas standing with a camera in his hand. Just seconds ago she'd felt bad about his lost recorder. Now she wanted to grab the camera, slam it to the ground, and stomp on it.

Instead, she grabbed it and stuck it in her pocket. "Get on the other side of the crime-scene tape and stay there," she ordered. "And if I have to point out one more stupid thing you're doing, you're out of here. For good. Contract or no contract. Understand?"

He blinked behind his glasses. For a second she tried to read his reaction—she picked up on a quiet anger—but then she filed him away as unworthy of the moment and a waste of her focus.

"My camera?" he asked.

"You'll get it back later. Once I erase the photos."

He still didn't leave, and now she was aware of David taking in the exchange.

"I'm supposed to shadow you," Jay Thomas said. "Everywhere."

"You are in my world, Jay Thomas Paul. And just because you're shadowing me doesn't mean you get a special pass to confidential information that could impact this case," Elise told him. "Anything confidential will hit your eyes and ears the same time the rest of the media gets it. At a press conference. Understand?"

He looked from her to David, then past them to the body on the ground. Temporarily defeated, he nodded, spun on his heel, and walked away, giving the crime-scene tape an angry tug as he ducked under it and vanished into the crowd.

Elise turned back to the body, David beside her, everyone else engaged in their jobs.

David pulled out his phone and snapped several photos of the victim. "It's not him."

His words cut through the chaos in Elise's head. She didn't even pretend not to know what David was talking about. Tremain. The Organ Thief. The guy who'd kidnapped her and defaced her body and sexually assaulted her.

"There are similarities." Her voice, as she attempted to control her emotions, was monotone. "The dark hair. The violence. The tape. The defacing of her skin with ink . . ."

"Tremain is dead." David spoke slowly and clearly, but with words for her ears alone.

"We don't know that," she argued. "Until I see his body on a slab in the morgue, he'll be out there to me. The possibility of his still being alive will haunt me." She hated the word "closure," but that was what she needed.

"I get it," David said. "I do. But I shot him. He was dead."

"Then what happened to his body?"

"Alligators dragged it away. Tide came up. Somebody found him and buried him."

Because David needed her to believe, she pretended. She pretended in the very way she'd been pretending ever since finding out Tremain's body had vanished from the island where they'd left it. And maybe, with time, the pretending would have worked. It might have eventually led to belief—belief that Tremain was truly dead—if not for these new reminders. If not for this person on the ground in front of her who'd most likely been tortured in much the same way Elise had been tortured. If not for the brutal assault and murder of two women in this beautiful city, both crime scenes deliberately creating an echo that couldn't be ignored.

Survivor's guilt. That was what a psychiatrist might say about Elise's reaction. And it was true. Elise felt guilty for being alive when two women were dead.

She wanted to go home. Just go home.

She imagined herself in the safety of her living room, feet tucked under her in one corner of the couch, a drink in her hand, soft music playing. And after that drink, another. Then bed, with covers over her head.

Even as she focused on the body, Elise's vision went half-dead in some unconscious primal attempt at self-preservation. She stared with clouded eyes, and her brain struggled to comprehend the shifting and melting in front of her. For a second she wondered if she was passing out.

Finally vocalizing her observation, she said, "The words—they're moving."

The letters on the body were changing, the black lines spreading against white skin. And then a cold droplet hit her cheek.

"Rain!" someone shouted.

Rain. Splashing on the body, washing the words away. Not only the words, but clues.

The careful control and methodical feel of the scene vanished. People scrambled to preserve as much evidence as possible.

A sheet of blue plastic appeared. As it was spread, the sound of the rain changed to the kind of silly noise that went along with frivolous pursuits like camping or a wedding that had gotten rained out. Not murder.

Elise found herself sharing a huge black umbrella of mysterious origin with David. The rain and the canopy created their own private world, but nonetheless David urged Elise away from the body in an attempt to find a spot of privacy. Once they were out of earshot of the other officers, he hunched his shoulders toward her and whispered, "Has Savannah ever had a serial killer?"

Serial killer. There it was. The words hung in the air. She wanted to grab them and stuff them in her jacket pocket, then burn the jacket once she got home.

She'd been head homicide detective a total of six months.

She looked up at David, at his blue eyes, his intense gaze, the jaw that always needed a shave, the dark hair, wet from the rain, hanging over his forehead. "I'm not ready for this," she whispered. A confession for his ears and his ears alone.

"Nobody is ever ready for this."

His words calmed the quaking in her bones. "Didn't you work a serial killer case before coming here?" she asked. "I know we had Tremain and the TTX murders, but those fell outside of what I consider a standard serial killer profile. Those were personal, for profit. This . . . This seems textbook."

An odd and unreadable expression flitted across David's features while she vaguely recalled something she'd heard about him before he'd come to Savannah.

"A couple," he said. "When I was with the FBI. I was called in to profile the Puget Sound Killer."

She nodded. "I remember that case. I remember being thankful nothing like that could happen here." God, she'd been so naive back then. "It was never solved, was it?"

"No." As if to reassure her of his skill, he went on. "We were closing in when he vanished."

"Maybe an alligator got him." The words were out before she could stop them. Not the time for sarcasm.

"Don't start that."

But she felt as though the alligator pitch in reference to Tremain was just as ridiculous. A weak attempt to placate. *There, there.* "What do you think happened to him? The Sound Killer?"

"Maybe he was arrested for another crime. Or he got sick and could no longer kill. Or died. Something that physically put an end to the murders."

"Like other famous serial killers," Elise said. "That's what people speculate, anyway. Because killers don't just stop killing. Something *stops* them from killing."

"Right." He glanced over his shoulder, toward the activity and the body, then back at Elise. "Look, I'm good at what I do. You know that, right? I used to be one of the most promising profilers in the FBI."

That was before.

"I'm just saying you aren't alone," he told her.

He was the stronger one right now. In this hour, this moment. "You should have taken the job as head homicide detective." She meant it.

"It wasn't offered to me. And even if it had been, you're the better person for the position. I'm not exactly the most stable guy in the world." Before she could either agree or argue, he added, "But I can be. When the situation calls for it. I can be."

What a pair.

They could do this, she reassured herself. And really, who better to catch the perpetrator than someone like her? Someone who'd suffered at the hand of just such a sick bastard?

Pep talk over, Elise squared her shoulders and turned back to the crime scene.

The rain was still falling. Not hard, but at a steady rate. The kind of rain she would have liked in any other situation. Coffee-shop rain. Curl-up-with-a-book rain.

Because of the weather, the victim had been quickly bagged, and John Casper was now overseeing the loading of the body into the coroner van. As Elise watched, a face in the crowd caught her attention. A gray-haired man in a shapeless canvas coat standing on an elevated piece of ground beneath a tree. Elise's father. Why was he here?

He might have everybody else eating out of his hand, but she didn't trust him. How could she trust a guy who'd lived a lie for so many years?

CHAPTER 4

Ten minutes later they were heading back to the police department, Elise behind the wheel, wipers going, all three of them silent, thinking.

"It's an Egyptian soul glyph," came a petulant voice from the backseat.

Elise glanced in the rearview mirror. "What are you talking about?"

"The body," Jay Thomas said. "The way it was laid out. An Egyptian soul glyph."

She and David shot each other a look, both knowing it unwise to discredit any input, even when coming from such an unlikely source—the pouting reporter in the backseat.

"I'll show you." Jay Thomas bit the cap off his pen. Head bent, he scratched across the surface of his tablet, then passed the tablet over the front seat to David.

"The head is the round section of the glyph, and the arms represent the soul," he explained, pointing with the pen. "The glyph itself represents life. Of course, I have no idea what it means in this context. That's why I wanted to get a picture. Glyph was the first thing I thought when I saw the body."

At the next red light, David passed the image to Elise, who gave it a quick perusal. It was a familiar design. Almost as familiar as a peace sign. "I see this everywhere," she said. It could very well have been something Jay Thomas had unconsciously spotted on a gawker at the crime scene. That was how this stuff worked, how the brain worked when it came to unreliable witnesses. They tended to pull up random information and spout it with a conviction that had to be considered with caution. "On necklaces in discount stores," Elise elaborated. "My daughter even has one."

"Just sharing my thoughts," he said.

She returned the notebook to him. "It's a stretch, but we'll keep it in mind."

"Something was written on her," Jay Thomas said. Paper rustled as he flipped to a fresh page. "I wasn't close enough to see, but it looked like the same word over and over. What was the word?"

Elise took a right and pulled into the department parking lot.

"That's what I'm talking about," she said as they slammed doors and headed for the police station. "That's exactly the kind of thing we don't want leaked to the press."

Pausing in the middle of the sidewalk, Elise went through the photos on Jay Thomas's digital camera. One boring picture after another. Once she was satisfied that he hadn't taken any of the crime scene, she passed it back to him. "Next time I'll break it."

He smiled at her, no annoyance or half-hidden anger in his eyes this time. "I think I'm in love."

David smirked. "Join the club."

CHAPTER 5

The next few hours were spent at headquarters. While David and Elise sat at their computers accessing databases, their new friend, Jay Thomas Paul, waited in line for lunch.

"Good idea to send Jay Thomas for food," Elise said as she stared at her computer screen, her damp jacket tossed over her chair.

"Genius to send him to Zunzi's."

They both laughed, knowing the popular sandwich shop would have a line a block long and Jay Thomas would be out of their hair for a couple of hours.

God, we're the mean kids, David thought, not with pride.

He finished composing a confidential e-mail to the handwriting analyst at the Georgia Bureau of Investigation, then attached a photo of the lettering he'd taken at the crime scene, plus an image from the first victim. Confident the script would be the same, he hit "Send."

"*Defaeco,*" he said. "Is that a place? A person?"

Elise clicked some keys as she did a quick search. "In Latin it means 'to cleanse or purify.'"

"Hmm." David leaned back in his chair. "How does that have anything to do with the word on the first body?" They'd speculated that the first word, *virgo*, had been a riff on the Zodiac Killer, but this new word made the Zodiac Killer nod seem less likely.

Elise did another search. "*Virgo* is Latin for 'virgin.' So the one thing they seem to have in common is Latin."

"The first victim, Layla Jean Devro, was a heroin addict and a prostitute," David pointed out. "Definitely no virgin. Someone who lived a darker existence. Certainly no innocent."

"Right."

"So virgin . . . cleansing . . ."

"Wish fulfillment?" Elise asked.

"Maybe. Virgin being the opposite of what she was. Or, if you consider this glyph thing your buddy was talking about, then it could be the killer sees these murders as a rebirth."

"Not my buddy," Elise said absentmindedly as she continued to stare at her computer screen. "I'm running the crime-scene photo through FACES to see if it can deliver a match."

Her landline phone rang. She glanced at the ID, then picked up. A brief conversation and she was done. "Avery. He's e-mailing a fingerprint from the morgue." Another monitor check. "Here it is." More key clicking.

David came to stand behind her, one hand on the back of her chair as he watched her transfer the JPG image to IAFIS, the fingerprint database.

What David hadn't shared with Elise out there in the park was that the Puget Sound murders had been the case that ruined his life. Not because the killer had gotten away, making David feel like a failure. Well, there was that. It had definitely knocked him down several pegs. But no, the Sound Killer had also ruined his marriage.

He was never home. His wife had been left on her own with their son in Virginia while David was in Washington State working on the Puget Sound murders. And when he did make it home, he spent every waking second on the case.

Beth began having an affair.

They warned you about that stuff when you were training at Quantico. How you had to protect the personal side of your life; otherwise it would go all to hell. He hadn't listened. He'd been cocky enough to think Beth would be there for him no matter what, because she'd been crazy about him.

In the beginning she'd done the pursuing. That was how it worked for him. *Except when it came to Elise.* Females chased him, and he didn't have to do anything. He could pretty much have his pick, so he'd thought Beth would always be around. Didn't even consider the possibility of her looking elsewhere. *Didn't even consider it.* Dumb, cocky bastard that he'd been.

"There!"

He and Elise spoke in unison, their eyes on the monitor.

An eight-point match. The fingerprint came with a mug shot they both recognized.

"That's our girl," David said.

"Victim has a record." Elise scanned the on-screen rap sheet. "Arrested several times for drugs, car theft, vandalism. Prostitution."

They knew prostitution and drugs often went hand in hand.

David dropped back into his chair and grabbed the landline phone. At the same moment, Elise said, "Call Strata Luna at Black Tupelo."

David punched in numbers and went for the lounge position: legs out, one hand supporting the back of his head. "Already on it."

When Strata Luna, Savannah's infamous madam, answered, David small-talked a few moments, then got to the reason behind his call. "Do you have a prostitute working for you named"—he motioned for Elise, who slid a piece of paper across his desk— "Portia Murphy?"

"No, honey, but I recognize the name. Bad news. Really bad news. She tried to get a job at my place, but she was an addict and probably carrying diseases. I think she worked with a pimp named John Riley Blackstone for a while, but no decent pimp's gonna keep a girl like that for long."

David decided it wasn't the time to point out that the words "decent" and "pimp" didn't belong next to each other in a sentence. "Okay. Thanks. Oh, and Strata Luna? Confidential conversation."

"I never heard a thing, sweetie."

"You're a doll." He smiled and hung up.

"Doll?" Elise asked, eyebrows raised.

"Criterion Collection. I'm slowly going through all the noir movies, and I'm kinda liking the period jargon. I invited you over for movie night," he reminded her. "You declined."

She looked at him a long moment. Those eyes. Those weird, weird eyes were just like her father's.

"Right," she said with feigned disinterest.

He knew this game. Knew it way too well. Enough to also know there would never be any winners.

"Who did you invite when I said 'no thanks'?" she asked.

Oh man. She'd heard something. But he couldn't keep waiting for her, waiting for something that was never going to happen. Love the one you're with. And yet he shouldn't have done it. He'd known better. And since Elise was bound to find out, he decided to confess.

"Major Hoffman."

She recoiled in shock, and then her eyes went flat.

He'd seen that expression on her face before—when she discovered he'd helped her dad find a place to stay. David didn't like that expression.

He could go into excuses, saying Hoffman came on to him—which was true. It was damn true. The woman wouldn't leave him alone, but still . . . Someone from work. His boss. *Their* boss. Not good. Not good at all. And it didn't escape him that it was close to the very excuse Elise had used for avoiding him. *Partners can't be lovers.* So maybe he was trying to prove she was wrong.

Don't look at me like that, David thought, then childishly added, *You didn't want me.*

Elise pulled in a deep breath and straightened in her chair. "The major is . . . nice." She didn't sound at all convinced by her own words, most likely because lately Hoffman had been summoning Elise to her office more than usual, and David could only guess there was jealousy at play there even though he'd never told Coretta how he felt about Elise. But of course she knew. Hell, the whole department probably knew.

"She's funny. Funny clever, not funny weird," David explained. His words were a weak attempt at convincing Elise that the fit wasn't bad. Maybe even a weak attempt at convincing himself. He had a sense of humor; Coretta had a sense of humor. Common ground. "You probably wouldn't know it since you don't see her much outside work, but—"

She cut him off. "I can imagine her letting loose."

David struggled to remain unreadable. Letting loose was right. The woman was a damn gymnast in bed—another area where she'd made the first move. He'd been thinking dinner and a movie. She'd been thinking dinner and sex. Lots and lots of sex.

Throughout this exchange, had Elise even blinked? Or glanced away? It came to him that this was how she cracked criminals. It also came to him that this was the method her father had been famous for back in the day, when it was said he could get anybody to confess to a crime. He'd put on his famous glasses with the blue shades, and people would spill their guts. Watching Elise, David decided the apple hadn't fallen far from the tree. If he wasn't careful, he'd soon find himself blabbing about every position he and Coretta had tried.

The door flew open, and their newly acquired friend with three first names burst into the room, wearing the scent of a diner, his arms loaded down with Styrofoam take-out containers, greasy paper bags, and drinks.

"The line was a mile long," Jay Thomas Paul said breathlessly. "But I pulled out my *New York Times* press ID, and some nice person let me cut in."

Praise the Lord and pass the sandwiches. David had never been so glad to see a reporter in his life.

CHAPTER 6

The city hall conference room had a vibe David could appreciate. Heavy gold curtains that went from ceiling to floor complemented pale lime walls and dark woodwork. Underfoot lay an elegant parquet, and behind the podium were flags of the United States and Georgia. In front of a bouquet of microphones, reporters jockeyed for the best spots, each one with a question or two for Mayor Burton Chesterfield.

Chesterfield was about fifty. Old money, if David recalled correctly. The man had always reminded him a little of Bill Clinton.

Once the mayor started talking, it was the typical bull—*isolated incidents, victim knew the killer*—which was exactly why David had tried to beg off the press conference, pointing out that his time would be better spent helping Detective Avery put together a task force. But Major Hoffman and Elise had insisted upon his presence, so here they all were, standing behind the mayor while the man reassured the public—people who'd voted him in and people who could vote him out—that things were under control.

David wanted to roll his eyes, but he restrained himself, aware of the cameras and the footage that would soon be hitting local and international feeds.

"If you aren't the demographic, then you have nothing to worry about," the mayor said. He went on to spew out the incorrect information that had been dumped into his brain and uploaded to the teleprompter just minutes earlier.

When the mayor was done, his press secretary stepped forward. "We're opening the floor for five minutes of questions," he announced.

Hands shot into the air. The mayor pointed. David followed the direction of his finger and shouldn't have been surprised to see a microphone jammed in the face of Jay Thomas Paul. "And what exactly is that demographic?" the reporter asked.

A decent question.

While the mayor paused to formulate a reply that wouldn't cast their fair city in a poor light, Jay Thomas continued with what David supposed could be considered a fill-in-the-blank. "Young women? Young white women?"

"No." The strength of that single syllable in no way reflected the shifting feet and the clenching and unclenching of hands the cameras couldn't see. "Our city is a safe city," the mayor insisted. "I want to reassure residents and visitors of that. At this point, the targets appear to be women involved in illegal activity. Prostitutes. Race has nothing to do with it. And after discussing the situation with professionals in criminal behavior, we feel that the two crimes are connected and are related to drugs, maybe drug deals gone bad. Granted, that's not anything to be proud of, but it serves as reassurance that these were not random crimes perpetrated on innocent victims. These were women involved in activities they shouldn't have been involved in, and these killings were retributions or warnings to others living outside the boundaries of the law."

David glanced at Elise in surprise. At no point during their brief conversation with the mayor had either of them intimated that the crimes were drug related, and at no time had they established a victimology. The mayor was rewriting history, had his own agenda, or had the ear of someone outside Savannah PD.

Or more likely, was covering his ass.

Since taking office, the mayor had cut police department funding, and the direct result was a drastic increase in crime. The seriousness of the numbers hadn't yet hit the general public, but once they did, a second term looked doubtful. The guy was all about damage control. And if damage control meant lying . . .

One of these days David would like to meet a politician who made his choices based on what was right, not on what was right for his wallet and ego.

There were more questions and more lies, followed by a few half-truths tossed in by Major Hoffman, along with some standard replies from David and Elise.

"We promise to do all we can do to bring this person or persons to justice," Elise said.

Then it was over. A crazy blur of activity and a room of highly charged people, then boom. Done.

"That was bullshit," David muttered under his breath as he and Elise headed out of the building and down the marble steps.

"I agree."

Elise paused in the middle of the sidewalk, obviously trying to remember where they'd parked. David pointed, and they resumed their departure. "When I was a kid," he said, "my mother used to tell us that a decent doctor could smell an illness and diagnose it from the odor."

Blow your nose, she'd once told David's pediatrician. *Maybe you'll be able to smell something.*

"I could see that being true in certain cases," Elise said.

They reached the unmarked car. Elise directed the key fob, and the doors unlocked. "I enjoy these little visits back to your childhood," she added, "but what does this have to do with our case?" They slid inside and simultaneously fastened their seat belts with firm clicks.

David wasn't ready to say it out loud, but the two crimes had a stench that made him uneasy. "Just small talk."

Elise put the car in gear and started to pull away from the curb when someone pounded on the trunk. She hit the "Unlock" button. A flurry of movement, then, breathing hard, Jay Thomas Paul dove into the backseat, slamming the door behind him. "What is it about shadowing that you two don't understand?"

Elise drove off for real this time. "Sorry." She sounded genuinely contrite.

"Good questions back there," David said, attempting to smooth over the awkwardness of forgetting Jay Thomas.

The reporter puffed up and smiled. "Where to now?" he asked.

Elise glanced at him in the rearview mirror. "The morgue."

Jay Thomas's smile faded.

CHAPTER 7

The morgue was its own private world. Bright and white and stainless steel, with polished cement floors and downdraft fans that did a fair job of keeping the odor under control. Fair. Sometimes Elise wondered if the smell of death was permanently embedded in her sinuses. There were times when she'd turn her head, or the wind would lift her hair, and she'd catch a whiff. And then she'd wonder if she'd absorbed the stench through her pores. And she'd wonder if anybody else could smell it. If so, was it strong? Stronger than she realized?

The Chatham County morgue was in a nondescript, flat-roofed building on the outskirts of town. David and Elise stood in the autopsy suite, an hour into the exam. The body had been washed, measured, and weighed, with eye color noted. The paper bags had been removed from the hands, and John Casper's assistant—a large, silent man who looked like he lifted weights as well as dead bodies—had collected detritus from under the nails to send for DNA testing. Superficial abrasions and contusions had been noted, along with the woman's physical condition: malnourished, her dental hygiene characterized by negligence and decay.

Elise wasn't sure what made her sadder: the murder, or the evidence of such a hard, cruel life. Some might argue that the woman had brought it on herself, but this was a time for sympathy, not judgment.

"Victim had a serious drug issue," John Casper said. "Beyond the obvious like meth mouth, I'm seeing signs of systemic damage."

The Y incision had been made, but the organs had not yet been removed, examined, or weighed.

"So she'd been at it awhile," David said.

"I'd say so."

"Cause of death?" Elise asked from behind her clear plastic face shield.

"Pretty straightforward strangulation. Like the last victim, the trachea has been crushed, causing bleeding into the tracheobronchial tree."

"The perpetrator needed to be fairly strong to accomplish that," David said.

Elise looked at him. "Or riding a wave of adrenaline."

"So maybe driven by anger."

"And fear," Elise said.

"Fear?" David asked.

"Of being caught. Or fear and horror at his own behavior."

"You give the killer too much credit," David said. "To feel horror, he'd have to feel he was doing wrong. These animals don't feel anything close to remorse."

"So you don't think they have any humanity in them?" Elise didn't believe that. Even after all she'd been through, she didn't believe it. Her faith in the smallest shred of something good was how she broke criminals; it was how she got them to confess. You find the good and you speak to it.

The cold body between them, David said, "No, I don't."

"Almost every killer has a line he won't cross," Elise argued. "You've said so yourself."

"That's true to an extent. But when they escalate, they push themselves to step over that boundary."

"I see no sign of escalation here."

"Not yet." The words came out as a threat, even though she knew he didn't mean them that way.

Elise dropped her gaze from her partner to the body on the metal table. "These bruises . . ." She pointed to the victim's arms, legs, and torso. "Precapture? Or later? I'd like to establish a timeline. When he picked her up. How long he was with her. Was the kill fairly quick, or did he keep her awhile? Did he torture her? More to the point, did the murderer know her?"

She knew she was too anxious to get answers they didn't yet have. Some of those answers the autopsy wouldn't even be able to supply.

"The bruises are a mix," John said. "Some are old, some look as if they occurred hours before death. As far as torture goes . . . nothing extreme."

"What about sexual?" Elise glanced up at the clock. They typically didn't remain for the entire exam, which could take four or five hours. She needed to get back to headquarters to see how Avery was doing putting together a task force.

"Bring me the rape kit," John instructed his assistant.

The kit appeared, and a few minutes later John said, "No sign of forced penetration." He swabbed the woman's vaginal cavity, passing the sample to the assistant.

"I doubt we'll find the killer's sperm," David said. "So far this guy has been pretty thorough when it comes to not leaving a trace of himself."

Elise agreed. "And if she's a prostitute, then she's been with multiple people."

"See this bruise?" John pointed to the throat. "Deep, with some bleeding. I thought maybe I could lift a print from it. No print at all. Sometimes extreme pressure will leave behind at least a partial."

"No surprise," David said. "We suspect he wore gloves."

"That would be my guess too."

Had she been beautiful at one time? Elise wondered. "So hard to tell what someone used to look like before the ravages of meth kicked in," she said, then added, "Meth being another thing the mayor thinks is no big problem."

David let out a snort. "He needs to get his head out of his ass and look around him."

John shut off the recorder he used to dictate his notes. "That might require some editing . . . ," he mumbled.

"It's true," David said in defense of his unprofessional comment. "The press conference today was irresponsible. I'm hoping that guy gets voted out this fall."

"Spoken like someone who's actually from here," John said with a grin.

"It's pretty easy to see he's gearing up for the next election and wants to give people the impression he's done a good job and made the city safer, when in fact crime has gotten worse while he's been in office."

A polite cough came from the corner of the room, where Jay Thomas Paul had collapsed earlier in a pool of sweat, pale skin, and trembling bones. They'd decided to let him in on the autopsy, thinking he'd either decline or leave the room as soon as the Y incision was made. Instead, he'd staggered away to drop into the first chair he found.

"Damn," David said. "He's like a fly on the wall."

Elise hated to admit it, but their new friend was one of those people you forgot was in the room, even when he was standing right in front of you.

"My earlier comment had better not end up in print," David told the reporter.

Jay Thomas adjusted his glasses. "I . . . um, can't promise that it won't make it into the story."

David bristled. "Get out."

Elise shot her partner a look of warning.

"If it's pertinent." Jay Thomas appeared to consider the possibility of just such a thing. "That said, I don't see how it has any bearing on the story I'm doing on you two." He got to his feet. "I don't write for the *Mirror*—I have integrity." He ripped off his disposable gown, tossed it in the bin by the door, and stalked from the room.

John looked up from his removal of the heart. "Since when did you become so explosive?" he asked David. "You were kinda hard on him."

David sighed. "I was just annoyed with myself for forgetting he was there."

"Mara will be nice to him," John said. "She's probably getting him a coffee and a cookie right now."

"How are the wedding plans going?" Elise asked. Change the subject. Always a good idea when things got tense.

John placed the heart on the scale. "Kinda wish we'd just decided on something quiet."

"Told you I could perform the ceremony," David said.

"I want you as best man."

Elise wasn't big on weddings, but she was looking forward to this one. Normally she sat in the pew, trying to gauge how long the people at the altar would remain married—most of the time giving them a maximum of three years. It would be nice to attend a ceremony where she felt the couple would be together for a very long time. Maybe even forever. Their devotion made her happy in a world where happiness wasn't always easy to find.

. . .

Mara offered a plate of cookies to the dejected man in the vest and glasses. She kept them handy for visitors, especially for the ones who burst out of the autopsy suite, their faces pale and skin clammy. "They're ginger," she said. "It helps the stomach."

From his seat near her desk, the man examined the plate of cookies, chose one with the care and thoughtfulness of a child, and took a bite. "They kicked me out," he said, his mouth full.

"Well, that was rude." David and Elise could be a little harsh, but kicking him out seemed excessive. "I think they're a bit on edge because of the murders."

He smiled at her. "You know how it is. Cops and reporters. Oil and water."

"Oh, so you're a reporter?"

"Yeah. *New York Times.*"

"Wow. That's impressive."

He laughed. "You're the first person around here to think so." His color was improving, and he allowed himself to sink deeper into the chair with the yellow slipcover she'd added to brighten up the place.

"Hey, is that the crossword puzzle?" he asked, spotting the folded newspaper on her desk. She noticed that he had a nice face, a kind face.

She turned in her swivel chair and grabbed it. "John and I usually do it together, but we're not going to have time today." She passed the paper to him.

He held what was left of the cookie between his teeth while retrieving a pen from his messenger bag. Removing the cookie to speak, he said, "I do the crossword every day."

CHAPTER 8

Standing in her recently remodeled kitchen in the Savannah Historic District, Elise drizzled olive oil over asparagus and looked out the window at her friends gathered on the patio. David, tongs in hand, stood in front of the grill, wearing a black apron that said, "Kill the Cook"—a joke from John Casper, who sat at the picnic table next to his fiancée, Mara. Across from her, rounding out tonight's group, was Detective Avery.

The cookouts had begun as an effort by Elise to create a life for herself beyond work and the Savannah Police Department. Funny thing was, the only people she really knew were cops and coroners. The other thing? They were the only people she really *wanted* to hang out with, other than her daughter, Audrey, and maybe Strata Luna.

Elise didn't do small talk, and her world was so exactly calibrated that anything falling outside her well-defined boundaries failed to light a fire in her. Her job had created a world that was small by unconscious choice—a common theme in her line of work. Few good investigators had much of a life beyond their cases, and that very insulation created a strange bond—a motley crew. Try as she might to expand her circle beyond homicide, Elise found this group of people to be her tribe.

Her phone buzzed. She picked it up. A text from Audrey.

Made it to the dance. Be home by 10. Maybe we can watch Doctor Who *when I get back.*

Elise replied with *Let's,* then hit "Send."

Elise rarely read, and she watched very little television. She regretted her disconnect with pop culture, but she understood that those things weren't part of her life right now. The one anomaly was the evenings spent watching *Doctor Who,* something Audrey had coaxed her into while Elise was recovering from the injuries she'd suffered at the hands of Atticus Tremain. At first she found the show silly, and her mind would wander, but somewhere along the way she'd gotten hooked.

She seasoned the asparagus with cracked pepper and sea salt, wrapped and pinched the foil, took the package outside, and handed it to David. He lifted the lid on the grill, placed the foil on the rack, and began removing the cooked chicken breasts, along with a tofu burger for Mara.

"I'm grabbing another beer." John Casper pushed himself from his chair and headed for the house. "Anybody else?"

Avery raised a hand.

The get-togethers might have started as cookouts, but they'd somehow evolved into weekends spent laying down brick to create the patio on which they now sat. Then came the card games—often poker for pennies Elise kept in a gallon jug in the kitchen. And now here they were. Over a period of a few months, her house had become their unofficial hangout, the place where they congregated.

Their visits were so familiar that everybody pitched in—cooking, preparing food, grabbing plates—until, like now, the tribe was finally settled at the wooden table, candles burning, food passed, wine opened.

A perfect evening. Humid, but cool enough for long sleeves, the air heavy with the intoxicating scent of gardenias and confederate jasmine, their floral perfume mingling with ancient wood and sandy soil. Live oak leaves drifted to the ground, whispering softly as they fell, creating a carpet underfoot. Put all of it together and the night was everything Elise loved about her hometown.

Once the food had been passed and served, Avery paused with a bite of grilled chicken on his fork, the sleeves of his plaid shirt rolled up to reveal freckled forearms. "So, anybody have any theories?"

By some unspoken agreement, they rarely talked about work at these dinners, so Avery's question took Elise by surprise. But they might as well discuss the case since it was on everybody's mind.

Mara, her smooth dark hair reflecting the candlelight, pointed to the ketchup, and David passed it. "Were both girls prostitutes?" she asked.

"Most likely." Without lifting his elbow from the table, Avery took a long drink of beer, then set the bottle aside. "And they both had a record, both did drugs, and they hung out in the seedier areas of town."

Elise refilled her wineglass. "At this point it looks as if he might have simply been targeting women who were easy prey."

"What about the writing?" Casper asked. "Any theories there?"

They all looked at David, who hadn't yet offered anything. Not now, and not to Elise in private.

"I'm still working on it," he said.

"Well, we're brainstorming." Avery's comment was an invitation for David to contribute.

"I don't know," David finally said. "Things don't make sense."

Elise was surprised by his obvious reluctance to toss around ideas.

"Does killing ever make sense?" Mara asked.

"Yeah." David reached for his beer. "It does. Repeat killers follow patterns, so you could call it 'making sense' in more of a formulaic way."

"Displaying them—that's a pattern," Elise said. "Writing—a pattern. Where are you seeing something that doesn't fall into a ritual? Seems pretty straightforward to me."

"Right now we're basically dealing with a list of what we don't have," David said. "And that very lack of clues was apparent at two crime scenes. No fingerprints, no matching DNA, no lead on the ink used, other than knowing it was most likely the same ink on both victims."

They were all aware that ink had a very specific formula, and each company and even every factory had its own secret sauce. The ink on the two victims had been identified as a formula from a washable marker mass-produced in Texas and sold in discount stores across the country. Not helpful.

"Why didn't he use something permanent?" Mara asked. "You'd think if he went to so much trouble to cover her whole body, he'd do it in something permanent."

The table went quiet. Forks paused in front of mouths.

"What?" Mara asked before realization dawned. "Oh, I'm sorry, Elise. I'm so sorry."

"That's okay."

Everybody was thinking of Elise's skin—and the ink that was permanent.

"But it's odd that he's using ink, too," John Casper said, backing up his girlfriend. "Surely somebody thought of that."

Avery pushed himself to his feet and headed for the house. In a hurry. Obvious alcohol run.

David made a frustrated sound, annoyed by what they were all implying. Elise had seen that annoyance before; she recognized it as his frustration at having been unable to provide her with the body of Atticus Tremain. On a practical level, she knew Tremain was gone. On an emotional one? Not so much.

"It's not him. It's not Tremain," David said quietly, smoothly, with a tone that meant, *Shut the hell up about it.*

"I'm not saying it is." Casper put down his fork. "But is this guy emulating him?"

"Coincidence," David said. "Two totally unrelated cases."

The screen door slammed as Avery returned from the kitchen with several bottles of beer. "So basically we got nothin'." He placed the beers around the table. Elise noted that there were five empties near Avery's plate. Unusual for him. He rarely drank more than two, and openly admitted to having had a drinking problem at one time. Nothing serious, but enough for it to play a part in his divorce.

"There's something weird about this that I can't put my finger on," David said. There was that odd reluctance again. "It's like I almost have it, almost see it, then I lose it." He waved a hand in the air. "Never mind. I'm talking nonsense."

Elise leaned back in her chair. "I have an idea." She paused, knowing it would be a tough sell. "We need information, and nobody on the street is talking to us." Even the younger officers had been unable to come back from canvasses with any leads. *I don't talk to cops* seemed to be the sentiment out there. *I ain't seen nothin'. I ain't heard nothin'.*

Drug addicts and prostitutes had their own code, and unless you had something to use as leverage, it was hard to get anybody to open up. There was nothing in it for them. Leverage was what they needed, and the information for leverage needed to come from somebody living the life. "I think someone should go undercover."

"What are you suggesting?" David said, without taking his eyes off Elise. "Savannah PD doesn't have undercover cops."

He knows, she thought. *He already knows what I have in mind.* She took a swallow of wine. "I want to do it."

The lines between David's brows deepened. He was practically scowling. "As a drug addict?" he asked.

"As a prostitute."

Ding! Now they were all staring at her with a mix of intrigue and horror.

"What?" she asked. "You don't think I can pull it off?"

"Well . . ." Casper looked doubtful.

"I can play a hooker," Elise insisted. "I can be a hooker. I'm a little older than our two victims, but not that much."

"Bad idea," David said.

"Good idea," she volleyed back.

"It hasn't been that long since . . ." His words trailed off. They all knew what he was going to say. No need to spell it out. *Since you were held captive and almost killed.*

"I'm the best there is at getting people to talk. You know that. Yes, we could send somebody else out to do it, but would they come back with any information?"

The discussion continued for ten more minutes before someone changed the subject. Thirty minutes later, plates were carried to the kitchen and food was put in the refrigerator. Mara and John left—autopsy in the morning. Elise walked them to the door and said good-bye. Moments later, she discovered Avery waiting for her in the dim hallway. Odd.

"I have to tell you something," Avery said with obvious agitation.

His words and body language made her uneasy; she tensed.

Arms at his sides, Avery listed forward like someone leaning into the wind. Drunk.

She rolled her shoulders and smiled, not in response to his drunkenness, but because she finally had a handle on the situation.

She understood why Avery was lurking in the hallway. He was drunk, and people who were drunk did things that made no sense.

"Diana couldn't handle being married to a cop," he said, nodding his head slowly. "Well, you know what I think?" He didn't wait for a reply. "I think it's better for a cop to be in a relationship with another cop."

Her smile wavered and her stomach sank. This couldn't be going where she thought it was going. *You wouldn't do this to me, would you? Don't do this to me.*

She was pathetically oblivious to these things. Subtle and even unsubtle hints of attraction. Had there been any signs?

He'd sent her flowers after her abduction. But she'd almost died. Why *wouldn't* he send flowers? Flowers weren't a sign. Were they?

What else? He'd come to see her in the hospital, had joked as he'd hovered near the foot of the bed.

Not so strange.

Avery was the one who . . . She guessed a person might call it a rescue. He'd ridden a boat through dangerous water to get to the island where she was being held captive. He'd carried her, cold and half-naked, half-dead, to the boat, and he'd held her to his chest as the craft struggled through the waves to finally make it to shore. High drama and high emotions and danger and life-and-death situations could create a strong, but unnatural, bond. It happened. All the time. She mentioned this to him. Softly, patiently.

Don't do this to me.

"That's not it," Avery argued. "I've cared about you for a long time. Back when I was still married. Back before the divorce."

She couldn't deal with this. Not now. Not ever. And she had to *work with him.*

Avery was a good cop. Getting better all the time, especially after his old partner transferred to New Orleans. Since then, Avery had blossomed.

Her mind jumped. Why did this seem so much worse than what was going on between her and David?

Because you care about David.

How did that make it any different?

God, relationships! She knew nothing about relationships, other than being pretty damn sure she was terrible at them and that it would be better for her to take an oath of celibacy than it would be for her to get involved with anybody in a serious way. Maybe she should tell Avery about the celibacy. Maybe she should tell him how, after what Atticus Tremain had done, the thought of having sex repulsed her.

Wait. Should she tell her shrink that? It hadn't been a real issue at first. In fact, the lack of issue was something she now put down to shock. That area of her mind had just shut off. She'd closed the door on what had happened. But now, months later, she still found herself jerking away when someone touched her. And that thing with Jay Thomas Paul had been a sign of post-traumatic stress disorder.

Avery reached for her, grabbed her by her arms, holding her firmly before she could flinch. Not Tremain's hands, but still not hands she wanted on her.

Avery bent a bit so they were face-to-face, his eyes locked intently with hers. And then he said it. The asshole said it. "I love you, Elise."

Her brain faltered. She struggled for words. *She* wanted to reassure *him*. How idiotic was that?

Now what? Make a joke of it? Probably the best approach. Shrug it off, then later treat it as if Avery had simply been unable to hold his liquor. And that could be the case. Maybe tomorrow he wouldn't even remember—a possibility to cling to.

She was about to say something like *Yeah, I love everybody when I've had a few beers*, when someone cleared his throat, and David's voice came out of the darkness. "Am I interrupting something?"

Avery released Elise while continuing to stare at her. His mouth opened, then closed. "Oh man," he said under his breath. "Sorry. I'm really sorry. I don't know why I did that."

One end of the hallway led to the kitchen and the lights that silhouetted David; the other led to the living room, darkness, and the front door. Avery spun on his heel and dove for darkness and escape.

Elise ran after him, catching the door as he strode down the walk. "You shouldn't drive!" she shouted. Without turning, unable to look at her, he raised one hand high in the air to indicate he'd heard. *Not to worry.* "I'll call a cab." He took a left and vanished behind the shrubbery, his footsteps fading to nothing.

"Sorry to break that up," David said from behind her.

"He was drunk." Elise turned slightly, and David stepped back. Did he know she needed more personal space today than she had months ago?

"He's going to be embarrassed as hell tomorrow," David said.

"More embarrassed since you heard him. And let him know you heard him," she pointed out.

"I thought you might welcome the interruption."

She felt old and haggard. Midthirties wasn't old, but in cop years she was a hundred. Bottom line? She felt unattractive. So why were David and Avery both making advances?

"Strata Luna," Elise finally said. Rather than finding herself annoyed, she relaxed—because she had an explanation. Strata Luna had done something. Spread a mojo in her doorway, some kind of attraction spell, and now here Elise was, getting the false attention of every single man who came in close proximity to her.

"It's not Strata Luna," David said, amusement in his voice. "I would list all the reasons Avery might have for being in love with you, but you wouldn't believe me."

"Try."

Why had she said that? "Wait. Don't try. It's this job. That's what it is." Earlier she'd been thinking about how nice it was to hang out with her tribe. Damn David. Damn Avery. "We're like a bunch of inbreds."

He let out a snort.

"So much for these dinners and our team bonding. It seems to have worked a little too well."

"Elise, if you invite a man to dinner, he's going to hope. That's all I'm saying."

"*You* don't hope."

"That's because I know better. I used to hope."

"But not anymore?"

He looked up at the ceiling, then back at her, a crooked smile on his face. "There's a little bit of hope left, but not much."

"I'm not a tease, am I? Am I sending mixed signals I'm unaware of?"

"You're just being Elise. Don't worry about it. Just keep being Elise. Everything else is our problem. Mine. Avery's. Probably a million other guys'."

Night scents drifted in through the front door, and a siren could be heard off in the distance, coming from the vicinity of River Street.

"Something weird's in the air," David said.

"There's always something weird in the air. This is Savannah."

He gave a slow and thoughtful shake of his head. "I don't know. I don't know if it's the murders, or . . ."

"Are you psychic now?"

Distracted, David looked toward the door. "You feel anything?"

"A nice breeze." She didn't add that he was making the hairs on the back of her neck stand up. Not because of his words, but because he was the one who'd said them. David wasn't given to the impractical or the fanciful.

"I've had this feeling before, and I don't like it," he said.

"When have you had it?"

"I don't remember, but it's familiar."

"Déjà vu."

"Yeah. Probably."

Had she detected a slight drawl? "Are you picking up a Southern accent?"

"Absolutely not."

"You are."

"Have you gone to see your dad?" Abrupt change of subject.

"No."

"Going to?"

"No."

"He wants to talk to you."

"I don't want to talk to him."

"Okay." David grasped her gently by the shoulders, leaned in, kissed her on the forehead, then released her. She flinched a little, but not much. And if he noticed, he didn't let on. "I'm taking off. Thanks for dinner. Thanks for the beer. Sorry about Avery. See you tomorrow. The hooker thing is a really bad idea."

And he left.

.   .   .   .

"It was okay," Audrey said. "Kinda wished I'd stayed home and hung out with you guys."

"You would have been bored," Elise told her. "We were talking murder."

They were standing in the kitchen, and Audrey had just gotten back from the dance. "Those girls?" she asked.

"Yeah."

"Kids at school are saying they deserved it."

"They're just repeating what they heard their parents say. Nobody deserves anything like that. Nobody." This was a hot button for Elise. There'd been times in the past when a murder wasn't treated with the attention it deserved because the victim was a drug addict or a prostitute. That attitude was one she planned to change now that she was head of homicide. In fact, it had been one of the deciding factors behind her taking the position. Equality for every victim.

"Even the ones who think it's awful are saying we don't need to worry. I mean, regular girls. What do you think? Is it only prostitutes and drug addicts that are getting killed?"

"That seems to be the MO."

"Kids are also saying it's a serial killer. Is that what you and David think?"

"We don't know yet, baby girl." Elise reached out and tucked a strand of hair behind Audrey's ear in a gesture meant to reassure. "I don't want to keep secrets from you about the case, but I really shouldn't be talking about this to anybody outside the police department."

Audrey backed into the counter and levered herself up to sit on top of it, legs dangling. "I won't say anything. Not a word."

"Your friends will try to pump you."

She shrugged and grabbed a bag of tortilla chips, removed the clip, and dug inside. "I won't say anything." She took a bite of chip.

"It's too early in the investigation to form any strong opinions." Elise didn't add that they had very few leads. No sense in causing undue alarm.

"But David . . . He's a profiler. Is he profiling?"

"He's working on it. We're at the brainstorming stage right now."

"He'll figure it out."

Elise smiled at Audrey's obvious favoritism. "And I won't?" she teased.

"You aren't a profiler like David."

Elise thought about David's last big profiling case. The killer who got away. She didn't mention that either.

"Ready for another episode of *Doctor Who*?" Elise asked.

Audrey folded the chip bag, replaced the clip, and jumped down from the counter.

Upstairs in bed, Elise turned on the television, hit the Netflix button, and scrolled to the *Doctor Who* icon. Audrey joined her, lying on her stomach, chin in hands, head at the bottom of the bed. When the episode ended and the credits rolled, Audrey looked over her shoulder at her mother.

"Dad called today."

Not unusual. He called Audrey a couple of times a week.

"He heard about the murders, and he wants me to move to Seattle to live with him. He says it's too dangerous in Savannah."

Elise's heart sank. She didn't want Audrey to leave, yet she understood the concern.

"What did you tell him?" Elise asked with caution.

"That I wanted to stay here."

Of course she'd want to remain near her friends.

"With you."

Elise released her breath. "If David or I feel you might be in danger, I'll consider Seattle, but right now I don't think it's something you need to worry about, other than taking the precautions anybody should normally take." Things she'd schooled Audrey about many times. And yet now that the idea of Audrey's leaving had been presented, Elise couldn't help thinking about possible dangers. Elise wasn't the best person to be around. She'd made a lot of enemies. She was still making enemies. "Safe" wasn't a part of her existence.

Audrey got up from the bed. All shiny hair and long, beautiful legs beneath her pink sleep shirt. Not a child, but a young woman. When had she turned into an adult? *Was* she in danger?

"And Grandpa's here now," Audrey said.

"Grandpa?"

"Your dad."

"You call him Grandpa?" Elise was appalled.

"He's my grandfather."

"Did he ask you to call him that?" And worse: "Have you seen him recently?"

"He didn't ask me to call him Grandpa. It was my idea. We've had tea together a few times. He was waiting for me when I got out of school one day."

Jesus H.

"He's going to teach me some stuff. Like rootwork. Maybe even some easy spells. He says it's time for him to pass the mantle, and since you aren't interested in it . . ."

Elise sat up straighter. "I want you to stay away from him."

Audrey's face darkened. "He's my grandfather, and I'll see him if I want to."

Elise couldn't deny that there was something compelling and mesmerizing about Jackson Sweet. Audrey probably felt flattered that he'd even noticed her, let alone spoken to her and taken her for tea. "We don't know anything about him."

"David thinks he's okay. Strata Luna thinks he's okay."

"He could be a very bad man."

"Guess I'll find out." Audrey flounced from the room.

CHAPTER 9

"Christ, Elise."

"What do you think? Too demure?"

Elise and David stood in their shared office. The only other witness to her outfit was Jay Thomas, who waited near the closed door watching the interaction with something that struck Elise as feigned disinterest. But there was one thing she was quickly learning about Jay Thomas Paul: he was always listening and watching.

"Those weren't the words that came to mind," David said.

Elise had decided against the tacky-hooker look and opted for somewhat tasteful but still sexy. Hopefully. Black high heels, bare legs, a floral dress that might have been considered sweet if not for a neckline that exposed more of her breasts than anybody other than her gynecologist had seen in ages, and a hemline so short, the dress could almost pass for a long top. Her hair hung loose and shiny; her bangs arranged above darkened brows. With Audrey's help, makeup had been expertly applied, and when Elise looked in the mirror, she didn't recognize herself. It was no surprise her own partner had done a double take.

Maybe she'd gone too far, but it had bothered her that nobody thought she could pull it off.

Couldn't blame them. She'd doubted it too. She'd never felt sexy and had never been one to turn heads, although upon occasion she'd been told she simply didn't notice the turning heads. Maybe that was true, especially in light of Avery's revelation.

In high school, she'd been consciously and subconsciously infatuated with all things root doctor. Because of that, she'd learned a spell she'd used to catch a boy—a boy who later married her. Maybe a shrink would say that was where her relationship problems originated, and that might very well be true. She couldn't say whether the spell really worked or if it had simply been a coincidence, but deep down it was now ingrained in her subconscious that the only way to attract a guy was for the attraction to come from somewhere else. A mojo. A love spell, like the follow-me-boy she'd used so long ago.

She wasn't a profiler, but in dealing with criminals, she'd learned that most of the behavior they exhibited began in childhood. She was no different. And now, with David gawking at her as if she'd suddenly turned into this sexual being instead of Elise the cop . . . well, it could almost go to her head.

Almost.

She went through the gaudy gold bag she'd picked up at Goodwill. Mace, handcuffs, her badge, gun, cigarettes, and red lipstick. Everything a girl needed. "Let's go."

Their destination was Jefferson Street, where the first victim had been known to hang out. Unmarked car. David at the wheel, Jay Thomas Paul in the backseat. Elise had decided a wire wasn't necessary. She had her phone and a gun, and David would stick close. This wasn't a sting operation; she was just after information. The last thing she wanted was to alienate the very people who might help them crack the case.

David pulled to the curb. She slid out, shut the door, then leaned in the open window.

She'd chosen one of the bleaker areas of Savannah, of which there were many. Where even the streets and buildings were sad and uncared for, littered with trash and graffiti, the weedy sidewalks claustrophobically narrow, butting up against windowless buildings of questionable purpose.

"Thanks, darlin'." She gave David a smile and an accidental view of deep cleavage. "Don't be a stranger."

She read his expression, could see he still wanted to stop her. She saw him clamp down on his response, give up, give in. "I'll be close."

She played along in case anybody was within hearing. "You're too damn sweet for your own good."

"I can be more than sweet."

"I'm sure you can. Next time." She straightened away from the car and he drove off, but she knew he'd circle around and come back to park at a safe distance.

A woman stepped from the shadows. Blond, limp hair with dark roots. Short denim skirt and black ankle boots. Hard to tell her age. She looked forty, but could have been twenty. Prostitution and drugs aged people.

"This is my corner," she barked in a smoker's voice. "Find another spot."

"I had to leave my street," Elise said. "Two girls were killed, so I'm looking for a new place. Something safer. I can move on, but I saw you out here and thought it might be better not to work alone."

The woman's tough attitude and hostility faded. "I heard about them girls," she said, with fear in her voice. "People are saying it's a serial killer."

"That's what I heard too."

"Nobody cares. The mayor don't care and the cops don't care." The woman waved her arms in frustration. "I'm sick of this town.

I just want to make enough money to get out. Maybe go to LA; I don't know."

Elise pulled out a pack of cigarettes and shook one at the prostitute, who took it. Elise lit her own, then passed the lighter. As she exhaled, she released an inner sigh—the cigarette tasted good. She remembered this feeling, and she hoped to hell a few drags didn't start something. She hadn't had a smoke in a year, and it had been several years since she'd been serious about it.

She took another deep drag. *Damn.* "Did you know them? Either of the girls?" she asked.

"Layla Jean. The first one, but not good. Like we didn't hang out or compare notes or anything, but I seen her around, talked to her sometimes. Just shoot the shit."

"Ever see anything suspicious?" Elise asked. "Like anything that just made you feel like something wasn't right?"

The woman laughed. "Honey, I see a lot of weird things. Girls like me are weird magnets."

"You know what I mean. That sixth sense that kicks in."

"What are you?" Her eyes narrowed in suspicion. "A cop?"

"Would that matter?"

Hesitant to be pulled into conversation with a possible officer, the woman grudgingly said, "We all got a sixth sense. All of us in this business. You gotta have it to survive. You learn pretty fast which cars to skip. You open that door and you look at the potential client and in a split second you make a decision. That one girl who was killed? The first one? I'm pretty sure she was a pro. I saw her cuss people out and flip 'em off. She was tough. She knew her stuff. So to have two girls fall for somebody—that's scary. Makes you think he doesn't come across as a creep."

Since the woman had already pegged her as a fake, Elise didn't try to play the part of a hooker. She talked to her the way she'd talk to anybody. "The worst killers are incredible actors," Elise said. "They convince people of their trustworthiness." Elise didn't add that it was the serial killer MO. "Killers can be extremely charming. You need to remember that."

"You *are* a cop, right?"

Elise took another drag. "How could I be a cop? You said the cops didn't care."

"Cop." Spit out with conviction. The woman moved closer. She looked over her shoulder, then back at Elise, seemingly prepared to share information, when the exchange was interrupted by a potential customer. A long black car crept up the street, then stopped. The back window dropped silently, and a man looked at them from the deep recesses of the backseat. Suit. Dark skin, immaculately groomed, about Elise's age.

The woman inhaled sharply, whispered to Elise, "That's Tyrell King. Layla Jean went with him the night she was murdered. He comes here a lot. Drug dealer. Pays with whatever you're lookin' for. Got some good stuff, that's for sure. He's the guy we all want. Nice body, clean, polite, doesn't go for anything too kinky. Sometimes all he's after is a blow job."

"You," Tyrell said. "Blondie. C'mere."

The prostitute hung back and grabbed Elise's arm.

"I said, c'mere."

Elise shook off the woman's hand and approached the car, stepping into a circle of lamplight. "She ain't feeling so hot."

The guy stared at her. "How 'bout you? You feeling okay?"

Elise took a drag from her cigarette and rested an elbow on her crossed arm. "I feel great."

The door opened.

She was poised to get inside when he stopped her. "No smoking."

"You live a clean lifestyle?"

He smiled. "Very clean."

She flicked the cigarette away and ducked into the car, closing the door behind her.

"Wanna drink?" Tyrell asked moments later. He was reclining in the seat, feet braced on the floor, one arm stretched toward Elise, the other holding a mixed drink. He smiled, and in the light of a nearby building she could see the diamond in his front tooth.

"I don't drink when I'm working."

He laughed. "Working's the best time to drink."

He drained his glass, then passed the empty over the front seat to the driver—an enormous, bald black man. Everything about him said bodyguard rather than chauffeur.

Tyrell settled back in his seat and eyed Elise up and down. Then finally he said, "I want a blow job."

That was when Elise reached into her bag and pulled out her badge. "I'd like to ask you a few questions."

He read her name and laughed. "Goddamn, if it isn't Elise Mansfield. I thought you looked familiar. I read about you in the paper."

Mansfield. Nobody had called her by her maiden name in years.

"We went to high school together," he explained.

She stared at him, trying to imagine this cocky, handsome guy in her school.

Seeing that she couldn't place him, he decided to jog her memory. "English. Mr. Monroe's class. I went by Harold Freeman then."

"Oh my God." Little wormy guy who wouldn't shut up. "You were always in trouble."

"Things don't change, do they?"

"Well, I never figured you for—" She stopped to measure her next words, unwilling to offend someone who might be beneficial to the investigation. "What do you consider yourself, exactly?"

"A businessman. An entrepreneur. And I never figured you for a cop."

It was odd running into someone who saw her any other way.

"You married Sandburg," he said. "Could you have found a whiter whitey? Like you were trying to get away from all that hoo-doo stuff your daddy saddled you with. So right out of high school you marry the whitest guy around. I figured you'd have three kids, drive an SUV, and go to soccer games. That's what I figured." He pressed deeper into the seat, continuing to size her up. "But my, my, my. Should have voted you most likely to get hot."

"You were the class clown." He'd made her laugh. Elise was a serious person. Too serious, but it suddenly occurred to her that she had a thing for guys who made her laugh.

"Not that you weren't attractive. Not sayin' that. But you weren't sexy. But now . . ." He pursed his lips and shook his head.

Yep, she'd overdone it. "This is a costume," she pointed out.

He let out something close to a giggle, his hand fisted against his mouth. "I don't care what it is. It's not the clothes I'm findin' interesting."

They talked about classes and teachers and crazy things that had happened—things they both recalled differently. Finally Tyrell said, "Are you sure we can't continue with our little rendezvous?" He glanced down at his lap, then back at her.

She chose to ignore his question, and instead introduced one of her own. "Would you be willing to come downtown to answer some questions?"

His face lost all friendliness, and the interior of the car took on a chill. "No."

"I heard the first victim was someone you knew," Elise said, pulling back on the threat of downtown. She wouldn't get anything out of Tyrell if she pushed him too hard. "I heard you picked her up the night she was killed. Is that true?"

He nodded. "I did see her that night. Like early. I gotta get my beauty sleep. I'm in bed by eleven."

"So when would you say you and she . . . hung out?"

He didn't answer.

"I'm betting the samples we took from her mouth and stomach would match your DNA."

Her words had the expected effect. "About ten o'clock," he said. "She gave me a blow job, I paid her, and she left."

"Paid her with crack cocaine? Because according to the autopsy report, she had coke and meth in her system."

"Does it matter how she was paid? I thought this was about murder, not drugs."

"I'm trying to let you know that we have enough to lock you up." But not enough to hold him long. She didn't tell him that. "And I'm trying to let you know that I'm willing to forget about that if you help us." She produced her card and handed it to him. "Here's my number."

He checked it out, smiled to himself, and tucked the card inside his jacket.

"This is serious, you know," she said. Tyrell had been polite to her. She got the sense that he respected women, all things considered. "Girls are being killed in the most brutal way. You don't want that, do you?"

"Hell no."

"So if you hear anything or see anything, call me." She directed her voice toward the driver. "Pull over, please."

Their speed didn't change.

"Pull over," Tyrell said, repeating Elise's command. This time the big guy responded and stopped the car. Elise opened her door and stepped out. "Call me night or day," she said.

"You like the symphony?" Tyrell asked. "I got season tickets. Good seats. I'll wear a suit and tie." He nodded at some thought in his head. "I look really fine when I get slicked up. And you could do your hair and wear some kind of red strapless dress. We'd make a good-looking pair."

"Not gonna happen."

"For old time's sake?"

"Not gonna happen."

He gave her a smile. "I'm not used to being turned down."

"I'll bet you aren't."

"What the hell was that all about?" David asked once she was back in the surveillance car with him and they were driving in the direction of the police station. "From my front-row seat, that appeared awfully chummy."

"Old school buddy. Used to go by the name of Harold Freeman, but he reinvented himself as Tyrell King. We reminisced a little. He asked me to the symphony."

From the backseat came the sound of Jay Thomas's scratching pen. Once again she'd forgotten about him.

"My God, this town is weird." David drove on in silence, then seemed to have an alarming thought. "Are you going?"

CHAPTER 10

Caroline Chesterfield adjusted her backpack and headed down the dimly lit street in the direction of home, her legs aching from standing on concrete for five hours. Such was the life of a waitress. Such was the life of an estranged child. But at least the scent of jasmine brought her a soft sense of comfort, and the dark and quiet were welcoming after the noise and overstimulation of the bar.

She considered herself a good girl, although other people had a different opinion. Her father, for instance. But she was no slouch. She'd been accepted to Harvard. Harvard! Wasn't that enough? she asked herself as she crossed the dark street. Wasn't that as good as actually going? An acceptance letter from freakin' Harvard?

"He's holding you back," her mother had told her, talking about Caroline's boyfriend. "You can be anybody, do anything. Why stay in Savannah? Why go to SCAD when you could go to Harvard?" In her mother's soft Southern voice, the word "SCAD"—as the art school was known both in and outside of Savannah—somehow managed to convey just the right amount of polite disdain.

Her parents had never taken Caroline's interest in art and music seriously, always treating it like a hobby. *Oh, isn't that cute?* The verbal equivalent of a pat on the head. They wanted her to be a doctor or a lawyer or whatever other prestigious occupation could be pulled from their butts.

Her daddy had been no more understanding than her momma. "We won't support you in this," he said the day Caroline confronted him with her decision to turn down the Harvard offer. They'd stood in his office in city hall. Flags in the corner, a photo of her on the wall behind his desk. "And by not support you, I don't just mean emotionally," her father had gone on to say. "I mean financially. If you attend Harvard, we'll give you a nice stipend. All you have to do is concentrate on your studies. If you don't go to Harvard, you'll get nothing. Nothing."

She'd recoiled in shock, his cold and unemotional tone impacting her more than the message itself. No discussion. No understanding. Handed to her like one of his mandates. But her mother's involvement, or lack of involvement, was worse. No sympathy there either. Just silence. The good wife, backing her husband's decision, no matter what.

So here she was, waiting tables five nights a week at the Chameleon in one of the shadier areas of Savannah, sharing a cramped apartment with two other students, going to school during the day, the boyfriend long gone. Her mother had been right about that. Once the plug was pulled on Caroline's money, he'd vanished.

Had she made a mistake?

She'd never admit it to her father, but she might have gone to Harvard if not for her boyfriend. And it pained and shamed her to know she'd stayed in Savannah for a guy. A loser. But none of that really mattered anymore; the biggest issue was the way her parents had treated her. Like a disposable child. The very people who should have loved her had acted like strangers, like business people she didn't even know. And now a year had passed since she'd talked to either of them. She was beginning to wonder if she'd ever see them again.

At the next street corner, light from a bulb high on a pole radiated outward, encompassing the intersection. The scene was blurry, and with annoyance—and, yes, self-pity—Caroline realized she was crying. She stopped to wipe her eyes with the back of her hand.

"Hey."

Startled, she turned.

A guy. In a car, the passenger window down as he craned his neck to look up at her, one arm draped over the steering wheel. "You okay?"

In the lamplight, she recognized him from the bar. He'd been polite and had left her a nice tip. Not the kind of guy you'd notice in a crowd, but someone a girl would feel comfortable around. Safe around.

"I'm fine," she said.

"You don't look fine."

She laughed, thinking he was probably talking about the mascara running down her cheeks.

"Would you like to grab a cup of coffee?" he asked. "There's a place on Abercorn that's open all night."

She didn't answer.

"I'm a good listener," he assured her. "And I have sisters," he added, almost as an afterthought, smiling at what having sisters implied. He understood young women. He understood this kind of breakdown.

It might be nice to talk to someone totally removed from her life. Her roommates didn't get it. Poor rich girl, reduced to working and living just like the rest of them. No sympathy there.

But it wasn't about the work. It was about the rejection.

She pulled in a stabilizing breath.

Footsteps drew her attention away from the guy in the car. She looked up to see a man heading down the sidewalk toward her, his gait uneven.

"And you really shouldn't be out here by yourself," the guy in the car said, not in a judgmental way, not in the way her parents would have done, but concerned. For her. And God, it had been so long since anybody had shown her any concern.

He leaned across the seat and swung the passenger door open.

The man on the sidewalk was getting closer, close enough for her to see his rough beard and tattered clothes. And he was coming *straight for her.*

The city was buzzing about the two girls who'd been murdered. Not smart to walk home. She'd taken a cab for a few days, but cabs were expensive. And anyway, in a recent televised press conference she'd been forced to watch in the bar, her father had stated that the victims had been prostitutes and drug addicts. No need for worry.

But the weird guy was still coming toward her.

Decision made, she dove into the car, slammed the door, and locked it. "Thanks," she said breathlessly.

Her rescuer smiled, put the car in gear, and pulled away.

CHAPTER 11

Body is no longer in full rigor mortis," John Casper said after a brief, preliminary on-site evaluation. "I'd say she's been dead close to forty-eight hours."

David's phone had rung at 6:30 a.m. with a report of another murder, and now here they were. Sometime during the night the nude body of the female victim had been displayed on a narrow strip of beach along the Savannah River, the body discovered just after dawn by an unfortunate group of Girl Scouts.

"Judging from the lividity, the victim was moved after death," John added.

"Seems like the killer might have waited until she was close to full rigor to display her," Elise said.

Early morning, a chill in the air, wind coming in off the water, sun still low in the sky, seabirds calling overhead while sandpipers scurried along the river's edge. Beauty and horror.

John nodded. "Looks that way."

Same MO. A young woman, nude, displayed in a public place. Body covered in a single word, just like the others.

"*Cupio.*" Coffee mug in one hand, David pulled out his phone and did a quick search of the word. "It means 'desire' in Latin."

Avery broke in. "Got an ID on the vic," he said with an odd look on his face. He lived closer to the crime scene and had arrived thirty minutes before Elise and David. "Caroline Chesterfield."

"The mayor's daughter?" Elise asked in disbelief. "You sure?"

Avery turned his phone so she could see the headshot of a young woman. Blond hair, smiling at the camera. "Matches the missing person report. We still need family confirmation, but I'm betting it's her."

Things were a little strained between Elise and Avery, but they were both doing a good job pretending the other night had never happened. She wouldn't mention it, and hopefully he never would either.

David lowered his coffee. "Who reported her missing?"

Avery pocketed his phone and flipped through his notes. "Roommate—after getting a call from the bar where the victim worked. She didn't show up for her shift. Roommate didn't report her earlier because she figured she'd stayed the night with someone. As far as a timeline . . . looks like Caroline was last seen two nights ago walking home from work."

"Have an address?" David asked. "I'd like to talk to that roommate."

Avery tore a sheet of paper from his small notebook and handed it to David, who examined the address before tucking it into his breast pocket. "That's a pretty shady area for the mayor's daughter to live." The whole story was odd.

"Excuse me."

David looked up to see a young female officer standing with one hand on her belt. "I overheard you discussing the identity of the victim," the woman said. She looked upset. "It's Caroline Chesterfield."

"How certain are you?" Elise asked.

"A hundred percent. I know the family. My younger sister and Caroline were best friends for years. She used to stay at our house. It's her."

"Don't release any information yet," Elise told both Avery and David once the officer left. "Until I break the news to the mayor." She took a deep breath and squared her shoulders. "Call me if you come across anything substantial."

Avery nodded.

Wanting to talk to Elise in private, David fell into step beside her as she headed for the parking lot, her car, and a waiting Jay Thomas Paul.

"The mayor's daughter," Elise said. "What the hell?"

"Think it's calculated?"

"Could be a coincidence. She was just in the wrong place at the wrong time."

"That would be a helluva coincidence. A dead girl who doesn't fit the victimology, who just happens to be the daughter of the mayor, who just happened to appear on the news a few nights ago talking about how everything was under control and the killer was going to be arrested at any moment."

They paused in the soft sand. David offered his coffee mug to Elise. She accepted and took a drink.

"I'm going to work on the assumption that this isn't random until we find out otherwise," David said. "There are few coincidences when it comes to serial killers. And there's a strange and rapid escalation to this that doesn't fit standard serial-killer profiles. This is more in keeping with a seasoned killer. The stakes are increasing too rapidly."

"Seasoned? What are you saying? That he's been doing this awhile?"

"I think this person is a pro, and I think he's got more than three kills under his belt. It's long been suspected that the most elusive serial killers don't stay in the same location. Our killer might have come here from somewhere else. We need to check all open serial killer cases around the country and see if we can find any with his MO." Not an easy task. At any given time there were at least twenty open cases in the United States, and that was probably being conservative.

"Is that all?" Elise eyed him with suspicion. "Is there something you aren't telling me?"

"Nothing worth sharing at the moment." He had his theories— theories he wasn't yet convinced weren't just part of his own hysterical mind.

Elise gave him a long look, passed the coffee mug back, turned, and headed up the wooden walkway, her black jacket and dark hair billowing in the morning breeze. From where he stood—just an ordinary day at the beach.

He watched as she spoke to Jay Thomas, words he couldn't hear. The reporter nodded, a solemn expression on his face. Then they both disappeared behind a row of trees.

David took a deep breath and turned back toward the crime scene.

CHAPTER 12

Elise maneuvered her blue Camry toward Bay Street, heading for Savannah City Hall and the mayor's office, Jay Thomas beside her in the passenger seat, thankfully subdued and not full of questions for once.

She parked on the street and left the reporter in the car, fearing he might put two and two together but hoping he didn't.

She planned to break the news to the mayor face-to-face, but if he wasn't in, a call would have to do because this kind of thing would hit Twitter feeds before the cops had the full story.

The mayor was in.

It wasn't until that moment—until she'd gone through the metal detector and walked past the cast-iron clockwork in the lobby—that Elise realized she'd subconsciously hoped to find him gone so this unpleasantness could be taken care of over the phone.

Coward.

Rather than take the cage elevator, she chose the privacy of the marble steps to the second floor. Down the hall, past the framed photos of previous mayors. Knocked on the dark door. That was followed by a secretary leading her to the deeper office and to the mayor, a Southern gentleman who got to his feet as Elise entered.

Mayor Chesterfield had a suave nature about him and that good-old-boy persona. Their few conversations had left Elise reluctantly charmed by his skill at manipulation and diplomacy. He was a true politician.

She saw from his expression that he expected news about the murder cases. *Good* news.

"Detective Sandburg!" He motioned toward the leather chair across from his massive desk. "Have a seat."

Behind him were photos of his family. *His family*. Beside the framed images were the requisite flags and maps and awards. Beyond those, the windows that revealed the street below. Cars and tourists moving along as if it were just another day. That was the thing about homicide. The world kept moving even when you felt deep in your heart that everything should stop for at least a moment of silence. Just a moment.

Elise sat.

She faced the mayor, hands clasped in front of her as if she were clinging to herself, holding so tightly her knuckles turned white. "I have some news," she said quietly.

He smiled from his seat across the desk.

His world was about to change, and he didn't know it.

Part of her wanted to give him this day. Postpone this moment. Maybe she'd suggest he take the afternoon off. He and his wife would go to Tybee Island and have a picnic. Watch the cargo ships go by and feed the birds. And then they'd come home, tired from a day at the beach, but feeling at peace, a feeling that was undoubtedly rare when you were the mayor. A carefree day. A day just for him.

Oh, how she wanted to give him that.

But it wouldn't happen. Maybe ten years ago a person could have gotten away with it. But today, with social media, every minute she wasted was a minute closer to his hearing the news from somewhere else.

"It's about your daughter, Caroline."

He reacted in the way she expected. The smile faded, and then came the fear.

The fear was the awful part of death and dying. The awful part of life. Thing was, death wasn't bad. It was the fear that came with it that was hard. The fear of how you would go on. The fear of tomorrow and the next day.

"I'm sorry to tell you this, but your daughter is dead."

Your daughter is dead.

Words that would bring Elise to her knees.

He struggled to put it all together. Fill in the plot holes. The how and when, all the while avoiding what deep in his heart he knew to be the cause of death—murder. He was on to the next step, which was clinging to the less awful of the awful. Death by anything but someone else's hand.

Looking as if his body had no bones, he shrank in his chair. "That can't be . . ."

"I'm sorry."

"How . . . ?"

This was where detectives had to spell it out very clearly and carefully; otherwise the loved one would grasp for something, anything, and cling to it. The false thing. The thing that wasn't true and wasn't real. She wanted to give him that false thing.

"Your daughter was murdered. Her body was found this morning." And now the cruelest part. The repeat pounding of the words in hopes of penetrating the roar in the survivor's head. "Caroline is dead."

Then came the shaking. Something so exaggerated it never looked real. It started in the mayor's core and radiated out, moving through his torso to his extremities until his arms were practically flailing, his legs shaking so violently, the pens in the cup on his desk began to rattle.

He stared at his arms. He stared at his hands as if he wanted to pour all of his attention into the strange phenomenon going on within his body. Focus on that and nothing else. Certainly not the pain. Certainly not the horror. *Not the fear.*

She reached across the desk and grabbed one palsied hand, gripping it tightly. Instead of stopping, the involuntary movement traveled from him to her, the shaking so violent that her own arm began to shudder.

His hand under hers turned into a claw, and as she held on, he pounded a fist against the top of his desk. That was followed by an inhuman roar that was half sob, half anger.

The sound itself seemed to startle and galvanize him. He thrust her hand away and sprang to his feet, eyes wild. "Where is she?"

"On the beach, but they'll be moving the body to the morgue soon. You can see her there."

"I want to see her now. I don't believe it's her. I think you're wrong."

This was the way it went. The denial. The brain struggling for an alternate route, finding it, clinging to it.

"She's not a drug addict." His spine straightened, and he looked at Elise with accusation, and then loudly and clearly, all tremors gone, he said, "She's not a prostitute!"

"I'll take you to her," Elise said quietly. There would be no belief until he saw the body, even though seeing her the way the killer had left her would be a thousand knives to his heart.

"Later today we'll need you to answer questions about your daughter. Details of her daily life," Elise told him.

He blinked, surprise pulling him away from his denial. He frowned, thinking. "I doubt I can do that," he finally admitted. "It's been a year since I last saw her."

"A year?"

They lived in the same city, and he hadn't seen her for a year? Of course Elise, of all people, knew that father-daughter estrangement wasn't uncommon. Maybe less uncommon than a lot of people let on. Funny how that was. The way people didn't want to admit they were no longer on speaking terms with close relatives, and yet in her years of homicide investigation, she'd discovered that familial breakups were almost epidemic.

"We had a falling-out," he said.

"About what?"

"School. She was accepted to Harvard. She was offered a scholarship. She didn't take it. She stayed here . . ." He stopped talking, going off somewhere in his head, then finally coming back. "I kicked her out," he whispered, his eyes connecting with Elise's. "I kicked her out." The words were a confession, everything he knew suddenly folding in on him as he found the person at fault here. The person at fault was always the survivor. "I kicked her out and cut her off without a penny."

The subtext and the horrified expression on his face said it all: if he hadn't kicked her out, she'd still be alive. And the worst part? That was probably true. But it fell into the brain game of what-ifs, and once you got going on that, it just didn't stop. *What if I hadn't turned right at that light? What if I hadn't gone out for a drink?* In Caroline's case—what if she hadn't chosen to take a certain path home from work? The randomness of life was unforgiving.

"Your daughter made an unwise decision," Elise said, speaking words that might have appeared to blame the victim. Not her intention. "She shouldn't have walked home alone. That was a poor choice on her part." She wouldn't mention that just days ago the mayor had reassured residents of Savannah they were safe. When would he make that connection? That his televised reassurance might have played a part in his daughter's death. That in this blame game he truly did have a role.

She traced the story back to its roots. If he hadn't disowned her, Caroline wouldn't have been living in a dangerous part of town and she wouldn't have been working at the bar. And she wouldn't have walked home alone late at night. He would always blame himself.

And maybe that was the lesson here. Love your kids, no matter who they are and no matter what choices they make. Respect those choices.

"I'm sorry," she repeated, recognizing the inadequacy of her words. And then she lied. For him, because what difference did the truth make now? "You aren't to blame."

If he heard those words a million times, he would never believe them. Because this story began with him. And he was to blame, however indirectly.

"I can take you there," she said. "To your daughter. To the park. My car is outside."

He gave her a numb nod, and together they left his office.

"Mr. Morris is here for his meeting," the secretary said as they moved past her desk.

A man in a suit got to his feet, a look of expectation on his face.

"Cancel everything," the mayor instructed. It was almost as if he'd forgotten he was the mayor, a job that no longer held any importance. He looked at the man. "I can't meet with you today. I'm sorry."

"An unexpected event has taken place that requires the mayor's immediate attention," Elise explained. Then she and the mayor left, heading for the beach and sunshine and immeasurable grief.

CHAPTER 13

I'm Jay Thomas Paul," the reporter said, introducing himself from the backseat where he'd relocated to allow the mayor to take the passenger side. "I was at the press conference a few days ago."

"Not a good time." Elise slid behind the wheel. Beside her, the mayor stared numbly through the windshield. Jay Thomas was unaware of the identity of the woman on the beach, but in another ten minutes the whole city would know—if word hadn't gotten out already.

Jay Thomas dropped the hand he'd extended toward the mayor. Picking up on the tension, he shot Elise a questioning look, and she gave him an almost imperceptible shake of the head. He didn't press it.

The mayor was silent on the way to the river. Upon arrival, before the car rolled to a complete stop, he bailed out and loped across the open sand in the direction of the yellow tape.

The scene had changed since Elise last saw it: now there was a crowd of about a hundred bystanders hoping to get a glimpse of something horrendous—as if their observation would protect them from ever experiencing anything similar themselves.

As the mayor moved awkwardly through the loose sand, people parted to let him pass. He was someone who'd always been accessible, a people's mayor. He rode his bike around Forsyth Park. He went to cafés and ordered his own coffee. He talked to people as he waited in line at the grocery store or while pumping gas. So when citizens saw him, they smiled. They waved and spoke to him.

Today he didn't see anyone. Smiles vanished, and people dropped out of his way. A few produced cameras and snapped photos of the odd expression on his face. The images would be hashtagged, and his grief would make fodder for mass consumption long before the next press conference. By the time reports of the murder hit the local stations, the crime would be old news.

Elise ran to catch up, scanning and assessing the scene as she moved. "Where's Detective Gould?" she asked a male officer.

"He's talking to the Scouts in the picnic area. They wanted to get the girls away from here."

The mayor ducked under the crime-scene tape.

A woman collecting evidence protested when Chesterfield charged forward. Then the evidence collector saw who it was, looked at Elise, looked at the mayor, got to her feet, and stepped aside.

"Don't touch the body!" Elise said.

The mayor ignored her. Or didn't hear. He scooped his daughter into his arms and hugged her to him, and it was all the more awful because the rigor hadn't yet left her body completely and her arms remained stiff and unbending. The grieving man let out the same sobbing roar he'd released in his office, rocking the girl's body against him as the people processing the scene tried to pull him away.

Finally, after what seemed like minutes, he let his daughter go, laying her back on the ground. He removed his coat and spread it gently over her. "You should have covered her up," he said. "She shouldn't be left like this."

"We're processing the scene." The words came from a young female wearing latex gloves.

The mayor zeroed in, directing his anger at her. "I don't care! Do you hear me? I don't care! My daughter is dead! Dead!"

The officer recoiled, opened and closed her mouth, and backed up.

John Casper stepped forward. "Sir?"

No response. John tried to get the mayor's attention once again. This time the mayor heard. His head turned slowly.

"I'm the coroner," John told him. "We're almost ready to take her to the morgue. You can see her again there."

John's white coat and the mention of the morgue seemed to send the mayor's emotions in a new direction. He showed a sudden comprehension of his surroundings. He spun around, arms limp at his sides. He spotted Elise.

"You."

She swallowed.

"Head of homicide." He spit out the words. "A third murder in less than two weeks. This should not have happened. My daughter wouldn't have died if you'd been doing your job."

"I understand," she said, attempting to placate him. Elise could imagine his tangle of thoughts, each tripping over the one before.

"Do you? Do you really? You have a daughter, right?"

"Yes."

"A daughter who's alive, right?"

"Yes."

"Then you do not understand."

"No."

"This is your fault. *Your* fault. My daughter's death is on your head."

It was common for survivors to go from blaming themselves to blaming the handiest person. Right now, that person was Elise. She might have been able to shrug off his accusations if she felt she'd done as well as anybody could have done under the circumstances.

But when people were still dying, the truth was, she wasn't doing her job.

It was entirely possible she *was* to blame.

"I'm calling the FBI," the mayor said. "I'm going to get some people down here who know what the hell they're doing. People who'll catch this person and put a stop to this so no one else will lose a daughter."

"I'll give you a ride to the morgue," she told him.

"No." His face was red. "I can't look at you anymore. I'd fire you this second, but who would we have left until someone with more experience arrives? Your partner?" He sneered.

What he did next took her by complete surprise. He put a hand to her chest and physically pushed her. Not hard, but a solid shove. People gasped.

And, oh God, she shouldn't have said it. It was horrible of her, but the words just came out. "You shouldn't have reassured the public that this was all under control."

Another gasp.

Everything from that point on was in slow motion.

A fist, coming at her.

In the back of her mind she remembered that he boxed. She wasn't sure how she knew that about him, but she suddenly recalled that he'd started an after-school boxing program for kids.

She attempted to duck and dodge. If she hadn't, he probably would have broken her nose. Instead, his knuckles connected with her cheek, the force driving her backward, her body airborne for a brief second before she hit the ground, the wind knocked out of her, the pain in her face creating a burst of light behind her eyelids.

He was still coming.

Like a charging bull.

Someone knocked him aside, bodies flying, his attack thwarted.

It took her a minute to realize who'd intervened. Jay Thomas Paul. He was on top of the mayor, pinning him to the ground, Jay Thomas's hipster glasses only slightly askew, his hair only slightly mussed.

The mayor pushed him away, or Jay Thomas allowed himself to be pushed. All three of them scrambling to their feet, Jay Thomas keeping a cautious hand to the mayor's chest.

"You're gonna be writing traffic tickets!" the mayor shouted, shaking a finger at Elise. "Traffic tickets!"

CHAPTER 14

Lemme see that again," David said.

Elise paused in the middle of the sidewalk to let him recheck her face. Nothing seemed to be broken, but her cheek was swollen and her eye was blacker every time she looked in the mirror.

"You need to put a bag of peas on it when we're done here," David said, then added, "I know I should feel more empathy for the mayor, all things considered, but seeing your face has effectively eliminated any slack I would have cut him. In fact, I want to work him over."

"I suggest just not voting for him in the upcoming election."

"The guy decked you."

"He was out of his mind."

"That makes it okay?"

"That kind of news can make someone act in ways that go against who they are," she said softy, reminding him of things that needed no reminding.

"Don't look at me that way." He began fiddling with his jacket pockets, searching for something. "Grief is weird. Believe me, I know that. But I also think it can reveal our hidden selves, our darker selves. Right now he's the guy who hit you, and I can't see past that. Maybe later I'll give him a break, but his actions today mean he's probably hit women before, and that knowledge effectively drives out any compassion I would have felt for him no matter how much we have in common."

She stared at him a long moment before deciding her expectations had been unfair. "You're right."

"We're cool?"

"We're cool," she replied.

"I'm surprised he didn't fire you. He has the authority." David found what he was searching for. He pulled the scrap of paper Avery had given him from his pocket, reread the address, and pointed down the block to a three-story house in need of paint. Together they moved toward it.

"I wouldn't be shocked if firing is just around the corner," Elise said. "Of course, the punch in the face might make it harder for that kind of action to stick."

"Right now getting fired sounds pretty good to me."

He had a point. "Are we the only detectives who talk about losing our jobs as if that would be a good thing?"

"It'd be great, right?" David asked. "We could freelance. We could open our own detective agency. We could take *a damn vacation*."

The apartment where Caroline Chesterfield had lived was in a crumbling building that should have been condemned long ago. Typical colonial wood-frame home, probably built in the late 1800s. Student shack.

"What do you mean *we*? Your job isn't in danger," Elise pointed out. "At least I don't think it is."

"I'm not sticking around if you're gone."

"That's sweet, but what about Major Hoffman?"

He scowled and ignored her question. "I can't believe Jay Thomas Paul came to your rescue."

"Speaking of the guy with three first names, where is he?"

"Said he was going back to his rental."

They took the stairs to the front porch. "Which means right now he's hunched over his laptop, typing up today's story about his heroics," Elise said. "And I'll bet he has photos." She tried to recall if he'd pulled out his camera. Couldn't remember. Everything had happened so fast. Didn't really matter. This wasn't anything they were going to be able to suppress. Regardless of Jay Thomas's contribution, the story would hit the media outlets fast. But, come to think of it . . . "People might be afraid of incurring the mayor's wrath, especially after what happened to me. The local paper might not run the story," she said hopefully.

"You're the closest thing Savannah has to a celebrity. Getting punched out by the mayor is going to be news. Mix that with his loss . . . Story will go national by five o'clock." He gave her a long look. "That's gonna be one of the best black eyes I've ever seen."

"Go big or go home."

"Yup."

David lifted the knocker on the door and let it fall three times. "What'd you say to piss him off?"

She told him. "I shouldn't have said it. He had a right to be upset."

"But he didn't have a right to hit you."

"You know what the focus is going to be now, don't you?" Elise asked. "The father-daughter relationship."

"People love that stuff."

He pulled out his phone and began poking at it. "Aha." He turned the device around, giving her a landscape view of a YouTube video. Of her getting knocked down by the mayor. Uploaded by someone named Streetsavannah. Might or might not have been captured by Jay Thomas. "The punch heard round the city."

She pushed the phone away.

He scrolled, coming across a close-up of her battered face. "What do you want to bet this was taken by your rescuer? If we dropped by his room, we'd probably find him in his lair, posting images—" He stopped. "Yep. His Twitter account. His damn Twitter account. Your name is hashtagged. That son of a bitch. I thought I saw him scurrying away from the crime scene like a spider clutching an egg sac." More scrolling. "And he's not being reticent about his role in the event. Takes credit for breaking things up and saving you from serious harm." He tucked away his phone. "A modest and noble man. A man I'm going to talk to."

"And here I've been feeling awful about not being nicer to him."

"Never doubt that sixth sense. It'll save your life."

The door was finally answered by a young girl with pink dreadlocks, a floral dress, and army boots. She'd been crying.

"It was the Savannah Killer, wasn't it?" she asked.

That was fast. Killers were given names by the media—not because people were trying to be clever or trying to diminish the horrific events or glorify the killer, but because a name made it quick and easy for the media and even cops to anchor the conversation or journalistic piece. There were a lot of killers, a lot of murderers out there, and a name simplified the discussion. Instead of "the killer who murdered the Murphy girl" or "the killer who left writing on bodies" or "the killer who did 'this' or 'that'" or "the perpetrator of the event on such and such a street," one universally used name brought clarity. It filled in the blank. Still, it bothered Elise, maybe because there was something immature and school yard about it. A nickname given to a buddy.

The Savannah Killer. She could live with that. It was better than the last one the media had come up with: the Organ Thief.

"Caroline was the sweetest person," the girl said as they sat down at a table that had been made from a door. "The sweetest. Like wouldn't hurt a fly."

Standard questions were answered. *No unusual activity. No unusual people around.* They asked to see Caroline's room and were led to a small space at the end of a hallway. Dark, with piles of clothes everywhere, and a floor that slanted toward the street, a clue that it had once been a porch.

"A really weird place for a mayor's daughter to live," Elise noted.

"Her father kicked her out," the roommate said from her position in the doorway, arms crossed at her waist as if she had a stomachache. "He cut her off completely. He was mad because she turned down Harvard to stay in Savannah and go to school."

David and Elise looked at each other. She could read his mind. *Yep, not who he wants people to think he is.*

The girl glanced around the room, then down at her feet. "Is it okay if I don't stay in here? I can't deal with being in her room right now."

David's expression went sympathetic. "Sure."

The girl left, and David said, "Mayor has a daughter. She's an embarrassment to him. Enter serial killer . . ."

"Are you implying that the mayor might have staged his daughter's murder to look like the previous ones? That's ludicrous."

"Parents kill," David said softly.

He would know. She shook her head.

"And with an election just around the corner . . ."

"I'm not buying that."

"Okay, if we back-burner the mayor for now, I say the killer, at the very least, knew her," David said. "Or rather, he knew who she was."

"We don't know that, but like you said, it does seem more than a coincidence."

They spent two hours digging through the girl's belongings, turning up nothing. When they were done, they bagged and attached an evidence seal to her laptop. At headquarters it would be combed for clues, with special attention paid to e-mails and social-networking sites. Then they left the building and headed for the bar where Caroline had worked.

"When she left, I thought she was taking a cab. Woulda given her a lift if I'd known she was walking."

Elise and David sat in a dark bar called the Chameleon. Both of them were drinking iced tea with pink umbrellas while interviewing the bartender, a guy of about thirty with a lot of face jewelry and a neck tattoo.

"Did anything unusual happen two nights ago?" Elise asked.

"It was pretty normal."

"Any interactions with customers that caught your attention?" David added. "Anybody you'd never seen in the bar before. Someone who might have struck you as a bit odd?"

"We get the regulars, but we also get tourists, so a new face isn't going to stand out, ya know?"

"Did Caroline mention anybody? Or act in the least unusual herself?" Elise asked. "We're looking for someone who might have been watching her, a person she might have served."

The guy thought a moment, then shook his head. "We were fairly busy for a weeknight, so I was focused on my job. I didn't know what was going on beyond filling my orders."

Elise gave him her card and told him to call her if he thought of anything.

"We're going to need copies of all your receipts for the evening," David told him. "We're especially interested in credit card signatures and the tables Caroline waited on."

"Each waitress has a specific number, so it'll be easy to sort out Caroline's."

While they waited for the owner to go through the receipts, they ordered sandwiches and fries. Someone turned on the television in the corner, and a short while later there was Mayor Chesterfield on the screen, a cluster of microphones in front of him.

"We're bringing in an FBI profiler," he said. "A specialist."

"I was under the impression the Savannah Police Department had its own profiler," someone said.

"We have an officer who used to be a profiler for the FBI, but that's no longer his job description. The expert we're bringing in is the best in the country." A close-up of the mayor. "I want to make sure another young woman doesn't lose her life. I want to make sure another parent doesn't lose his daughter to this madman."

"Would you care to comment on what took place today at the crime scene with Homicide Detective Elise Sandburg?"

"That was an unfortunate incident that I deeply regret," the mayor said. "And I hope Detective Sandburg will accept my sincerest apologies when I next see her."

"Can you give us the name of the FBI agent you're bringing in? The specialist?" a woman off-screen asked.

"Special Agent Victor Lamont."

David inhaled sharply.

"Know him?" Elise asked.

"We trained and worked together at Quantico. Roomed together for a while too." His voice was strained.

"Is he good?"

"He thinks so." David tossed his pink umbrella aside and took a long swallow of tea. Elise got the idea he would have liked for it to have been something stronger. He put the glass down but didn't look at her. "An arrogant prick, unless he's changed."

"I don't care how obnoxious and arrogant he is if he can help us catch this guy."

After a long silence David pushed his half-finished sandwich away and dropped back in his chair. "I don't think I'll be able to work with him."

"You'll have to put aside your differences. Be adult." She pinched her straw between two fingers and looked up at him. "What did he do? Short-sheet your bed?"

"No." The next words came as a reluctant admission. "But he slept in it."

She let go of the straw.

"When I was in Washington State working on the Puget Sound case, that bastard was back in Virginia sleeping with my wife."

CHAPTER 15

Vic Lamont.

It was a name David had hoped to never hear again, the man himself someone David sure as hell had hoped to never *see* again. But the biggest shock of the day wasn't finding out that Lamont was coming to Savannah; it was finding out that the mere mention of the bastard's name made David's heart pound and his mouth go dry.

Savannah was miles from David's old life, both literally and figuratively. He'd planted new roots here. Started over. He had friends, and, except for the constant ache caused by the loss of his son, he thought he'd put the past behind him.

Enter Vic Lamont.

People trick themselves into thinking they've moved on. That's what it was. David had made progress during his waking hours, but sleeping was another story. He dreamed about the people who'd caused him so much pain—those people being his now-dead ex-wife and Lamont. And in that dream, David was a hero. He saved his son's life over and over, arriving home in time to pull him from the tub, alive and breathing. Good versus evil, and good won.

But the blackness was back, eating a hole in his gut so it could live and sleep and spread dark thoughts. It had been close to two years since David had felt this bad. Shaky and helpless and distracted, while at the same time wanting to drive a fist through the wall. In the past, the things he turned to were prescription drugs, alcohol, and sex with strangers. All seemed nice choices right now.

In an attempt to distract himself from impulses that in the end would only make things worse, David lay down on the couch and grabbed the remote control. His Siamese cat, Isobel, jumped on his stomach and settled herself on his chest, just below his chin, purring loudly while David worked his way through channels until he came to the last five minutes of the eleven o'clock news. Footage of the crime scene. A bit about the mayor and Elise. The female anchor didn't come right out and say that the mayor had struck the head of homicide.

"Public disagreement," she called it. The report concluded with the Twitter photo of Elise. It looked like a mug shot.

David shut off the television and was contemplating taking Strata Luna up on her open offer to send him a prostitute, when his phone rang. He checked the screen, saw a photo of Elise's unbruised face. He didn't answer. She was too perceptive. Back there at the bar a few hours ago she'd tried to get him to spill his guts, but he'd told her nothing other than the few words about Lamont sleeping with Beth. That was all she needed to know.

The phone stopped ringing. A minute later the screen brightened and a banner appeared, indicating a message. He was about to listen to it when the phone rang again. Knowing Elise wouldn't give up, he answered this time.

"Want to talk about it?" she asked.

David struggled to pull himself out of the black pit. He made an attempt to sound adequately level, a combination of chirpy and irritated. "If I wanted to talk about it, I would have talked about it earlier. No, I don't want to talk about it."

"Just checking. Did you see the news?"

"Caught the tail end of it. They're calling it a public disagreement."

She let out a dry laugh. "I heard that. Are you home?"

"Yes."

"Alone?"

"Yes."

A pause. "Maybe you shouldn't be by yourself."

Damn. She knew he was fighting a meltdown. Was she calling to lend an ear, or make sure he didn't arrive at work tomorrow with a hangover or still drunk? He was struggling to formulate a casual and reassuring reply when a knock sounded on the door. Isobel let out a cry of alarm, jumped off David's chest, and vanished into the bedroom. Typical MO. Figuring it was Elise outside his apartment, he said, "You didn't have to come over." He got up from the couch and opened the door, the phone still in his hand.

Not Elise.

But close.

Standing in the dark hallway was Jackson Sweet. The man had stopped by a few times, but not often, and never this late.

"Gotta go." David ended the call before Sweet could say anything and alert Elise to the visit. She was already upset enough over David's association with her father, slight as it was. David, of all people, knew what betrayal felt like, and he didn't want to be the one serving it to Elise, but he also wasn't going to ignore someone in need.

Without invitation, the older man stepped inside.

Sweet's clothes had a limp, unwashed sheen; he needed to shave, and he smelled like a trash fire. Was he no longer staying at the shelter? David wondered. But lacking a permanent address and looking like a street person didn't diminish the power Sweet projected.

The folklore about Elise's father was that he had a hard-to-define thing about him. A *thing*. People talked about how his presence filled a room. That was true. But it wasn't overt. And it wasn't anything he deliberately projected. It wasn't calculated. It just *was*. A kind of cool and laid-back quality that emanated from his pores. It took a lot to impress David, but Sweet impressed him.

The man closed the door, then pinned David with eyes reminiscent of Elise's. "I've been following the news about the murders," he said with a voice that was slow and deep and as Georgian as a Southern plantation. "I want to help."

"I appreciate the offer," David told him, "but we typically don't use anybody outside the department unless they're FBI or Georgia Bureau of Investigation."

"I can interview witnesses and suspects. That's my strength."

Oh man. Elise would love that. "Probably not a good idea," David said.

Getting straight to the point, Sweet said, "Coretta contacted me."

David frowned in surprise. "And?"

"She asked me to come in tomorrow. I just stopped by to let you know. I thought maybe you could break it to Elise."

Holy hell.

David had long suspected that Coretta hadn't left her Gullah heritage far behind, so it shouldn't have been a surprise to find that she'd reached out to Jackson Sweet in a time of crisis. But to bring him in to help with the case? Maybe interrogate suspects? Somebody wasn't going to be happy about that. Hell, *David* wasn't happy about it.

David offered Sweet something to drink and eat, but the man declined and didn't hang around. Once he'd vanished into the dark hallway and the door had closed shut behind him, David called Coretta, hoping there'd been some mix-up.

Nope.

"We have to use whatever resources are at our disposal," she said.

"Involving Sweet is a bad idea." It felt weird and wrong to be talking to Coretta about work outside of headquarters. Which was probably a sign that their relationship, or whatever it was, shouldn't be happening.

"I didn't ask for your opinion," she said, clearly angry that he was taking what she probably considered Elise's side in this.

He was tempted to bring up the fiasco that had been the press conference, but he decided her chilly response wasn't inviting any more criticism.

"I want you and Elise to go over the details of the case with Mr. Sweet," Coretta told him. "Bring him up to speed."

"Even the information we haven't yet released?" This was getting odder by the second. He didn't want to think it, but he'd sensed that Coretta was jealous of the relationship he had with Elise. Was Coretta doing this to torment her?

"Yes. Everything. And David? I'll break the news to Elise tomorrow morning at a meeting in my office. I want you and Jackson Sweet to be there."

David disconnected and headed for his bedroom and hopefully sleep; he was dreading tomorrow. But the Jackson Sweet twist had brought with it an unexpected consequence. David was no longer fixating on Vic Lamont.

Standing in the kitchen, Elise contemplated going to David's apartment to make sure he was really all right, but she'd have to either leave Audrey alone or drag her out of bed to bring her along. Both bad ideas.

Instead, she dug out the business card Jay Thomas had given her the day they met. She hadn't bothered to enter his number into her phone. She did so now, then called him.

A groggy voice answered, and she checked the clock: 11:35 p.m. "This is Detective Sandburg." She heard rummaging, heard the click of what sounded like a lamp switch, and imagined him in bed, dressed in striped button pajamas, fumbling for his glasses.

"Has there been another murder?" Jay Thomas asked, his voice edged with sleep.

Elise opened the refrigerator, stared at a few shriveled oranges and a pizza box, then closed the door. "No." At least not that they knew of. "I'm calling for a couple of reasons. One, to thank you for intervening earlier today. And two, to tell you to remove the YouTube video you posted." She found a bag of chips in the cupboard, set her phone aside, and opened the package, corn tortillas scattering across the counter.

"That YouTube video isn't mine," he said. "I swear. I wouldn't do that."

"But the Twitter photo is?" she asked, grabbing the phone.

"Um, yeah."

She'd tell him to delete his post, but the damage was done. The photo was trending.

"I already talked about this with Detective Gould," Jay Thomas said.

"You're talking about it with me too." She scooped most of the chips back into the bag and folded the top down. "Are you writing a piece on what happened today? Because if you are, let me remind you that you have a contract."

"This doesn't fall under the boundaries established in the agreement I have with the police department. It's current news."

"You wouldn't have been privy to it if you hadn't been with me."

"I disagree."

"I've felt bad about treating you with suspicion. Not anymore."

"I'm sorry, but I have a job to do. Report the news. I could have sold that photo of you, but I didn't. I posted it to Twitter to circumvent anyone else who might try to do that."

"Noble of you." Pure sarcasm. "If I see a sensationalized story about the altercation with your byline, we're done. Don't expect to get in a car with me again."

She disconnected and began eating chips off the counter.

CHAPTER 16

Elise dreaded being summoned down the hall to Major Hoffman's office. The visits were known to involve a reprimand, often dealing with something David had or hadn't done. And now, since David and the major were dating—well, that put a new spin on things.

Unlike some police departments where walls were glass and afforded little privacy, most offices in the ancient building that housed the Savannah PD were private and full of dark wood and high ceilings. Even the newer updated areas were nothing like the contemporary spaces portrayed in modern cop shows.

The building was old and not very functional, but Elise couldn't picture herself in a modern office on the outskirts of town. It wouldn't feel right. She liked the brick building and the location. She liked being in the heart of the city; she liked that the station was a part of the neighborhood. Whenever anybody brought up the topic of moving, Elise would point out that having a police department downtown established a stronger police presence.

Or maybe she just disliked change.

Major Hoffman's door was as old as everything else. A window of beveled milky glass was held in place by rusty nails from another era. Elise knocked and received the standard invite from the other side. Stepping into the room, she was fully braced for an awkward encounter. What she wasn't prepared for was the sight of her father sitting in one of the heavy wooden chairs positioned along one wall.

Much like the first time she'd seen him, not that long ago, he was dressed in faded jeans, scuffed and ancient work boots, and a button shirt, the cuffs frayed but clean. He was thinner than she remembered, his face more gaunt. Beside him sat David Gould, his hands clasped between his knees, eyes trained on the floor.

David, Jackson Sweet, and Coretta Hoffman.

What the hell?

David looked uncomfortable, Sweet unreadable, and Hoffman, sitting behind her desk, had that air of authority she never seemed to put aside.

"Detective Sandburg," Major Hoffman said in formal greeting. She was dressed in a blue suit that complemented her skin tone. Nearby on the wall was a framed photo of her with a white dog that looked like a miniature poodle. Elise had a hard time imagining David in that picture. "I'm sorry about your black eye and the circumstances under which it came about."

Elise touched her face, feeling the stickiness of the makeup she'd applied earlier to hide the bruise.

"I heard Jay Thomas Paul broke it up," Hoffman added.

"I think it would have ended the same way regardless of his presence." Elise would have felt better about giving him credit if not for the Twitter business.

Hoffman motioned to an empty chair. "Sit down."

"I'd rather stand."

"Suit yourself." The major shrugged. "As you already know, we've contacted the FBI to request their aid in solving the murders of these young women. After much discussion with Detective Gould about the case, I've decided to also enlist the help of someone else."

After much discussion with Detective Gould.

Really?

Jackson Sweet was watching Elise with silent intensity.

The man had a strange way of unplugging from his surroundings. Just a body in the room. So deceptive, because he seemed to be able to turn himself on and off. Kind of like a cat that could wait hours without moving. And then something imperceptible shifted, and even though there was no discernible change, his presence expanded. Just sitting there, hardly moving, watching her.

Had she imagined the change? Then she had another thought. David, powerful in his own right, dimmed next to her father, dimmed and almost vanished. Her father would be in his late fifties now, yet she could feel his power. It was something charismatic leaders had. Something serial killers had.

Then Major Hoffman dropped the bomb, and the room got weirder. "Mr. Sweet has agreed to consult on the case."

Now both men were staring at her, David with the look of someone braced for conflict, Sweet with something more like a smirk of defiance.

Elise thought about how her father had snuck around behind her back to meet with Audrey after school. And now . . . Now he was worming his way into Elise's work life. He'd also been at the Murphy crime scene. Why? Curiosity? Or was it more than that? Another question: Had *he* approached Major Hoffman?

"That's ludicrous," Elise said. Maybe not the best choice of words, and certainly words she shouldn't have spoken to the chief of police. "He has no qualifications," Elise went on to explain, speaking as if her father weren't in the room. "Unless being dead for thirty-some years qualifies him." Now it was her turn to smirk.

"I shouldn't have to remind you that Mr. Sweet was a sheriff years ago," Hoffman said.

"That's right," Elise told her. "Years ago. The world was different back then. This is like calling in a psychic, or . . ." She locked eyes with David. "Did you know about this?"

Hoffman answered for him. "It was my idea."

"Do you know what the press will do with this information when they find out?" Elise asked. "They'll say we've called in a witch doctor to help with a case we can't solve."

Hoffman sat up straighter in her chair. "I'm hoping we can keep it quiet for a while. And if the press finds out—which they will—we'll deal with it. It won't be the first time they've ridiculed us, and it won't be the last."

"I can't be a part of this," Elise said.

"You don't have a choice," Major Hoffman told her. "The mayor wants this case solved immediately. Immediately, or heads are going to roll. He's already reached beyond Savannah for help, but now he's threatening to get rid of all of us. Everybody. You, me, Detective Gould, and Detective Avery. We'll all be out."

So in desperation she'd called in a flimflam man.

"I want you to make a copy of the case file for Mr. Sweet. Everything. Every minute detail. I want him to be privy to it all."

Elise was beginning to doubt the major's sanity.

She made one final attempt to reason with the woman. "So what if he was some sort of self-proclaimed sheriff for a few years, back before cell phones and the Internet? That's nothing. Hell, he could be a suspect. Did you think of that? This all started after he decided to return from the dead. And the way he's been lurking around crime scenes . . . suspicious."

"That's enough, Elise," Hoffman said, her tone a warning.

But Elise was winding up. "The man's been living underground for decades." She pointed at him without looking in his direction. "Things have changed. Yes, he has a reputation for getting the truth out of people, but I call BS on that. You're grasping at a myth. You know how it is here. People embellish. People make heroes out of criminals. And the stuff about Jackson Sweet? It's *folklore*. Nothing but folklore. Bringing him in on the case is like calling in Harry Potter."

David let out a loud snort—his first comment. The sound had her spinning around in time to see him put a hand to his mouth to hide a smile.

Ass.

"This is a waste of time," Elise said. And David. His betrayal was so deep. Her father. His relationship with Hoffman. They all seemed a tidy little group, and she was on the outside looking in.

She had to get away from them before she said more she shouldn't say. "Is that all?" she asked, trying to keep her voice from shaking.

Hoffman gave her a long look, then replied, "Yes."

Elise turned to Sweet, whose only movement since she'd stepped into the room had been a slight turn of the head. "I'll get everything to you by tomorrow."

Then she left, David on her heels.

"Elise."

She ignored him and kept walking, down the hall to her office.

David followed her inside. She slammed the door, spun around, and without a hiccup, shoved him, a hand to each of his shoulders—the kind of attack she'd never launched on anyone until recently. First Jay Thomas, and now David.

"Why didn't you tell me about this?" Elise demanded. "How long have you known? Was it something you and Hoffman cooked up?" With each question, she shoved.

"Stop." David didn't fight back, and that annoyed her even more. And he'd been uncharacteristically quiet in Hoffman's office. That annoyed her too.

She shoved him again. Not like a cop, but like some kid in the school yard.

"I said, stop," David said.

She shoved.

In an exasperated movement, he grabbed her, spun her around, and pressed her face to her desk, her arm pinned behind her. He didn't apply much pressure, just control. She could continue to fight him, but the undignified position reset her brain.

"Ass," she muttered, her mouth against the morning's folded newspaper. "You ass."

"It wasn't my idea," David said.

"Bull."

"Hoffman asked me what I thought about her decision to bring your father in. I told her you wouldn't like it."

She believed him, even though Hoffman had called the conversation she'd had with David a discussion. Even though she'd made it sound as if he might have played a part in Sweet's presence here today. But Elise had never known David to lie.

"Did you get eight down?" David asked.

It took her a few beats to realize he was talking about the crossword puzzle under her nose. She laughed. Bless her own heart, she laughed. Leave it to David to defuse a tense situation.

"The last passenger pigeon," David said. "That was the clue."

"You'll have to talk to the guy with three names."

"Are you gonna quit shoving me?" David asked as he loosened his hold on her.

Elise nodded, and he released her. She straightened, rotated her shoulders, and adjusted her neck. Then, without looking at him, she walked away.

CHAPTER 17

Vic Lamont.

It didn't sound like a real name. What it sounded like was one of those names Hollywood studios gave their actors back in the fifties. But you could bet David had done his research on his ex-partner. Birth name. Parents were Lois and Harvey Lamont, second-generation United States citizens, Victor's French grandparents having immigrated in the late 1800s. Lamont himself was known to toss some French around, but David always suspected he knew about ten or twenty words, total. And now the ass was droning on and on about the killer's profile.

It was the morning after the meeting about Jackson Sweet. Fifteen minutes earlier Major Coretta Hoffman had introduced Lamont to the room—a crowd made up of about twenty officers plus Jay Thomas Paul and Jackson Sweet, Sweet standing against the wall in the back of the room, hands in his pockets, Jay Thomas sitting next to Elise. Jay Thomas and Elise occupied the front row, smack in the center, like a couple of good students, while David sulked in the back, yesterday's unfinished crossword puzzle braced against one knee, the printed profile Lamont had supplied abandoned on the floor beside David's chair.

If David were to pick it up and look at it, he knew it would say the same stuff Lamont was going on about. Killer was a white male, about thirty years of age. Probably had a couple years of a trade school but dropped out before he finished. Blah, blah, blah. Profiling 101. And then Lamont went on to embellish his description, from the way the guy dressed to the kind of movies he watched and the kind of books he read and the kind of car he drove.

"Chevy Caprice. And as far as personality traits—this is a guy people made fun of, someone who would never in a million years attract the attention of the women he's killing."

And everybody ate it up. Just *ate it up*. David wanted to kill someone himself.

He'd tried to get out of coming to the briefing.

"Just grab a copy of the profile for me," he'd told Elise when they'd discussed it earlier in their office.

She'd given him that look that said she didn't want to get all bossy on him. And then Hoffman had sent him a text, telling him she'd see him there.

Coretta didn't know about Lamont. Didn't know about the history he and David shared. Why? Because when David had applied for the job at Savannah PD, he'd left out that stuff, of course. And David was pretty sure he wasn't going to tell her now either. Which went to show just what kind of relationship he had with the major.

Not wanting to make things worse than they already were, he'd come to the briefing. But he'd taken a seat as far from the podium as possible and only glanced up once or twice, enough to note that Lamont hadn't gotten fat and bald the way David had hoped. He was trim and in shape, and he seemed to have a full head of dark brown hair. But there was still time for hair loss. Always time for hair loss.

"David."

The sound of Coretta's voice cut through his childish thoughts. He looked across the expanse of people seated in front of him to lock eyes with Coretta, while trying to ignore the man standing beside her. "Yes, Major?"

"Do you have anything to add to Agent Lamont's profile? Or anything you want to add to the conversation?"

He sometimes wondered if she went out of her way to publicly humiliate him in order to squelch any rumors that they might be sleeping together.

"No."

He looked back at the crossword puzzle. Eight down: *The last passenger pigeon.*

What the hell did that mean? Last passenger pigeon?

Extinct?

No, that was seven letters. He needed six.

"Are you sure?" Coretta asked. "I couldn't help but notice that you've been busy jotting things down."

David reluctantly tore himself away from the folded newspaper. Coretta was waiting. Damn, he could get himself into some messes.

His gaze tracked to the left, enough to take in the crisp jacket, the white shirt, the maroon tie. There was that clean jaw, plus that rigid and unreadable expression on Vic Lamont's face. Old-school FBI. David wanted to jump to his feet and shout, *You fucked my wife!* Instead, he tucked his pen behind his ear and leaned back in his chair.

He was pretty sure he was the antithesis of Lamont. And maybe that was his reaction to his days in the FBI. Rather than crisp and tidy, David's white shirt with the turned-up sleeves was rumpled, and his jaw needed a shave.

He nodded as he gripped the newspaper with both hands, hands that were shaking a little. Just a little. "Eight down. Do you know the answer to eight down?"

Lamont's demeanor shifted slightly. Taken aback. Confused. "Eight down?"

"*The last passenger pigeon*. And it's not 'extinct.' Too many letters."

While he said this, David kept his eyes on Lamont. Never blinking, never wavering. And he sure as hell didn't look at Coretta. He didn't want to know what kind of expression she had on her face. And he sure as hell didn't look at Elise, who was probably at this very moment furrowing her brow and shooting him a harsh warning.

He and Lamont didn't break their gaze. It was like high noon and each was waiting for the other to draw. And while they waited, time spread across the floor. Not only spread, but moved backward. David recalled when he and Lamont had worked cases together *while Lamont was sleeping with Beth*. If David followed the thread all the way to the beginning, Lamont could actually be indirectly blamed for the death of David's son.

Lamont told Beth he wanted her, but he didn't want a kid. So Beth took care of that little problem.

A hesitant voice broke the silence. "Martha."

That came from the guy with three names.

"What?" David asked.

"The last living passenger pigeon was Martha."

The tension broke, and David pulled his gaze away from Lamont to focus on Jay Thomas Paul. "Martha?"

"She died of old age in 1914 in the Cincinnati Zoo. Some people said she was twenty-nine."

David plucked his pen from behind his ear and bowed his head to scrutinize the paper in his hands. He filled in the squares. "I didn't know she had a name."

"Oh yeah," Jay Thomas said, eager to share his knowledge. "She's famous."

Somehow talk of the last passenger pigeon, along with the presence of Lamont, someone from David's old life, someone David had talked and joked with before Christian's death, someone who'd played a role in that awful thing, no matter how unwittingly—all of those things took the time that was now spread across the floor and folded it back on David.

A beautiful son with golden hair that smelled of soap and childhood filled David's head, and his arms felt the weight of his child as he'd carried him to his bed at night and tucked him in, leaving the night-light on because Christian was afraid of the dark.

I'm scared, Daddy.

David would always reassure him that there were no monsters in their house. *No monsters.*

In truth, the monster was down the hall, asleep in her bed.

"I was asking what you think about the case, not about today's crossword puzzle," Coretta said. And man, was she mad.

"Believe me, you don't really want to know what I think."

"Yes, I do. We all do."

"Okay." He adjusted his ankle on his knee. "I think the profile is bullshit. That's what I think."

A few gasps. Mouths dropped open. A fresh wave of irritation flashed across Coretta's face. "Okay, this meeting is over unless anybody other than Detective Gould has something to add."

People got to their feet, clutching and folding the profile that had been supplied to them. David was almost out the door when Coretta put a hand to his arm, stopping him. "My office," she said.

Yeah, they should probably break up.

.   .   .

"I'm not sure what's going on with you." Coretta grabbed a package of crackers from her desk. "But I can guess. You're jealous of Lamont."

"Jealous?" David blew air out his nose.

"He's an FBI agent. A profiler. You used to be an FBI agent and a profiler."

"Oh, right."

"So just shut it off." She couldn't get the package open. She gave up and tossed it down on her desk, then said with anger, "You can be so childish."

"I try."

"That's what I'm talking about."

"Okay, okay. I'm sorry." He swept up the crackers, tore open one end of the package, and handed them to her.

Her anger evaporated so quickly, he wondered if she'd really been mad in the first place or merely doing her job. "Will you stop by tonight?" she asked, smiling as she accepted the open crackers.

His phone announced a text message. He checked the screen: *Elise.*

"I'll make a low-country boil," Coretta said. "You bring wine."

"You just said I was childish." Had his voice sounded a bit petulant there?

She abandoned the crackers, circled the desk, and pressed herself against him. "I like immature men who act like boys." She unzipped his pants and stuck her hand inside, grabbing him.

He let out a gasp. "Isn't that a bit like pedophilia?" he asked, holding his breath while he spoke.

She laughed. "You're darling." Her laughter faded, and her expression became serious. David was pretty sure she wanted sex. Right now, right here.

He held up his phone with the text message. "Gotta go. Detective Sandburg wants to discuss Lamont's profile with me."

She backed off, and he quickly zipped his pants before she got any more ideas.

"That's adult of you." She sounded disappointed.

CHAPTER 18

Alarm set, Elise stepped out the back door. Gripping the handle of her briefcase, insulated coffee mug tucked under her arm, she removed the key from the lock and hurried down the steps in the direction of her car and the small parking spot next to the garage. Audrey was already off to school, and even though the day had hardly begun, Elise was running late.

A movement in the shrubbery caught her eye. And there she went again. All reflex and no thought, she dropped the mug, lid flying, coffee splashing her black slacks as she pulled her weapon.

Another trembling of branches and Jackson Sweet emerged, a backpack draped over one shoulder. "I've gone over the case files," he said in a deadpan voice, as if he'd stepped through an office door instead of emerging from greenery, as if his stalking behavior weren't in any way unacceptable, "and I'd like to talk to you about a few things."

She exhaled and returned her gun to her shoulder holster. "What are you doing here?"

"As I'm sure you already know, I've been trying to catch up with you." His voice was thick with his low-country accent. Like hers, but stronger. "At the police department, and last night—knocking on your front door. You don't seem to be all that willing to talk to me."

No surprise. At the Savannah PD, she'd ducked into the restroom and also done an about-face to head for the stairs when she spotted him coming her way. Last night when he knocked at the front door, she'd turned off the porch light.

"I'd suggest anything you want to discuss you discuss with David Gould or Major Hoffman," Elise said.

"You're the head of homicide."

Elise was still trying to figure out how Sweet had managed to insinuate himself in her life. "You went to Major Hoffman, didn't you?" she asked. "You suggested she put you on the case."

"So what if I did?"

"I don't know what you're doing or why you're doing this. You and I—we don't have a relationship." She thought about picking up the mug, thought about going back inside and getting more coffee, but gave up on both ideas. She'd get the mug later. She'd get coffee at headquarters. "We will never have a relationship," she said. "And I want you to leave Audrey alone. I don't want you hanging around her school, waiting for her to get out. Do you understand?"

"A grandfather taking his granddaughter out for tea—that's harmless."

"Nothing about you is harmless."

"I plan to keep seeing her."

"Then I'll get a restraining order."

He smiled. "You have no grounds."

"I know people."

His smile faded. He understood she would do whatever it took to keep him away from her child.

"So you don't want to hear any of my theories?" he asked.

"Talk to David. Talk to Major Hoffman. Stay away from me. And stay away from my house."

"I don't blame you. I really don't, but this is more important than your hatred of me. Lives are at stake. A killer is out there. Can't we put our history aside, at least for now?"

"David. Major Hoffman."

"I admire your unwavering dislike. I'd probably feel the same if I were in your position. You're tough. Like me."

"I'm *nothing* like you. Nothing. We wouldn't even be having this conversation if I'd died in that cemetery where I was left as a baby. All because of you. It's hard to let go of that kind of history."

"I'm sorry it's made you so bitter, but believe me when I say your heritage and what happened to you have made you the strong woman you are today."

Elise let out a snort. "So I should *thank* you?" She looked down at her black slacks and coffee splatter. "I have to go." She hit the "Unlock" button on her key fob and charged for her car.

He followed.

Opening the door, she tossed her briefcase across the console to the passenger seat.

"Wait, Elise. Please wait."

She'd planned to hop in the vehicle and not give him another glance as she pulled away, but the desperation in his tone caused her to hesitate.

"There's something I need to tell you." He planted his hands on the hood of the car and looked into her eyes, seeming to come to a decision. "What I'm about to share can't go beyond you," Sweet said. "No one else can know. Not David or Audrey or Strata Luna."

She almost rolled her eyes. This was where he'd tell her he had another family somewhere in Mexico. Or this was where he'd make up some wild story about being chased by a band of zombies.

He circled the car to stand three feet from her. He checked behind him, then leaned in close. "I was recruited. By a secret government organization." He paused for her reaction. He didn't have long to wait, because his "revelation" was more ridiculous than she could have imagined.

"Oh my God." Why hadn't she driven away when she'd had the chance? "Can't you just tell the truth for once in your life?" she asked. "It's not like you have anything to lose in this relationship. Why not just tell me you have a wife and family in another part of the country, or whatever it is you're hiding?"

"I'm *trying* to tell you."

"I have to go."

"Please. Two minutes."

She blinked. "You told me you left to protect me. Now you're saying that was a lie?"

"Oh, there was that too. Listen, I want to help."

"Why?"

As he spoke, he placed a splayed hand against the hood of the vehicle. "What kind of question is that?"

"You want to know what I think? I think you're using this case to hang around me."

"I like to stop bad men from doing bad things."

"That's funny, because as I understand it, *you* are a bad man."

"It takes a bad man to know a bad man."

No argument there. "You've killed people."

"Where'd you hear that?"

"Around." More of the folklore.

"I *have* killed people."

His admission surprised her. Not that he'd killed, but that he'd admitted to it.

"People who needed to die. Not innocents." He looked over both shoulders, then refocused on her. "Before you were born, I already had the reputation of being able to extract confessions from criminals," he said in a low and confidential voice. "But that didn't always work. A few times, when I didn't get the proof I needed to put someone away, I took care of it myself."

Judge, jury, and executioner. She could read between the lines. "You mean you killed a suspect."

Tip of the head, eyebrows raised. Affirmative. "These were bad people, Elise. People who couldn't be allowed to continue inflicting harm."

"More than one." A statement. "You killed more than one."

"Yes."

He didn't appear remorseful. She had a psychopath hanging around her daughter.

"You have to understand. These were men who'd done terrible things to children. And women. They needed to die."

"That wasn't for you to decide."

"Why not me? Why not the person who had an unfiltered view of what was going on, and not some chosen jury listening to sifted and diluted evidence that might or might not put someone away? Especially if that someone had money and influence."

Elise resented his ability to upset her. He didn't deserve that kind of power.

"There was one particular man," he said. "A case you won't find anywhere because all records have been destroyed. He was almost the end of me. I have to admit, by that time I was getting careless and cocky and sloppy. And yes, I started thinking I was above the law. After I killed him, an investigation was launched, and it wasn't long before they were getting close, and I knew I'd probably end up with the death sentence."

"So you ran."

"I thought about it, and I probably would have. Just hop a train and live on the rails and in the street. But I was approached by an undercover branch of the FBI. In return for my cooperation, I was given full immunity, and the case was not only closed, all records were destroyed. They helped me fake my own death. They helped me disappear."

Now she did roll her eyes. "And what was this fabricated position? Why did the FBI want you so desperately, enough to destroy evidence to a homicide?"

"I broke people."

"Tortured them?"

"That usually wasn't necessary, but . . ."

"I'll ask David about this secret group, this secret FBI club."

"Go ahead, but he won't have heard of it. I worked for them for ten years. Then I left. Or I should say, they let me leave. But I was still dead to the rest of the world."

"Why are you telling me this now?"

He ratcheted things up. "I'm dying. For real this time."

If anybody else had spoken those words, Elise's heart would have broken a little. But she wasn't an idiot. He was playing her. When she didn't swallow his FBI story, he pulled out something else. Only a naive child would fall for his act, so she steeled herself against any shred of sympathy she might feel. "We're all dying."

"Believe it, don't believe it. It's your choice. But I wanted to see you, and I wanted to see Audrey and Strata Luna."

"Before you died?"

"Yes."

"You didn't have to get involved in this case to see us."

"You needed help. I get the truth out of people. And I'm telling the truth."

"Oh, I don't doubt that you've killed people." She could feel it in him.

"And you haven't?"

"No. Never."

"What about Marie Luna?"

Elise inhaled.

"My daughter," he reminded her. "Strata Luna's daughter." He was watching her closely now. "Your half sister."

"I did not kill Marie Luna." That honor went to Detective Avery, but she'd been there.

"You would have, so don't tell me you don't believe in killing when it's necessary. Don't tell me you wouldn't have done exactly what I've done. Don't tell me you wouldn't have killed your half sister."

"Not the same."

"Exactly the same."

His rationalization was similar to a serial killer's. "Marie Luna was killed to save a life," she said.

"That's what I mean. We do what we have to do. You're just like me, Elise. Just like me."

No.

He pushed himself away from the car. "I would advise you to not mention this conversation to anyone, not even David Gould."

"Are you threatening me now?"

"I would never do that. But saying anything could put your life in danger."

Anger exploded in her; words came rushing out. She shouted, not even sure of what she was saying. Something about how blood didn't make family; that loyalty and love made family. And something about how he had no right to haunt her the way he was, and he had no right to see Audrey. "You are nothing to us. *Nothing.*" Those were the awful things that poured from her mouth, each sentence seeming to beat him down a little more.

She, more than anyone, knew how words had power. Words could hurt more than a physical blow, but it surprised her to see that *her* words could hurt *him*. That *her* words had any impact at all. But they did.

She calmed down enough to notice that his breathing was shallow, as if inhaling and exhaling were too much work. He tilted a little, then reached out and grabbed for something that wasn't there.

In the short time he'd stood behind her house, he'd seemed to shrink, and the force that emanated from him had dimmed. Now he looked like a pathetic old man.

How had he gotten there? Walked? More to the point, was he really sick? "Do you want me to call a cab?" she asked.

He shook his head, turning his back to her. "I won't bother you again," he said over his shoulder as he took one faltering step after the other.

A trick? A final attempt to garner sympathy?

The man's entire life had been a lie, so how was she to know? And the truth was, she knew absolutely nothing about Jackson Sweet other than the legend of exaggerations and half-truths that surrounded him.

Moving down the alley, he stopped, teetered, and dropped to his knees. A second later he pitched forward.

She watched him for several heartbeats, waiting for him to get up, waiting for the scene to correct itself. It didn't. He lay there, unmoving.

Heart attack?

She ran to him and fell to her own knees beside him, rolling him to his back.

His face was gray, his lips blue.

She pulled out her cell phone and called 911. The dispatcher led her through a list of instructions. She checked his vitals. He had a weak, irregular pulse, and his breathing was shallow.

The ambulance arrived within minutes. An oxygen mask was put in place, and Sweet was lifted to a gurney while Elise gave them what details she could supply—which amounted to pretty much nothing.

"You can ride in back with him," one of the EMTs told her.

Ride with him? "That's okay. I'll follow in my car."

Fifteen minutes later, Elise was in the ER waiting room. She took a seat. As she sat there, she went through possible people she could call to relieve her of this duty. The list was short. David, Strata Luna, and Major Hoffman, the major seeming the most unlikely.

This episode put a new spin on things and carried a new tide of resentment combined with fear. Was Sweet really dying? If so, why her fear? What did she care? How would his death change anything, since he'd been dead all of Elise's life until a short time ago? And more to the point, why was she feeling anxious as if deep down she'd taken some weird sense of comfort in knowing he was alive and nearby even if she wanted nothing to do with him?

Confused emotions battled it out as a young doctor appeared, his gaze sweeping the waiting room and settling on her as he approached. "Are you Jackson Sweet's daughter?"

It didn't get much more personal. A daughter waiting anxiously to hear how her father was. If the doctor only knew.

She got to her feet and nodded.

The doctor came closer and hunched his shoulders, the action seeming to create privacy in a public place. "As I'm sure you know, your father's condition is serious, but then we *are* talking about cancer."

"Cancer?" Her heart thudded.

"You didn't know?"

"We aren't close."

"It might seem strange, but it's not unusual for a parent to keep this kind of news from a child. Parents want to protect their children, and they don't want to be a burden."

No need to explain the details of her relationship with Sweet to a total stranger. "What kind of cancer?"

"Hodgkin's lymphoma. The prognosis for this type is fairly good because it tends to respond well to chemotherapy, but home care is essential, especially with his heart condition."

The bad news just kept coming. "What kind of heart condition?"

"Arrhythmia and mild congestive heart failure. He needs to take care of himself, and he apparently hasn't started chemo. Says he has no plans to get it. That needs to be remedied. With it, his chances for survival are decent. Does he live by himself?"

"Yes."

"Right now we have him on IV fluids because he's severely dehydrated. I want to keep him several hours for observation. If he's stabilized by late afternoon, we'll release him. But I can't release him without assurance that he won't be left alone."

Elise shook her head. "That's out of the question." Apparently he didn't know who they were. Maybe she and her dad weren't as locally famous as she thought. Or maybe the doctor was new in town.

"We sometimes send recovering patients to a place that's voluntarily run." He could see she wanted no part of Sweet's home care. "I might be able to get him in there."

She grabbed at the idea. "Please look into it."

The young man didn't try very hard to hide his disappointment in her. She, not Sweet, was coming across as the bad guy here. "He's not my father," she found herself saying. Not a lie. What she meant was that he might have been her biological father, but he wasn't a *father* father.

"I could have sworn he said you were his daughter."

"He likes to think I am."

"I'll see what I can arrange." The doctor vanished, then returned ten minutes later. "We got lucky, and they happen to have an empty bed just vacated today. I spoke to the woman in charge, and they'll save the spot for him. We'll take care of everything, including getting him there." He handed Elise a piece of paper with an address and phone number. "In case you want to stop in and see him."

Elise checked the address, recognizing the location as a high-crime and drug area, but that was where free beds were located.

CHAPTER 19

On her way home from work, Elise pulled out the address the doctor had given her that morning. Earlier, Elise broke the news of Sweet's illness to David and Major Hoffman.

"Let's keep this to ourselves," Hoffman had said, making it clear she still wanted Sweet involved in the case. If a cancer diagnosis didn't change the woman's mind about bringing Sweet on board, nothing would.

As expected, the voluntary care center was a sad place, a dark place, probably fifty times as depressing as David's apartment, and that was saying something.

"I'm here to see Jackson Sweet," Elise told the woman sitting in a metal folding chair at the rummage sale desk near the front door.

"Up two flights of stairs, down the hall, third room on the right."

"Thanks."

The wooden stairs were bowed and bare in the middle where a million feet had worn the paint away. The building smelled like urine and feces and food you wouldn't want to look at, let alone eat. She passed windows on the way up, but was unable to see through glass that hadn't been cleaned in a century.

She knew the history of the space. A crack house where there had been a bust almost every week and almost as many killings.

The city finally kicked everybody out and sold it to a nonprofit for a dollar. It didn't appear that they'd done much more than bring in patients.

She made a mental note to look into it, see who was behind the nonprofit, see if it was legit, and see what could be done to improve the overall situation. The mayor would be the person to contact, but that wasn't going to happen, not now, probably never. Elise would try city council members.

She found Sweet in his room, sitting in a chair, a thin cotton robe around him as he stared out opaque glass. She rapped lightly on the open door, but he didn't turn his head.

"Now I know there are worse things than dying of cancer," he said without movement. As odd as it seemed, seeing her nemesis brought down so cruelly made her sad. This place might have been okay for some people. Others could have endured it, but for someone like Sweet . . .

"Maybe you could go to Strata Luna's." If she knew he was living in such a state, the Gullah woman would be there in a second.

Her comment about Strata Luna woke him up. "No!" He turned his head, and his eyes held some of the old fire. "I don't want her to know about the cancer."

Elise stepped deeper into the room, taking note of the uneaten food on the plastic tray. Green gelatin, macaroni, and some kind of meat that looked like it had come from a can.

"So the cancer is the reason you came out of hiding?" she asked, finally ready to converse with him without being on the defensive. Maybe she'd learn something. Or maybe not.

"I didn't know it was cancer at first," he said. "I just knew something was wrong, and I knew I couldn't live like I was living, hopping trains, sleeping in shelters. One day I just couldn't do it. Didn't have the strength to pull myself into a car."

"When do you start chemotherapy?" She knew the answer but wanted to see if he could be straightforward with her.

"I'm not getting it."

"The doctor said your chances of survival are good—if you have chemo."

"I don't care."

"Are you afraid? I've heard the treatments get rougher as you go along."

"Thanks for the pep talk. And no, I'm not afraid. Not trying to be melodramatic, but I just don't see the point."

He'd been telling the truth about dying. Had he also been telling the truth about his job with the FBI?

She opened a cupboard. Inside were his jeans, shirt, boots, jacket, his backpack. Decision made, she tossed the jacket over her arm and gathered the rest of his clothes, boots on top. "Are these all of your things?"

"What are you doing?"

"Taking you to my place." Maybe Audrey would have more luck convincing him to get the cancer treatment.

CHAPTER 20

Jay Thomas was feeling lonesome, feeling sorry for himself as he sat in the establishment where the mayor's daughter used to work and where she was last seen.

He'd taken a spot at the end of the bar on a stool in what had been Caroline Chesterfield's section. David Gould had mentioned that killers liked to return to the scene of the crime to relive and savor the events of the killing. The Savannah PD even staked out the place for a few days. Nothing had come of it, so Jay decided to take it upon himself to investigate the bar, see what was going on. He considered himself lucky to find an empty seat in the dead girl's section, but then maybe nobody wanted to sit there. Like maybe the killer would return and decide to replay the night.

Not much of a drinker, Jay still managed to polish off two beers. Unfortunately, the alcohol made him feel even more sorry for himself, and the resentments he'd been trying to push aside now became this big neon sign in his brain.

Truth was, shadowing Elise Sandburg and David Gould made him feel like a grade-school kid all over again. The dork wanting to hang out with the cool kids.

His hamburger and fries arrived.

He ate, not with relish and hunger, but more like a spoiled brat who really wanted pizza.

Maybe he *was* immature. Maybe the problem *was* with him. Maybe it had always been with him. They treated him like a pain in the ass and a fool, and it might be possible that he didn't deserve their respect.

A depressing thought.

Another beer later and he wasn't feeling much better. Looking for a diversion, he pulled the day's newspaper from his messenger bag, folded it to the crossword puzzle, and began filling in the squares.

Minutes later someone asked, "Do you compete?"

Jay heard the words, but he figured they weren't for him.

"Do you compete?"

This time Jay looked over to see a tall white guy perched on the stool beside him. Hadn't noticed him sit down. And he must have been there awhile, because he had a half-finished drink in front of him. Something in a short glass, something on ice. Something someone cooler than Jay would drink.

"The crossword puzzle," the guy explained. "I couldn't help but notice how fast you finished it, and I thought maybe you competed in crossword puzzle competitions."

Jay gave him a bashful glance and hunched his shoulders. "No, I just like to work them."

The man was probably several years younger than Jay. "It's popular because of the sly humor," he said.

Jay pegged him for a salesman. Maybe somebody who golfed, but instead of the requisite polo, he wore a white dress shirt, tie removed, collar rumpled. He had one of those haircuts that was precise and tidy and needed to be touched up every couple of weeks, everything topped off with the kind of cologne that smelled like money and sleek cars.

"The puzzles are popular because of the sly humor," the guy repeated, this time with more authority. "There's the surface stuff . . . but then, when you look deeper, there's more."

Wow. He got it. He totally got it.

"Yeah." Jay tried to control his excitement. "It's always there. Even when you think it's just a normal puzzle."

Jay had tried to talk about this very topic to Elise and David; they weren't interested. He'd tried to talk to other people about the deeper meaning of the puzzles. Nothing. So to be sitting in a bar and have a stranger come up and immediately start in on the very thing he'd given up trying to discuss—it made Jay feel good. It fixed the day and it fixed the week.

"I couldn't get six across," the guy said. "Did you get six across? Beanie?"

"Dink," Jay said.

"Never heard of that."

"It's a tough one," Jay said.

"Humorous, though."

"Right."

"What do you think the underlying theme of this puzzle is?" Jay asked, admiring the finished piece, admiring the design and pattern of the layout. Because that was important too. He loved seeing the squares filled in with large capital letters, but he also enjoyed admiring the pattern. That was part of the satisfaction of a completed puzzle. Seeing the design was almost like looking at topography from an airplane.

"I don't know." The guy moved Jay's pen aside, picked up the paper, and scrutinized it. "Fifties slang?"

"Oh, right."

The more they looked, the more they found.

"You obviously aren't from here," the guy said. "Your accent isn't local. I'd peg you as being from New York."

"That's right." Jay went on to explain about his job and how he was shadowing Elise and David. "I thought it would be a fun gig, but they don't like me very much." He couldn't believe he'd confessed something so personal. He picked up his glass, realized it was empty, and put it back down. "But it's not a journalist's job to be liked."

"What *is* a journalist's job?"

Without pause, Jay said, "To tell the truth."

"Whose truth? Yours?"

"What do you mean?"

"My truth might not be the same as your truth. Aren't you really telling your own truth when all is said and done?"

"I suppose so. If you want to get all existential about it."

"Didn't mean to bum you out."

"No, that's okay."

Was he hitting on him? Guys so good-looking and charming didn't ordinarily hit on him. Jay was attracted to both males and females, but he tended to prefer males. Maybe that was just a cop-out on his part, but he found both sexes intriguing in different ways.

"Name's Chuck," the guy said. "Can I buy you a drink?"

Yep. Hitting on him.

"I'll have whatever you're having."

It turned out Chuck was in town for a convention. And yep, a salesman. Salesmen were like sailors, seeking comfort and companionship in any port. Jay didn't blame them. Everybody needed comfort. Everybody wanted to be held.

They talked for hours, so lost in conversation that neither noticed the time.

"Locking the front doors in five minutes," the bartender said.

Jay checked his watch. Almost 3:00 a.m. It seemed like he'd been there only a couple of hours, but when he did the math, he realized it had been more like five.

Once outside, he looked at the guy in the khaki slacks and white shirt. Before he knew it, Jay was asking him if he wanted to come by his motel for another drink. Was there any alcohol in the room? No. He corrected his invitation. "Or coffee."

The place where he was staying had one of those plastic coffeemakers with packaged grounds. Up until now he'd thought there was no way he'd rip one of them open.

The guy smiled. White teeth that practically glowed in the dark. "Sure."

They drove separately, with Jay's new friend following him to a more-than-scummy motel that rented by the hour or the week, located in a questionable neighborhood. They parked on the street and walked through the lobby together.

Would Chuck stay the night? The whole night? In the morning, would they order room service and work the crossword puzzle together? That would truly be a culmination of a perfect night, the working of a crossword. And maybe that was also the appeal of puzzles. They were things people did alone, but a crossword was also something you could share with someone. It was almost intimate.

Inside the room, Jay turned off the bright ceiling light so a single lamp illuminated the space. Like someone on a first date, he fumbled with the coffeemaker, searching for a filter, looking at the cups to see if they were clean, all the while aware of his new friend standing behind him.

His hand shook slightly as he removed the carafe. Turning, he passed Chuck, afraid to so much as glance at him, at the same time enjoying the scent of his cologne, which didn't completely mask male skin and alcohol.

"I'm not sure how this thing works." Jay poured the water into the plastic reservoir, placed the carafe on the warming plate, and hit a small button. A few seconds later the coffeepot made a sound, and a burst of steam and a trickle of water dribbled into the filter where he'd forgotten to put the coffee.

He touched his fingers to his lips, wondering if he should admit his mistake, when a pair of arms wrapped around him and his new friend pressed his body against him. Chuck's erection jabbed into the curve of Jay's ass, making it obvious that neither of them cared about coffee.

"Did you know that a young woman was murdered leaving the Chameleon just a few nights ago?" Jay asked, reaching behind him to dig his fingers into his new friend's slacks.

"I do," Chuck whispered, his breath hot against Jay's cheek. He spun Jay around and threw him down on the bed.

CHAPTER 21

To say it was weird having Jackson Sweet around would have been an understatement.

After his first night in the guest room and first full day at Elise's house, Sweet sat on her blue couch with the ornate wood trim, his cheap hospital slippers protruding from underneath the blanket Strata Luna had spread over his lap earlier when she stopped by to bring him a key lime pie and a mojo that was supposed to return him to excellent health. The mojo was now stinking up the room with something that smelled like mint and urine.

At this point, per Sweet's wishes, Strata Luna didn't know about the cancer, but Elise could tell the Gullah woman suspected Sweet's collapse was due to more than just exhaustion and dehydration. And why wouldn't she? He looked like hell. He was pale, and his arms below the sleeves of the white T-shirt were thin. An old man.

He'd spent the day going over the case files once more while Elise worked the street with David. Home now—for how long she didn't know—Elise took a seat in an overstuffed chair, tucking her bare feet under her while at the same time reluctant to get too comfortable in Sweet's presence. It might make him feel welcome.

"You haven't brought many people in for questioning," he said, closing a manila folder and tossing it aside.

Was he criticizing her? Or just making an observation? "People are afraid to come forward," she said. "If anybody saw anything or heard anything, they're unwilling to share it."

"I can make them talk."

At the moment, he didn't look like he could make a nun raise an eyebrow. And it was no surprise that he'd zeroed in on their lack of witnesses, since Hoffman wanted him involved in the interrogation process. Elise was hoping his poor health might be enough to keep him away from performing that duty.

"We're offering a reward for information leading to the capture," she told him.

"That'll just get you more false leads you'll have to wade through."

The reward had been the mayor's idea. Ten thousand dollars. People would be crawling out of the woodwork for a chance at that.

Elise checked the clock on the wall. Audrey, who was thrilled about their houseguest, would be home from school soon. Elise had some interrogating of her own to do before that. "What were you doing at the Portia Murphy crime scene?"

Late-afternoon light poured in the long front windows of Elise's Victorian home. Even in poor health Sweet's eyes radiated a multitude of strange colors as he watched her. "Am I a suspect?" he asked.

"Shortly after you got to town the murders started. You were at the second crime scene—typical behavior for serial killers. And now you've insinuated yourself into the investigation. And you've admitted to killing people. What do you think?"

He held up a sheet of paper. Lamont's handout. "I don't fit the FBI profile."

"Profiles aren't foolproof."

"So why am I here if I'm a suspect? Keep your friends close and your enemies closer?"

"That's right."

"You aren't thinking very clearly, baby girl. I'm a weak man. The person who did this—" He riffled through another folder and pulled out a color eight-by-ten of Portia Murphy. "Whoever did this was strong."

"You might have had help."

"Don't let your dislike of me send you down a wrong path."

"The word 'dislike' . . ." She paused.

"Too harsh?" he said hopefully.

"Too mild."

He laughed a real laugh. She'd never heard him laugh for real. In fact, she'd hardly seen him smile. "So why are you doing this?" she asked.

And then she had another thought: "Is this about the cancer? Do you think that helping to catch the killer will keep you from going to hell, if you believe in such things?"

"I don't. Believe, that is."

A rap at the front door saved Sweet from further interrogation. It was David. Instead of inviting him in, Elise joined him on the porch, closing the door behind her, out of earshot of Sweet.

"What am I going to do with him?" she asked, unable to keep the panic from her voice.

"He can come to my place, but you know how small it is." David leaned against the wooden railing, hands braced on either side of him. He looked tired. "He can have my bed, and I'll take the couch."

David needed decent sleep when he could catch it, not a few hours on a short, uncomfortable couch. "That's no solution."

He seemed relieved. "What about Strata Luna? Since they're old chums."

"I thought that too, but he doesn't want her to know about the cancer. And I'm not sure it would be a good idea, anyway."

Elise had come to realize Strata Luna wasn't as tough as she led people to believe. And like Sweet, much of her was about creating a persona built on folklore and legend. "I suspect she was in love with him years ago, and I don't think she ever got over him. No need to reopen that wound."

"Yeah, well . . ." He crossed his arms over his chest and looked off in the direction of the street. "Love is weird."

She decided to share what was front and center. "I swear to God he's just doing this to get to me."

"The cancer?" David smiled a little. "That would be devious of him."

"You know what I mean. It's left me with no choice."

"We always have choices."

"Right. I could just put him out on the street, or back in that awful place where he was yesterday."

"You could."

She frowned at him. "But I won't."

"You won't."

"Damn."

"What's that look?" he asked.

She was thinking about how it was too late to have any kind of undamaged relationship with her father. "Do we always want what we can't have?"

"Always."

The turn in conversation made her think of Vic Lamont's profile. "Lamont thinks the killer is someone people made fun of, someone who would never in a million years attract the attention of the women he's killing. But you don't think that, do you?"

"No, I don't. And Lamont's profile is all about pattern. I disagree."

"Have you ever known a serial killer to break pattern?"

"It happens. The Zodiac Killer."

"My theory is that the kills that broke pattern weren't those of the Zodiac Killer," Elise said. "They were simply attributed to him."

"I've had that theory too. It's a sound one."

"So where's this coming from? The idea that the girls aren't a pattern?"

"The mayor's daughter doesn't fit."

"Of course she does."

"She doesn't, and that's what worries me. This was not some random girl, a crime of opportunity. You suspect otherwise, but I still think he knew who she was."

"We don't know that."

"We can't afford to assume otherwise."

"Was he escalating?"

David rolled his eyes.

"What?"

"Let's just leave all that profiler BS out of this. It's deceptive. And in this case, I think completely irrelevant."

"You're letting your feelings for Lamont cloud your judgment."

"I'm not."

"You are. Everything he's saying—you're saying the opposite."

"That's because he's wrong," David said.

"You haven't done any real profiling in years. You used to be one of the best, or so I've heard, but—"

"Or so you've heard?"

"You're the one who keeps telling me that."

"And I'm lying?"

"No, I'm just saying you might be rusty, at best."

"Okay, I'm done." David raised his hands in frustration. "I'm gonna go inside and say hi to your dad. Then I'm out of here."

"Don't call him my dad."

"Okay, I'm gonna go inside and say hi to the voodoo man in your living room."

CHAPTER 22

A few days after stopping by Elise's to visit Jackson Sweet, David jogged down Oglethorpe. As he jogged, he imagined a calendar hanging on the wall, a very specific date circled with a heavy red Sharpie.

It always started as an unnamed dread—until it hit him that this was *the* month. After that, he became acutely aware of the ticking clock as the darkness and sleepless nights increased until the worst day of the year arrived.

The day his son died.

No amount of therapy, no amount of running or drinking or drugs or sex could dull the pain. You had to meet it head-on. You had to embrace it. Accept it. Wear it.

Nothing wrong with sorrow.

But he wasn't there yet. Not this year. He hadn't fully embraced the pain, and right now he was teetering on the edge of going full-blown batshit, the rhythmic slap of his feet against the sidewalk not a sedative but an irritant.

Pack it in.

He cut through Forsyth Park, past the fountain, the shadows of live oaks undulating on the ground in front of him. Back in his apartment, he showered, refreshed Isobel's food, jumped in his car, and headed for work. As he walked to the building, his message alert went off. He silenced it and checked the screen. Text from his mother.

Thinking of you today. I'll call you later.

He appreciated the text and appreciated knowing he wasn't alone in his hurting, but he didn't want to talk to her. Her anniversary-of-death calls made things worse. He knew she'd start out very cool and in control, but then she'd break down. They'd both break down. They always broke down.

Before the day was over, his sister would send him a message followed by an e-mail. Not because she didn't want to bother with a call, but because she understood that he couldn't talk. And maybe she couldn't talk either.

In the office, David wondered if Elise was aware of the significance of the date. Probably not. She didn't seem to be a person who clung to dates. He wished he could be that way, but as the day progressed, his agitation increased. If things had been normal, he wouldn't have come to work at all, but with a killer on the loose, nothing was normal.

He wanted to leave. Just walk out, get in his car, and drive to the nearest bar. Once there, he'd drink himself under the table. Black out. That was the best way to handle these things. Knock yourself out until the day was done.

May twelfth. Just a date.

That was what he always told himself.

Christian was dead. He'd been dead yesterday and he was dead today and he would still be dead tomorrow. So what difference did the date make? It didn't. It shouldn't.

But it did.

David must have been acting weird, because off and on throughout the morning he caught Elise giving him odd glances.

At one point he even caught Jay Thomas shooting Elise a mimed question to which she replied with a shrug.

"Are you okay?" she finally asked once they were alone together.

Should he tell her what day it was? Nah, because then he'd have to go through the sympathy stuff. He hated the sympathy stuff. It was weird, because in some way his strong reaction to this date was almost like saying he didn't grieve for his son the rest of the year, when in truth he ached for him every second, with every breath. The loss of Christian was the blackness David would carry in his soul every moment for the rest of his life—a hollowness that would always be there. Today was no different from yesterday. Somebody had just turned on the spotlight.

Instead of cutting himself open in front of Elise, he said, "I'm feeling a little off, that's all." Then he excused himself and left the office.

Maybe he should have stayed, because upon stepping out the front door of Savannah PD, he almost crashed into Vic Lamont, who was heading inside.

"Hey, Gould."

Up until that moment, David felt he'd done a decent job of keeping his feelings about Lamont to himself. But now, seeing the guy like this, breezing in as if he belonged there, David said, "Your profile is bullshit."

David didn't slow down, just kept walking in the direction of Colonial Park Cemetery behind the police station.

Even though David knew it wasn't fair, he'd always hold Lamont indirectly responsible for Christian's death. Follow the thread, and the thread led back to Lamont's sleeping with David's wife. Maybe he should bring that up, David thought. About how today's date might not have any significance if Vic Lamont hadn't told Beth he would have taken their relationship to the next level if not for her kid.

Angry footsteps told David that Lamont was following him. In the cemetery, David turned to see the guy barreling down on him, his face red. Not a surprise, considering Lamont's massive ego.

"I'm here because *you* can't do your job." Lamont pointed at David's chest. "And the only reason you're here is because you're sleeping with the boss."

Ooh-hoo!

"Yeah, that's right," Lamont said. "It's no secret. Know what else? You were never a good profiler. You blew that case in Puget Sound. You should have had that guy. And your wife? Don't get me started about that. About how you were *living* with her and didn't see what she was. So shut the hell up about my profiling. If you were as good as you think you are, your kid would still be alive."

For the past few years, David's entire existence had been about control, or rather about always feeling on the verge of a meltdown, always feeling he was just one breath away from losing it.

It felt good to let go.

To finally just say, *Come on. Jump. Fall. Stop fighting yourself. Let it happen.* He had just enough cognizance to realize that this was how murderers felt. This was how it happened. It wasn't that one day they just decided to do something aberrant. No, it was that one day they decided to *no longer stop themselves.* And once they experienced that total release, the total embracing of who they were deep down and dark, they realized they were free.

To finally punch that asshole Vic Lamont in the face? It felt great. Should have done it years ago.

And to see the expression on the guy's face? That comical look of shock, followed by indignant anger? Oh yeah.

It was a solid hit, but David was still surprised when Lamont went down, landing with a loud exhale, laid out flat on his back in the grass.

David had little time to enjoy the scene, though, because Lamont didn't stay down. He scrambled to his feet and charged, not with any technique, but rather an angry animal kind of thing, his head aimed at David's stomach.

This time they both crashed to the ground. And damn if every punch of Lamont's fist didn't feel good. After a point, David wasn't even sure if he was hitting back anymore. Maybe he was just lying there, enjoying being pummeled.

It didn't take long for the commotion to draw the attention of more than just tourists wandering through the cemetery, cameras in hand. Pretty soon officers in blue were running toward them. Hands pulled Lamont away, and David almost laughed at the looks of astonishment when they saw that David was the one getting the shit beaten out of him.

"That son of a bitch attacked me," Lamont said, his arms pinned, jacket torn, nose bleeding.

David panned the crowd from his position on the ground, stopping when his gaze landed on Jay Thomas Paul. Big eyes—and that goddamn camera. David made a mental note to delete the journalist's files. Or maybe just smash his camera.

"Did you attack him?" The question came from none other than Major Hoffman, undoubtedly alerted by the noise.

David wiped at his nose and checked the back of his hand for blood, happy to see quite a bit. "Yep," he said. "I threw the first punch." He felt euphoric.

"In my office. Just you." Hoffman turned and strode away.

This wouldn't end well.

David stumbled to his feet, lurched forward, steadied himself, then aimed for the police station.

He felt better than he'd felt all day. Better than he'd felt all week.

"Shut the door behind you," Hoffman said once they were both inside her office. The sound of the closing door was even more ominous than usual. There would be no reaching into his pants today.

Hoffman sat at her desk, her expression stern. "Badge and gun."

"What?"

"I want your badge and gun. On the desk. Now."

"Isn't that a bit of an overreaction?"

The anger in her face increased, and he could almost hear her teeth gnashing. "You know why we hired you?" She answered her own question. "We hired you because we couldn't afford anybody else."

"Ouch."

"Ex-FBI was better than no FBI. Or at least that's what I thought at the time." She opened one drawer, searched for something, opened another, slammed it. "Your entire history wasn't included in your file. I didn't know everything about you until you got here. By then I thought you might as well stay."

Another drawer. Pale blue bottle he recognized as antacid. She uncapped the lid and took a swig. "I have to admit that once I saw you, I decided to keep you for a while."

Harsh. Nice-looking people had a whole other kind of bias to deal with.

"You ended up surprising me." She recapped her drink. "You screwed up sometimes, and you've been on probation more than I can count, but you got a lot of things right. The press even called you a hero a few times. That was generous, but it reflected well on the department. I liked it." She dropped the bottle back in her desk and slammed the drawer. "But I'm done. Take two weeks, and I'll

rethink this once I've cooled off. But, David, I'm afraid you aren't a
good fit here. I'm sorry."

She didn't look sorry.

"Is it because of us? Is that why you're doing this?"

"Us?" She let out a scornful laugh. "There is no us. It was fun
for a while, but people are talking. I can't have that. I'm not looking
for a relationship. I've had those, and I don't want any more. What
you and I had was handy for me. Sex, with no strings. I knew you
weren't looking for commitment either. At least not from me. But
it was a bad idea, sweetie." Her face softened on the "sweetie." He
wasn't sure she'd ever called him that, even in the throes. "Throes."
What a weird word.

"I'm giving you fair warning." Her eyes narrowed, and her
severe expression returned. "There's a good chance you won't be
coming back."

CHAPTER 23

I'm outta here," David said.

Without looking up from her computer screen, Elise said, "Just a minute. I have a few e-mails I need to read that might be pertinent to the case. We got a handwriting match for Devro and Murphy. I'm still waiting to hear back on Chesterfield." Apparently she'd somehow missed the drama in the cemetery.

"I'm not heading out to interview people," David said. "I'm *leaving* leaving. In fact, I think I might get a drink."

"It's not even noon." She spun around in her chair, took in the condition of his face and clothes, and barely blinked. Another day at the office.

That was when he gave her an abbreviated version of what happened in the cemetery, leaving out the words Lamont had spoken to instigate the attack.

"Hoffman put you on temporary suspension?"

"Yep. Two weeks."

"Now? With a murderer out there?"

"You've got everybody you need. You've got the handsome and not-yet-balding FBI profiler, you've got the reporter from New York, you've got an old man with cancer who will most likely crack the case with some kind of hoodoo voodoo mojo mind-expanding spell. You'll be fine." He grabbed his jacket off the chair and flung it over his shoulder to demonstrate how carefree he was.

"You have blood on your face."

He rubbed his jaw and checked his fingers. Blood crumbs.

She handed him a bottle of water and a tissue. He uncapped the bottle, wet the tissue, and began blindly cleaning his face.

"Here." She took the tissue from him, wet it some more, and wiped the side of his cheek and under his nose, then tossed the tissue away. "You might want to change your shirt before you go to a bar."

He looked down. "Oh, right." Then, "Maybe people will just think I'm a sloppy eater."

"Did you two break up?" she asked.

She was thinking the same thing he'd thought, that Hoffman was doing this out of spite.

"There was never anything to break up," he said.

"That's not what I heard."

He gave her a crooked smile. "Word gets around in a small town." A rueful shake of his head. A thought about how quickly the day had changed. And how he somehow still felt better than he'd felt an hour ago. "I don't think it was anything to do with that."

"Then what?"

"She's just sick of my behavior, that's all."

They'd done this before. Elise knew the drill. "I'll keep you in the loop," she told him.

"I hate to leave you hanging, but right now . . . Not sure I want to be in the loop." For the last year Elise had talked off and on about quitting. Funny that he might be the one moving on.

"You'll be back. I'll bet by tomorrow she comes around. It's not like you shot somebody. And she's not following any protocol."

He didn't feel like going into the other stuff Hoffman had said. "Thanks for the bath."

"I'm going to talk to her," Elise said. "This is unacceptable."

He smiled. "We made a good team."

"Not made, *make*."

"Okay. Whatever you say."

He liked that she was going to battle for him regardless of the inevitable outcome. "Now it's my turn to talk about opening a coffee shop. I'll work on a name." His hand was on the doorknob when he stopped. "Have you done the crossword for today?"

"Not yet."

"Me neither."

She gave him a long, penetrating look, one meant to get a suspect to confess. "Why'd you hit him?"

The question was so Elise, and it was a question Hoffman hadn't bothered to ask. Elise wasn't mad at him for punching Lamont. She just wanted to know why. "He had it coming. And I'd do it again."

Out of the building and in his car, David stopped at the first bar he saw. Closed, so he hit the liquor store. Better anyway, especially when he planned to black out.

CHAPTER 24

After David left, Elise met with Major Hoffman, but the woman wouldn't budge.

"You've got the team you need," Hoffman said. "Victor Lamont has been given the okay to stay on for a couple of weeks. He'll be reporting to me, and I'll be reporting to the mayor. Detective Avery will continue to run the task force downstairs, and you've got Jackson Sweet."

"You know how I feel about Sweet," Elise said.

"Get over it. I want Gould's desk cleared so Agent Lamont can set up there, and I want you to make your father welcome, and I want him involved. And if you ever find a suspect to question, I want Sweet to do the questioning." Hoffman's voice, upon bringing up their lack of suspects, was snide and accusatory.

Had the woman totally lost her mind? First firing David, then this stuff with Sweet? "I'm the best at interrogation," Elise reminded her.

"Not anymore. I've been too lenient, and I have to confess I'm beginning to regret giving you the position as head detective."

"I didn't ask for it."

"Which I should have heeded. You didn't want it. You made that clear. And now here we are with the mayor's daughter dead and all our jobs on the line."

Ah, so that was it. Major Hoffman was concerned about losing her job.

"I think it's a bad idea to remove Gould from the case," Elise said.

"His attitude toward Lamont was seriously hindering the investigation. Hopefully I can talk Lamont out of filing assault charges, because that's the last thing we need right now. Admit it, Elise. Gould is a detriment."

It was true. "Yes," Elise said with reluctance.

"See that Agent Lamont is moved from the task force station into your office as smoothly as possible, and let's catch this killer. Not tomorrow and not next week. Now."

The next couple of hours were taken up with getting Lamont settled in. He was smirky and cocky about it, and Elise was glad David wasn't there since he would've punched him all over again.

Strange how one person could change the feel of everything. Lamont exuded a man's-world vibe, and Elise got the sense he didn't consider her on his level, but then maybe that was typical FBI behavior.

By the time evening rolled around, the day felt wasted. In the parking lot, Jay Thomas Paul was waiting next to her car.

"I thought you'd left for the day," Elise said when she spotted him.

"I didn't want to talk about this in front of Agent Lamont, but is it true about Detective Gould? Did he get fired?"

"I suspect he'll be back." But as she spoke the words, she had her doubts.

"I was writing a story about the two of you . . ."

"Oh, that's right." She made a face. "I'm sorry."

"What was the fight about?"

"Will that end up in your story?"

"Maybe. This is what I do. I can't shut it off."

"I appreciate your honesty." Annoying Twitter photos aside, she'd started to like Jay Thomas Paul. He'd never pretended to be anything he wasn't.

"Would you like to grab a bite to eat before heading home?" he asked.

"Not tonight."

He immediately looked embarrassed.

"But thanks for asking. Maybe we can get a drink sometime."

That cheered him up.

While Jay Thomas walked away, a bit of a bounce in his step, Elise called home. Audrey answered to tell her Strata Luna was there, cooking.

"Cooking?" Elise asked. "Strata Luna?"

"Well, her houseboy is cooking. Strata Luna is bossing him around." Mother and daughter laughed. "She says she has to fatten Grandpa up."

Elise cringed whenever Audrey called the man staying with them Grandpa.

"How'd his chemo go?" Unbelievably, Audrey had been able to talk him into getting it. She'd apparently inherited his power of persuasion.

"He seems normal. Like it was nothing. He even met me after school." Her voice dropped. "He still doesn't want Strata Luna to know. I feel weird about that."

Had he even gotten the chemo? Elise wondered. The plan had been for him to take a cab to the hospital and back once a week for five weeks, and he'd insisted upon going by himself. "Don't hold dinner for me." She'd deal with Sweet later. "As long as everything's under control, I'm going to stop by David's." Even before the incident with Lamont, David had been acting strange. Few realized it, but he was fragile.

CHAPTER 25

At David's apartment, located in a dark and foreboding building called Mary of the Angels, Elise's knock went unanswered, so she pulled out her mobile phone and hit "Speed Dial." From the other side of the door came the sound of a ring tone.

David didn't pick up.

His car was outside. He might have been jogging, but that didn't fit his routine. She rattled the knob and pounded, this time shouting his name. Could be he just wanted to be left alone, but his volatile behavior at the police station worried her. Added to that were past mental issues and his predisposition to breakdowns.

After another minute of no response she took the stairs to the caretaker's apartment on the first floor.

"I can't let you into someone's rental," the old man said. He was as decrepit as the building itself, and Elise seriously doubted there was much care going on at Mary of the Angels. She hated to do it because it was so needlessly dramatic, but she pulled her jacket aside and flashed the badge on her belt.

"Oh yeah. Now I remember you." He was referring to an unpleasant incident that had almost led to David's eviction. Getting kicked out seemed to be a recurring theme in her partner's life.

"I wouldn't do this if you weren't both cops," he let her know as they rode the ancient elevator cage to the third floor. At the apartment, he turned the master key in the lock and swung the door wide.

David's cat, Isobel, let out a hiss, skidded around the corner, and disappeared down the hall in the direction of the bedroom.

Barefoot, dressed in a gray T-shirt and faded jeans, was the man of the hour. From his sprawled position on the floor, he turned his head in an attempt to see who'd invaded his space. "Oh, hey."

It was hard to believe this wasted David had come about in just a few hours. He looked like he'd spent the last week living on a deserted island.

"He's drunk, that's all," the caretaker said with a tone that conveyed satisfaction and maybe even approval. Yeah, cops let go sometimes.

David's place was small, probably not much more than four hundred square feet. The combined living room and kitchen made it impossible to miss the evidence of his one-man party—which amounted to an uncapped half-empty fifth of vodka on the kitchen counter and a glass on the floor.

Standing in the doorway, the caretaker said, "He looks pretty happy to me."

"He seems to be good at finding his happy place," Elise said with distraction as she eyed a brown prescription bottle next to the sink.

From the floor, David let out a chuckle while the caretaker shuffled away without further comment and Elise stepped inside and closed the door.

At the sink, she read the label on the prescription bottle. "Did you take any of these?"

He blinked and narrowed his eyes, trying to bring the thing in her hand into focus. "Don't know. What are they?"

"Sleeping pills. Slumberon." She recognized the name. A newer sedative that had been getting negative press. Like some other sleep aids, it was said to cause sleepwalking and sleep driving, among other alarming types of behavior.

"Don't think so." He groped the floor beside him, found what he was after, and lifted a short glass to his mouth, looking like an invalid giving himself a much-needed sip of water.

"You're not an attractive drunk."

He let out a snort and sprayed vodka, most of it landing on his chest, where it left a dark splotch on his T-shirt. "That's funny as hell."

"Just being honest."

He raised the glass to his mouth again for another attempt. She thought about telling him it would be easier if he sat up but decided that would only encourage him.

"Where's your coffee?" She opened a cupboard, closed it, opened another.

"I don't want coffee. I worked hard to get to this point. I don't wanna come down."

"Are those song lyrics?"

"From my brain to your ears."

She found the coffee, popped the top on the plastic canister, scooped some grounds into a paper filter nestled inside a cheap plastic coffeemaker, added water, and turned on the machine. While it dripped and made agonized sounds, Elise kicked off her shoes and curled up in the corner of the couch.

It looked like he'd been working at some point before the vodka—the table between them was strewn with papers and photos.

The squeak of couch springs transmitted a signal to the normally antisocial Isobel, who came sauntering out of the bedroom.

"I'm sorry about Major Hoffman," Elise told David as the cat jumped on her lap. "About you and Major Hoffman."

"You think that's why I'm arse over tit?" He lifted his glass high in a salute to his drinking.

That's exactly what she thought. Spurned lover and all that. "Okay," she said, petting Isobel. "Then the job."

"It's not the job and it's not Hoffman. Well, unless I'm celebrating."

That surprised her. Had he broken up with Hoffman instead of the other way around? Probably not. Hoffman would have felt compelled to end it if she'd suspended him.

Expecting to see crime photos, she shifted her focus to the table, and her petting hand went still. A few heartbeats later she picked up one of the images and stared at it. "He's beautiful." Blond curly hair and blue eyes. Even though the hair was unlike David's, she could see a resemblance in the face.

David rolled to his side, head braced against his hand, elbow on the floor. "I like that you used present tense. Most people don't."

She examined the photo more closely. "He looks so alive."

Elise knew David's son had died in May. She wasn't sure of the date, but she had a suspicion. "It was today, wasn't it?"

Heavy eyes locked with hers, and his freshly awakened pain made her breath catch. "Don't take me there," he whispered.

She almost wished she hadn't come. Not because she didn't want to see him like this, but because until her interruption, he'd been able to numb that pain.

It was weird when she thought about it. About how he'd brought some levity into her life when she'd needed it, and yet his own life was so tragic.

"I don't know why I care about dates, because dead is dead," he said, shoving the now-empty glass across the table. "I wish I could wipe the date from my mind, but I can't."

The coffeemaker let out one final burst of steam, indicating it was finished. Elise unfolded herself from the couch, walked to the kitchen area, and went to work filling a couple of mugs. She carried them back to the living room and handed one to David. "Careful. It's hot."

He took a cautious sip. "Sweet kitty, that's strong."

She tried hers. "And it tastes a little like plastic."

"My mother bought the coffeemaker. She was wailing about how it didn't look like anybody lived here, so she went shopping for that nasty thing. Nothing like the taste of plastic to say home sweet home." He took another sip, made a face, and put the cup aside.

Reluctant to leave him alone considering his state of mind and the bottle of sleeping pills on the counter, Elise texted Audrey, letting her know she wouldn't be home for a few more hours.

Audrey replied, telling her Jackson Sweet was in the bathroom throwing up. Sad face. *He couldn't eat the food Javier fixed. Strata Luna got mad. Told Grandpa to tell her what was going on, so now she knows. Relief.*

So he did get the treatment, and it was apparently hitting him harder than anticipated. But then again, doctors always downplayed side effects and recovery.

Do you need me there? Elise asked.

No, Strata Luna and Javier are going to put him to bed and give him his antinausea pill.

Okay. I'll be home later. Love you.

Despite the coffee, David fell asleep, only waking when Elise gave him a nudge. A couple of hours later, after more coffee and no more vodka, he appeared sober enough for her to leave.

"You're going to have to move," Elise told Isobel.

David eyed the cat on Elise's lap. "I'll bet she saw him die."

Maybe he wasn't as sober as she'd thought. "What are you talking about?"

"Isobel. I'll bet Isobel saw my son die. She was his cat," he went on to explain. "One day when I was driving home from Quantico, I found her along the road. Thought she'd make a nice friend for Christian."

His eyes became unfocused as he traveled back in time. "He loved that cat, but maybe I should have gotten him a dog, you know? A dog might have protected him." He went through the motions of taking another sip of coffee, then replaced the mug on the table. "Dogs are smarter. But Isobel . . . She probably just watched it happen, hoping she'd get some salmon when it was all over."

There were no words that would help, but Elise tried anyway. "No matter how much we think we know, we can never be prepared for aberrant behavior in the people closest to us. You've seen it again and again in interviews with the families of killers. Most of them have the same response—they just couldn't think their son or husband could possibly have done such an awful thing."

"Yeah, but when you *press* them, they usually say there was something there."

True.

"Isobel." He patted the floor. "Come here."

The cat jumped from Elise's lap to join David on the floor, curling against his stomach.

"It's usually just a feeling. Killers are good at keeping secrets from the people who think they know them best," Elise said.

"I appreciate your attempt to reassure me, but I should have known. It's my job. Lamont's profile might be off, but he was right about me. I was a profiler. I lived with her. I lived with evil."

"Okay, I'll quit trying to convince you of the human flaw that blinds us to the people we love. The reason I stopped by was because I want you to know you're still my partner. No matter what happens, I still want your input on this case."

"You shouldn't listen to me. You should listen to the asshole. He's the expert. I don't know what I'm talking about."

Several times over the past two weeks he'd been evasive when speaking about the case, even though she knew his focus was on nothing else. "You're thinking something you aren't sharing."

"Haven't you heard? I'm off the case."

"I don't care." She wouldn't tell him Lamont was using his desk. If he found out, there might be another death in the city.

"You could be fired," David said.

"Has that ever stopped me before?"

He shook his head and smiled slightly. "My idea—it has no foundation."

"Let me decide."

Careful of Isobel, David got to his feet and sat next to Elise on the couch. With the back of his hand, he swept the photos aside, clearing a spot. Then he opened a yellow legal pad and flipped through the pages until he came to a blank sheet. Settling the tablet against his knee and uncapping a pen, he began to doodle. She'd witnessed this many times. Doodling helped him think.

"We agree that this person is a pro. He's killed a lot, and he's perfected his style," David said. "For him it's not about method. Everything he's doing is deliberate. Everything he's doing is designed to lead us just where he wants to lead us, to make us believe whatever he wants us to believe. And Lamont has walked right into it. That's what I think."

"Let's say this is a valid theory. How is it different from Lamont's profile?"

"For one thing, the guy is older. For another . . . Lamont is wrong about the killer's motivation. The mayor's daughter? That was all about us. All about getting our attention. Understanding motivation is everything if you want to get ahead of this guy."

She didn't like where this was going. The majority of serial killings were ones of opportunity. David was telling her that this was different. "Then who's next?"

"Let's just say I don't think it's a bad idea for your father to be staying at your house."

Her heart pounded in alarm. "You're thinking Audrey?" Would her job always put Audrey in danger?

"You can't be too careful. No more going out with her friends at night. She should be taken to and from school. I know you aren't crazy about having Sweet at your house, but I think his presence is a good thing. I don't have any doubt he'll protect her."

At least there was that. Elise might not trust Sweet, but she didn't believe he'd harm Audrey. Otherwise she'd never have allowed him into her home.

"Profiling 101 isn't going to cut it anymore," David continued. "Lamont is still working by the same curriculum we trained with. It's old. It's outdated."

"A killer is a killer."

"No." David shook his head. "That's what everybody thinks, and the FBI keeps churning out these profilers and profiles, never considering that killers have adapted. The killers of today aren't the killers of our grandparents' generation, and they aren't the killers of fifteen years ago. They've *evolved*, and a lot of that evolution is due to the Internet and media. Most killers still crave the attention, but they're also better equipped to manipulate the system—and to manipulate by-the-book thinkers like Lamont."

It made sense. And in a weird way, it tied into thoughts not yet fully formed that were lurking in the back of Elise's mind like some unnamed dread—a feeling that something simply wasn't right.

Now that the tablet was filled with swirls and random words and lines, David tossed it down on the table. "But that's probably all bullshit and you should forget it, because the most obvious and banal observations could be accurate. And right now you can't afford to be wrong."

"So you're doubting yourself."

"That's why I've been reluctant to say anything. Because I have nothing to back up this theory."

"Other than the fact that it makes perfect sense."

"Does it? I don't even know anymore. About anything. I thought it made sense a week ago, but now . . ."

"You have to let go of the toxic self-doubt your wife left you with. Don't let that poison you."

"Too late."

"Then drink the poison and survive it. Use it."

"Don't go all Yoda on me. I hate that stuff. And things like 'Tomorrow will be better.' And 'Everything happens for a reason.'"

"I'd never say that to you. Killers don't kill because there's some life lesson to be taught."

"I know they don't, and I know you wouldn't."

"If you step away from this, our chances of catching this guy decrease. Look at my team. Lamont, Avery—who seems a bit shaky lately—the guy with three names, and Jackson Sweet—cancer patient."

"Don't put too much faith in me. I don't have any leads. It's more about the *process*. It needs to change. It's more about tossing out the instruction book and starting over, this time with the realization that we've supplied the killer with everything he needs to know to evade us."

Chilling words.

As she was leaving, David grabbed a key from a hook near the door. "So the caretaker doesn't have to let you in next time," he explained, tossing it to her.

CHAPTER 26

An hour after Elise got home from David's, a crash downstairs woke her. The bedside clock read 11:02 p.m. as she grabbed her gun and tossed back the covers, her ears tuned for any additional sound. Wearing pajamas dug from the closet two days earlier, she made her way across the wooden floor, each step eliciting a creak from the hardwood under her bare feet.

She looked in on Audrey. Asleep.

On the first floor, she made a sweep of the house, checking front and back doors, plus the windows. The alarm was still set.

Through the kitchen and down the hall to the guest room. "Sweet?" she whispered. Getting no reply, she felt for the wall switch and turned on the overhead light. The bed was empty.

Yards away, the guest bathroom door was ajar, the room dark. She smelled vomit.

Elise flicked the wall switch.

Sweet, wearing nothing but a pair of boxer shorts, was curled in a fetal position on the floor. "Off." He squinted up at her.

She placed her weapon on the vanity, stepped over him, and flushed the toilet. "Did you take your antinausea medication?"

"Can't keep it down."

Sweet probably weighed 170 pounds; she wasn't sure she could get him back to bed by herself. Briefly, she thought of yelling for Audrey, but Elise didn't want her daughter involved in the disturbing scene, and she was sure Sweet wouldn't want his granddaughter to see him this way.

"Turn off the light and go," he said.

"You can't stay on the floor."

"I've slept in worse places." The words came out in a breathless exhale.

Severe illness reduced everyone to this. To the humiliation of being found on the bathroom floor.

She gathered up bedding. Returning to Sweet's side, she slipped a pillow under his head and another at his back. She covered him with blankets, wrapping them around him as best she could in order to protect him from the cold floor. Then she brought him a glass of water and his pills, placing them within reach.

"For later, when you think you can take a drink."

He gave her an almost imperceptible nod, too nauseated to speak.

Gun in hand, she turned out the light and left him there.

CHAPTER 27

Since first laying eyes on him, Coretta Hoffman had dreamed about getting David Gould into her bed—but acting on that fantasy had been a foolish thing to do.

Just sex. That was what she'd told herself. Maybe one night, maybe two, then done. Out of her system. But once she started, she found she couldn't stop, even though she knew people were talking, knew she was jeopardizing her already shaky career.

Stupid, especially once the mayor began watching her so closely, watching *all* of them.

Now it was done, over, but she wasn't relieved.

She'd miss Gould.

Maybe it had been an irrational move on her part, but she'd felt the only way to get him out of her system was to go cold turkey. And the only way to do that was to suspend him, which was really just a step toward firing him. They both knew it, because no way would she be able to see him in the hallway of the Savannah PD and not want to call him down to her office and rip off his clothes and have him work her over right there on her desk.

Because, Lord, that man was fine.

Oh yeah, she'd fantasized about the desk. Many times.

Even tonight, twelve hours after kicking him out of his office, she was so crazy about him that when a knock sounded and Trixie barked and ran for the door, Coretta found herself hoping it was

Gould coming to her house in the middle of the night like he'd done many times. Once inside, they'd shed their clothes and have sex on any handy surface, even the floor. Especially the floor.

In the semidarkness of the living room, she set her wineglass aside—how much had she consumed? She lifted the second bottle. Half-empty. She'd pay tomorrow.

The dog kept barking. Frantic, excited, scratching at the door as if she knew who was on the other side. Coretta felt the same way. Like scratching on the door in excitement while she made pathetic whimpering sounds.

She had no shame.

No self-control. That was what had gotten her into this mess.

She pushed herself off the couch and tightened the belt on her red silk robe. Maybe kicking him out of his office and her life had been a mistake. Maybe he was worth everything she'd lose. Worth losing her job over, if it came down to it.

No.

Because Gould would never truly care for her. Maybe that was really why she'd kicked him out. Because he'd never love her, not when he loved Detective Sandburg.

Take that man and run, woman.

She'd once gotten up the nerve to ask him if he'd ever slept with Elise. Coretta figured they'd at least spent a few weekends together. But no. If he was telling the truth, they'd never had sex.

Elise was a fool. Or something was wrong with her. Or she preferred women. But even at that . . .

Coretta unlocked the dead bolt and opened the door, a smile on her lips.

She was the chief of police, but she hadn't gotten there the usual way, not by coming up through the ranks, starting out as a patrol officer. No, she'd slept her way in, launching herself with a secretarial position. It had happened so long ago that the whispers and jealousy had long since died, gone out the door with the retirees and the people who'd simply become sick of law enforcement.

But regardless of how she'd arrived, Coretta was good at her job, maybe because she'd always been in administration. She could get people to do what they were supposed to do.

Still, the downside about coming up from the secretarial pool was that she knew little about protecting herself, other than the common things like eye gouging and a knee to the crotch. So when she opened the door with a smile on her face and an ache between her thighs, she was unprepared for the figure in the black sweatshirt, hood pulled low, face in deep shadow.

Before she let out a full gasp, a hand clamped down over her mouth, silencing her and shoving her deeper into the room. The door slammed behind her; the dead bolt turned.

In drunk confusion, she tried to change the scene to the expected, to David coming inside and the shedding of clothes and the crazy sex that would end with her telling him she was sorry about suspending him, and David telling her it was okay, that he understood.

That didn't happen.

With a vicious swing, the man—it was definitely a man—kicked her feet out from under her. She fell, hitting her head on the end table. Glass shattered, a lamp crashed to the floor, and the room went dark.

Her dog was no longer barking, probably cowering in the corner. "Don't hurt her," she said. A silly thing to say when she should have been begging for her own life.

She figured the intruder for a thief or rapist or both. "I'll give you whatever you want." She sounded pathetic, so unlike her strong self.

"Yes, you will." His voice was smooth. Southern? She wasn't sure.

"I don't have much money in the house, but you can have my bank card and PIN." *Always give them what they want.* It was one of the few things she did know.

He was on top of her, pressing her to the floor. "I don't want your money." His breath was hot against her cheek.

Sex. So it was sex.

She kneed him.

He let out a roar of pain and anger that she hoped the neighbors would hear. But she had little to do with her neighbors. Would they even care what was going on next door? Would they even notice?

"Bitch," the man said.

He moved quickly, shifting his weight, fumbling inside his clothes.

She expected him to spread her legs and bury himself inside her. Instead, she felt a deep pain in her neck, followed by a warmth across her throat. Blood filled her mouth—blood she realized was her own.

Had he cut her throat? No, that couldn't be. That was ridiculous. Surely a sliced throat would hurt more than this pain that was already ebbing. Surely she'd know without a doubt.

In the light filtering in around the curtains, Coretta tried to get a better look at him, for some reason feeling it was important. For some reason thinking she'd have to remember what his face looked like so she could report him.

She didn't like that gurgling sound. She wished it would stop.

Weird that she was both warm and cold at the same time.

Now she understood that this was not a robbery gone wrong. This was not a rape, although maybe that just hadn't happened yet.

Did she even care? She just wanted to sleep. On some level she recognized the seriousness of the situation, but she felt relaxed and sleepy. More at peace than she'd felt in years.

But something inside told her to stay awake. To keep her eyes open, to look at the man hovering over her.

Dark hood. Dark clothing.

Maybe she imagined it, but she could suddenly see a face. Someone who was rather nice-looking. Kind-looking. Sweet-looking. Not the face of a killer . . . Or was she hallucinating? Yes, she must have been, because suddenly the sweet face became David's face.

Trixie was barking again, and this time it was a fearful bark, a worried bark.

She should have gotten a breed that was more protective. Like a German shepherd or something. But miniature poodles were cute.

She'd have to tell David about this. All of this.

About the man she let into her home because she thought it was David at the door. That was funny. Horribly funny. They would laugh about it together, and then they'd make love.

CHAPTER 28

David knocked on the door. Coretta's dog, Trixie, let out a series of barks from the other side.

David sure as hell hadn't expected to stop by Coretta's house today, but Elise called, asking if he'd mind checking on the major because she hadn't come to work. A little past noon, the rest of the day stretching in front of him, David agreed, even though Coretta was the last person he wanted to see right now.

Earlier, in his apartment, she hadn't answered her phone, so he'd left a voice mail. No reply. He'd sent her a text. Same thing. And now she wasn't answering her door.

No surprise, really. She probably wasn't crazy about the idea of seeing him either.

Her house was located southeast of downtown, on the way to Thunderbolt. Ranch-style homes with palm trees in the yard. Kinda bland, but one of the safer areas, unlike Elise's downtown neighborhood, which had seen an uptick in crime over the past year thanks to Mayor Chesterfield.

Coretta, for all her tough exterior and ravenous sexual appetite, was pretty average when you took away her authority. David felt bad for even thinking such thoughts, but he couldn't help it. Nothing about Coretta had been a surprise, other than how boring she was.

He circled the house. In the backyard, he looked in the garage window. Her car was there.

Now he was beginning to worry.

Up the sidewalk to an area of flowers. He searched, finally finding a rock with a fake bottom, just the way Coretta had done one night not long ago when she'd locked herself out.

He didn't know the alarm code, but to hell with it.

He turned the key and opened the door.

No alarm sounded.

Trixie heard the door and came running, whimpering and whining in excitement. David bent down to pet her. "Hey, girl."

Her white coat was dirty and matted in places. More disturbing—the matting appeared to be dried blood.

He scooped the dog under his arm and shot upright. "Coretta?" He shouted as he strode through the kitchen. Paw prints on the floor were the same shade of burgundy as the stains on Trixie's white coat. Holding the dog like a football, David hurried down the narrow hall to the living room.

Lamp on the floor. Broken wine bottle.

And Coretta.

Lying on her back, eyes open, staring at the ceiling, her throat sliced from ear to ear, a pool of coagulated blood around her.

It was easy to see where Trixie had been and what she'd been doing. She'd pawed at the unresponsive Coretta, trying to wake her up.

Coretta was never waking up.

David staggered back into the kitchen. Numbly, he reached for the blue leash Coretta kept at the back door. He snapped it to Trixie's collar, carried the dog from the house, and put her down in the backyard. She immediately squatted. She'd probably been holding it for hours.

David tied the leash to a railing, then returned to the house and filled a metal bowl with dog food. Back outside, he untied the dog and sat on the step, watching her while she wolfed down the food.

It was strange how the mundane became a comfort in times like these. He'd forgotten about that. How when his son was murdered, it was the mundane that kept him going those first forty-eight hours. Just a simple human going through the motions of everyday life. Getting dressed. Taking a shower. Pouring coffee. Those things filled the space in a person's head, pushing out the horror and pain. Feed the cat. Feed the dog. Don't think about anything else.

Maybe he should take Trixie for a walk. She'd probably like that. But Trixie was evidence. He knew he shouldn't have even carried her outside, should have shut her in a bedroom and kept her contained, but . . .

Dogs weren't as ruthless as cats. That was what David found himself thinking. If David died in his apartment, he was pretty sure Isobel would eat him once she got hungry enough.

Where would she start? His face? His fingers?

But a dog . . . David was pretty sure most dogs wouldn't resort to eating their masters.

He pulled out his phone and realized his fingers were sticky. He unlocked the screen, tapped the green and white receiver icon, and called Elise.

"You'd better get over here," he said when she answered.

"Over where?"

It was good to hear her voice. "Coretta's."

"What's wrong?" She sounded alert, concerned. That kinda killed him.

He couldn't say it. He couldn't tell her. His throat tightened as he thought about the words, and he might have made an odd, strangled sound of despair. "Just get over here, Elise. Come around back. I'm around back."

"On my way."

He blindly returned his phone to his pocket, let out a tremulous breath, braced his elbows on his knees, and looked up at the blue, blue sky. *Come on, Elise.*

CHAPTER 29

Where you off to?" Vic Lamont asked as Elise reached for her jacket.

"Forgot something from home." She wasn't exactly sure why she lied. Maybe because she didn't want to share anything about her partner to the man partially responsible for getting David suspended, but the bigger reason was that she wanted to know what was going on before telling anyone else.

David was upset.

Hoffman was involved.

Lamont was already looking for the slightest infraction to make sure David never came back to Savannah PD. No need to give him any ammunition until she knew what they were dealing with.

Major Hoffman's house was fifteen minutes from downtown if the traffic was decent. Elise had been there once a few years back, to attend a strange and uncomfortable Christmas party. It had been interesting to finally see Coretta in her element. Elise didn't know what she'd expected, but a suburban-type house wasn't it. The kind of place where families settled to raise their kids away from the heart of the city, out of danger. But Elise was fairly certain Coretta didn't have kids.

On the phone, David had been distraught. Had Hoffman had a meltdown? That seemed the most likely scenario. Pressure from the mayor to find the killer, combined with her breakup with David.

.   .   .

Elise found David on the back steps of Major Hoffman's house. Beside him was a poodle he petted with unawareness.

Her heart sank: she did not like what she was seeing.

She'd visited enough scenes of tragedy to recognize the absence of expression; the blanket of numbness that served as protection when reality was too much to bear.

"David?" She whispered his name.

He responded with a series of small jerks—that robotic reaction when the body can no longer move in one fluid motion because the brain is misfiring.

In this type of situation, calm was needed, because there was no telling how the victim, or relative of a victim, would respond. Whispers and short sentences and eye contact. That was what the situation called for. She thought these things while understanding that David wasn't a victim of a crime, but instead he was the witness, the person who'd discovered the unbearable.

"Major Hoffman?" Elise asked.

David looked down at the dog leaning against his thigh, its tongue out, dark stains on its white coat. She was pretty sure what those stains were.

"Inside," he said.

Elise went up the steps. David shifted slightly as her leg touched his arm. He didn't follow her.

She remembered the kitchen. People drinking wine and eating cheese and crackers. Music playing from another room. A party with such a strange feel to it, almost as if the house had known this day was coming.

Through the kitchen, to the living room.

Signs of struggle. Broken lamp. Broken bottle.

And then Elise saw her.

Poor Coretta. Poor, poor Coretta.

Elise crouched and felt the dead woman's arm. Cold as marble. And the smell. She'd never get used to the smell of so much blood. A person could almost taste it.

Elise straightened, unsnapped her shoulder holster, and pulled out her weapon. The killer was probably gone, but a sweep of the space was necessary.

Blood was everywhere, in every room.

The dog had gotten blood on its paws and tracked it through the house. There were paw prints on the white front door where the dog had scratched to get out. Paw prints on the floor. Paw prints down the hall and in the bedroom where the animal had repeatedly walked back and forth on a white duvet cover.

During Elise's cursory inspection, she saw no signs of burglary. Hoffman's laptop and cell phone were on the dresser, the clothes she'd worn that day tossed over a chair, as if Coretta had arrived home, dropped her things, and changed her clothes.

But it could have been staged.

Ten minutes later, once Elise was confident the house was empty, she visually examined the murder scene.

The killer most likely exited through the back, because the front dead bolt was locked. Elise's sweep had revealed no broken windows or signs of forced entry.

Meaning Hoffman had most likely known her assailant.

Elise slipped her gun back into its holster, pulled out her phone, and dialed the Savannah PD. She gave them instructions, then finished with "No sirens. Come to the back door. It's already been compromised."

After that, she called John Casper and told him she needed him.

"Dead body?" he asked.

She stared at Coretta. Her red robe had come open in the struggle, or maybe she'd been sexually assaulted. Elise wanted to cover her. To find a sheet and cover her body before officers got there—before John Casper came and the crime team began snapping photos.

Something they did at every scene. But this was Coretta.

"Yes. A body."

Elise couldn't cover her. She couldn't close eyes that were now dry and turning opaque. But the urge was so overwhelming that Elise walked away before she did what she couldn't and shouldn't do.

In the kitchen, on the refrigerator, was a photo of David, taken on the deck in the backyard. He was sitting near where he sat right now, but in the photo he was slouched in a chair, a smile on his face and a beer resting against his leg.

Careful not to touch anything, Elise looked out the window. David was still on the deck steps, the dog beside him. She thought about the sound David had made on the phone. A kind of choked sob. She felt the threat of that same sound welling up in her, tightening her throat.

She had to be strong.

One of them always had to be strong.

With the house still empty, she knew she should take this time to go through it again, looking for any missed detail, but she'd wait. Instead, she joined David, sitting down beside him on the steps and putting a hand on his leg.

He was shaking. Not a violent thing. Not a shaking you could see, but she felt it shuddering through him like an electrical current.

"They're coming," she said.

He nodded. "Good."

She was sorry she'd called him. Sorry he'd been the one to find Coretta. It would have been better if he'd heard about it. It would have been better if he'd never seen her like that.

There was something about a sliced throat that was especially hard to get out of your head.

Did it have anything to do with the current rash of murders? Elise wondered. Not at all the same MO, but maybe someone, a relative of a victim, was angry that the case hadn't been solved. Grief made people do strange things.

She'd told them no sirens, so the first thing she heard was the sound of engines, then footsteps and voices.

The dog barked a halfhearted bark, and David tensed.

"I don't think I can be here," he said.

"You were the first on the scene," Elise reminded him. "Someone will have to question you."

CHAPTER 30

Someone equipped with a lack of squeamishness and no emotional attachment to the victim might note a certain beauty in the precision and symmetry of movement that descended upon Major Hoffman's house in the hours directly following David's discovery of the body. Elise always thought of it as a dark dance. If someone were to overlay the scene with music, the sound would be soft and tender and haunting.

The lot upon which the house sat exuded a solemn funereal tone as yellow crime-scene tape was stretched from tree to tree, blocking off the front yard and creating a barrier for the people in the street who stood with hands pressed to their mouths in horror while at the same time hoping for a glimpse of something tantalizing.

The crime-scene team was on the property, and cops had begun their canvass of the neighborhood. Two of the teams were setting up a grid search. John Casper's white van, with the words "Chatham County Medical Examiner" on the side, waited patiently in the driveway.

The dead were in no hurry.

Vague and incorrect stories were already circulating. Thirty minutes after Elise placed the call to Savannah PD, discussion hit social media in 140 characters, and news reporters were now on-site, Jay Thomas Paul included. He seemed to have finally learned his lesson, though, and was hovering on the edge of the yellow tape with everyone else.

He spotted Elise and gave her a big "c'mere" wave.

Elise joined him at the perimeter, going so far as to lift the yellow tape—an invitation to join her. Surprised, Jay Thomas ducked under the tape and, side by side, they moved away from the watching and waiting crowd.

"Is it true?" he asked in a hushed voice. "Was Major Hoffman murdered?"

The day was bright and getting hot, the sun beating down on Elise's head and bare arms. Earlier, she'd removed her jacket, exposing her shoulder holster and handgun.

She didn't know much about the major's personal life, but the woman surely had family out there somewhere. If so, it looked like they'd be hearing about this from the media. Not good.

Ordinarily Hoffman made decisions about press conferences, a job that would most likely fall to the mayor now. Elise couldn't believe it, but she was actually considering giving Jay Thomas Paul the story to break before reports got out of hand. Jay Thomas was controllable, and she sensed he wanted to please her.

"I'll give you the details for a piece," Elise told him, coming to a decision. "Don't go anywhere you aren't invited, and don't touch anything. I'll let you know what you can and can't take a photo of."

He nodded and tucked a pen behind his ear and a tablet into a pocket of his vest. Clutching his camera with both hands, he asked, "How about you? Can I take a photo of you? Here? In front of the house?"

"Go ahead." Her reply was distracted.

Two clicks later, he lowered the camera and asked, "Is it true Detective Gould found her?"

"I'll fill you in later, but I want no slant to this story. No per-
spective. Just the facts."

"Just the facts."

A car pulled up in front of the house, parting the group of
people in the street. The engine shut off, a door opened, and FBI
Agent Lamont stepped out. Dark glasses and a dark coat, despite
the warm day. He flashed his badge at the officer manning the
perimeter. The cop stepped away. Lamont ducked under the tape
and strode toward Elise.

He was pissed.

"We'll talk later," she told Jay Thomas. "I'll give you preliminary details you can take to *Savannah Morning News*."

Jay Thomas nodded and moved away, but not before snapping
a photo of Lamont.

"Why didn't you call me?" the FBI agent said.

"This crime is unrelated to the Savannah Killer. Not really your
jurisdiction."

"I just got off the phone with the mayor. A dead chief of police
is just as high profile as the Savannah Killer. He wants me involved
in every aspect of this new case, and I've gotten the okay from the
FBI."

He didn't waste time. Hearing that David found the body probably had him salivating.

"Where's Gould?"

"In the backyard. He's pretty shaken up."

"I plan to shake him up some more."

Exactly the problem. "I don't think you're the person to conduct an interview with him."

"He was first on the scene. I need to talk to him. Now. While
it's fresh in his mind."

Elise doubted the events of David's discovery were going any-where soon. "You aren't the person to speak to him, considering your history," she said.

"And who *is* the person to speak to him? You? Avery? Your father?" The last word came with a sneer. "I'm the *only* person for this."

Unfortunately, he had a point.

Feeling she couldn't leave Lamont unattended, she joined him as he strode through the house as if he owned it.

Inside was the typical scene, one she'd witnessed many times before. John Casper, along with the crime-scene team, attended to the body. Cameras were in action; evidence cards were placed about the room; samples were being collected. John, his face pale and strained, spotted Elise and looked ready to say something, then noticed Lamont and clamped his lips together.

The agent bent over the half-nude body. "Sliced throat," he said, taking strange note of the obvious. "Ear to ear." He straight-ened, hands in his pants pockets. Without moving, he perused the room. "Forced entry?"

The presence of Lamont once again left Elise with the urge to cover Hoffman. "It doesn't look like it," she said.

"So most likely an acquaintance killing."

"That's my guess, but it's too early to speculate."

"I like speculation. It can often lead to the truth."

This wasn't the time to get into it with him. "No sign of forced entry, so yes. Could very well be someone Major Hoffman knew."

"Any sign of sexual assault?" he asked John Casper.

"No scratches." John lifted one of Hoffman's hands. "Nothing under the fingernails. I'll know more once I perform an autopsy."

"Care to guess time of death?" Lamont asked.

"Body is in full rigor," John said. "That, combined with air and body temperature, puts the approximate time of death between eleven p.m. and one a.m., May twelfth to thirteenth."

Lamont nodded. "We need to get a list of close acquaintances," he said.

"Avery's on it," Elise said.

"I'm ready to talk to Gould," Lamont told her.

Elise's emotions were overriding common sense. She wanted to cover poor Major Hoffman's body, and she wanted to keep Lamont away from David, but she couldn't shield or protect either one of them.

"He's in the backyard."

She might not be able to protect David from Lamont, but she wasn't going to let the man do the questioning without her.

David was right where she'd left him, this time without the dog. In another area of the yard, a crime-team member was working on the animal, collecting samples. Elise doubted the dog would provide them with much, if any, information, but the animal itself was still considered collateral evidence.

Lamont positioned himself at the bottom of the steps so he was face-to-face with David, elbow on his knee as he leaned in close. Threatening interrogator body language, which might set David off since he'd know exactly what Lamont was doing. The first person on the scene was a suspect until proven otherwise, but it was hard not to miss the gloat surrounding Lamont. He wanted to take David down.

Lamont jumped right in. "Where were you last night between the hours of eleven p.m. and two a.m.?"

"Home."

"Alone?"

"With Isobel." David, even in his stunned state, saw where this was going.

"Isobel?" Lamont pulled out pen and paper, poised to jot down information. "I need her full name and phone number."

"She only has one name," David said. "Isobel is my cat."

Lamont's jaw tightened, but he plunged on. "You and Coretta Hoffman were in a relationship, isn't that right?"

"Your line of questioning is inappropriate at this time," Elise said before David could reply. "I suggest you focus on the details of Detective Gould's discovery of the body and not his personal life."

"That's okay," David said. "I have nothing to hide."

Lamont asked more questions—these fairly typical, with answers Elise already knew. She was beginning to relax, when Lamont turned things upside down.

"Weren't you somehow attached to a similar murder?" Lamont asked David. "One that took place two years ago?"

David stared at him.

Lamont flipped through his tablet. "A woman named Flora Martinez?" Pause for effect. "Her throat was sliced too. Ear to ear." More gloating.

"What are you getting at?" Elise demanded.

"I'm saying it's awfully strange that two women Gould was dating ended up dying in the exact same way. That's what I'm saying."

"An odd coincidence," Elise said.

"Or a pattern."

"I wasn't dating either of them." That from David, who still didn't seem upset by Lamont's accusation.

"Okay, sleeping with," Lamont said. "Let's put it that way."

Now David seemed to connect. "Fucking them? Is that what you mean? Like you were fucking my wife?"

Lamont's face turned red. "I'm gonna take you down, you son of a bitch."

"Okay, that's enough," Elise said, afraid of another brawl. "This isn't the time or the place."

Lamont cooled off a little, tucked his tablet inside his jacket, and wiped at the sweat on his forehead. "I'll see you downtown," he told David.

Elise took Lamont by the arm and led him aside, away from David. "This is exactly what I was talking about. You can't interrogate him."

"You're not seeing what's right in front of you," Lamont said. Briefly distracted, he squinted up at the sky. "Man, it's hot." He broke down and removed his jacket. His armpits were circled with sweat.

"The pattern is more than just the murders," he said. "Look at the dates of the homicides. May twelfth. Both of them. Come on, Detective Sandburg. I know he's your partner, but don't be blind. The guy's not right in the head. I'm not saying he doesn't have his reasons to be out of his mind. He does. But this is my theory: this death anniversary rolls around, he loses it, and he kills the handiest person in the room, who just happens to be the woman in bed beside him."

"What about last year? There was no murder last May."

"None *that you know of.* Murderers often get away with second and third and fourth killings that go undocumented. Common knowledge. And that's cool as long as we get the asshole off the street."

He was confusing her.

"Think about it. That's all I'm saying. This is more than a coincidence. This is an MO."

"The Martinez murder was committed by the TTX Killer, who ended up being Marie Luna," Elise argued.

"Can you be sure of that? The TTX Killer is dead."

He was right. Dead, with no confession.

"I read the report," Lamont went on to say. "No evidence to connect the killer to the crime. Another thing? The Martinez murder didn't fit the TTX profile."

He was right about that too. He'd done his homework, and she couldn't help but feel that nothing could make Lamont happier than to tie David to not only one but two murders.

"Hell, Gould might not even know he's doing this crazy stuff. That's what I think. Maybe he goes into some kind of state. I've seen it before. Or maybe he took something. You know that prescription medication that makes people sleepwalk and do all kinds of crazy stuff? There are several documented cases of people doing some seriously bad things when taking that new drug. What's it called?"

"Slumberon?" Elise tried to keep her face and voice neutral; inside, her mind was reeling.

"Yeah, that's the one." He seemed happy to see that she was considering his theory. "So he just goes off and releases himself by killing. Or sometimes killers reenact an event, kind of like a flashback where they actually act it out."

She glanced over to where David sat on the step, just sitting there in the bleeding sun, still dazed. She thought about taking him to her place, but then she thought about Audrey.

In that moment, she realized Lamont had succeeded in planting doubt. She didn't want David in the house with her daughter.

"We need to bring him in for questioning," Lamont said. "Hopefully we'll find enough evidence to hold him. You have to help me do that."

"It's not David," Elise whispered. But heaven help her, her words held no conviction.

"You're making an assumption based on emotions. I understand. I get it. Think about it, Elise. That's all I'm asking. Think about it." Lamont's phone rang. He checked the screen, then answered, moving away for privacy.

Seeing Lamont leaving the vicinity, David got to his feet and crossed the yard to join Elise. He looked a little better. His face wasn't as pale and his gait was normal. Those were the things she noticed. "Am I done here?" he asked. He looked down at his blood-stained shirt. "I want to go home and change."

A female officer appeared with the poodle in her arms. "What are we going to do with her?"

All three of them stared at the dog.

"What about Major Hoffman's family?" Elise asked.

"I'm not sure she has any close family," David said.

"A will? Maybe she made provisions for the dog. Some people do." But Elise's mind wasn't in the conversation. She was thinking about what Lamont had said.

"The dog needs a place right now," the officer said.

"I'd take her, but I've got a cat." David reached out and petted the animal, his blood-caked hand stroking the dog's curly white coat. "What about you?" he asked Elise. "You're always saying you should get a dog."

"That's more talk than anything. I don't know anything about dogs. And if I did get a dog, I was thinking a puppy. I was thinking something that's not a poodle."

"Poodles get a bad rap," David said.

"They aren't very protective." She couldn't believe they were having a somewhat normal conversation about dogs when she was wondering if David was a murderer.

Elise thought about what having a dog around would involve. Feeding it, taking it for walks, Audrey getting attached. Then she thought of the alternative—a shelter. "Give me the damn dog." She took the animal and tucked it under her arm. It squirmed a little before settling down. "Come on. I'll walk you to your car," she told David.

They circled the house.

In the time they'd been in the backyard, the crowd in the street had tripled. They had to work their way through bodies to reach David's vehicle.

Wind blew the scent of something sweet in their direction. A new form of sorrow pushed down on Elise, and it came with the suspicion Lamont had cast. She was a decent cop, and she knew that what he'd said made sense. If it was true, she didn't know how she'd carry on.

"Go home. Take a shower," she told David as he ducked into his black Civic. "Eat something. Try to get some sleep. I'll stop by later."

"What's going on, Elise?" Brittle and gutted, he'd still managed to pick up on her unease. "You're sad."

"Major Hoffman is dead. I *should* be sad."

"Right." But he wasn't convinced. He continued to watch her, and for a moment, just a moment, she felt a surge of fear. Ridiculous. David would never hurt her. But if he'd killed Martinez, and if he'd killed Hoffman . . . that meant she didn't know him at all. It meant she'd never known him.

"Don't leave town," Elise warned.

You'd think she'd slapped him.

David's eyes narrowed. "What did Lamont say to you?"

"That you're a suspect," she said, trying to divert the conversation. "We're just following protocol."

David slammed the car door and rolled down his window. "You think I might have done it, don't you?"

"Just don't leave town. I'll check on you later."

Before he could press her more, she turned and walked back toward the house and crime scene.

Her phone rang. Securing the leash, she put down the dog and pulled her phone from her pocket. Checked the screen: *Mayor Burton Chesterfield*.

She'd had little contact with him since the day his daughter's body had been found, choosing to let Avery handle interviewing the mayor and his wife. No sense inviting trouble.

She answered the phone.

"So it's true?" Chesterfield asked. "Major Hoffman is dead?"

"Yes."

"Murder?"

"Yes."

"Jesus Christ." A long pause, then: "Is there any chance this has something to do with whoever murdered my daughter?"

"Highly improbable. The MOs are nothing alike. This looks like an acquaintance crime."

"Any suspects?"

"Not yet."

She could feel him thinking.

"We're without a chief of police," he said. "We can't be without a chief of police with the city in crisis."

"I'm trying to keep on top of things, sir."

"That's good, because I'm making you interim chief."

Surely there had to be a better choice. "I can't—"

"I'm not asking you, Detective Sandburg. I'm telling you. You know the drill. Set up a press conference and get back to me with the time. The public is waiting." He disconnected.

CHAPTER 31

"I don't want to be here," Elise told John Casper as they suited up in the prep room. Five hours had passed since the discovery of Major Hoffman's body, and the autopsy was about to begin.

"Nobody wants to be here," John said.

"I think *he* might." Tying her yellow gown, Elise nodded in the direction of the guy on the other side of the glass, already waiting and eager in the autopsy suite. Victor Lamont. Despite Elise's arguments, the FBI agent had conducted an in-depth interrogation of David at the police station, but as good as he thought he was, he hadn't hit upon anything significant enough to hold or arrest Elise's partner. It was obvious Lamont hoped the autopsy would remedy that. She'd never been around anybody so eager to see a body cut open.

"That has to be tough, working with someone you aren't crazy about," John said. "Any idea when David will be back? With your being interim chief of police, I'd think you could reinstate him."

John was a good friend, but Elise was keeping the suspicions about David to herself for now.

How did he do it? she wondered. How did he always remain John? He was young, yes, and he had a fiancée he loved, but how did it not get to him? In an attempt to evade his curiosity about David, she asked the question aloud.

"Death is a part of life," he told her simply.

She slipped on elastic shoe covers. "Not murder."

"Even murder."

Yes, but she could argue that *he* didn't have the responsibility of keeping people alive. That might have been the difference between them. For her, every day was a day of failure, and that knowledge weighed heavy on her. And if her partner turned out to be a cold-blooded killer? She was done. She was over it. All of it.

"Why do you do this?" she asked.

John smiled as he snapped on his second pair of latex gloves. He looked as young as the day she'd first met him when she'd mistaken him for a kid making a delivery in his ragged jeans and red Converse sneakers and his wildly curly hair.

"When I was little, I used to take things apart," he told her. "Radios, TVs, anything I could get my hands on. It drove my mother crazy. But I had to know how things worked. Later, I was diagnosed with obsessive-compulsive disorder, so that plays into the how and why. Some medical examiners are fascinated by death. I won't lie about that. But most of us have an overwhelming desire to solve puzzles. I want an answer, and each body tells a story."

"That's kind of beautiful."

John handed her an elastic cover for her hair. "I know it's weird," he said, "but I love what I do."

"I wish I could say the same about my job."

"Don't beat yourself up. You bring compassion to the role. We sure as hell don't want somebody like that guy as head of homicide." He nodded toward Lamont, who was staring at them through the glass, impatience on his face.

Glad he couldn't hear them, yet wondering if he could lip-read, Elise said, "I don't know. I'm starting to feel kind of sorry for him."

John laughed. "That's what I'm talking about. Compassion."

The door burst open. "Are you two ready?" Lamont asked.

Normally a high-profile murder would fill the suite with a number of people from various departments. Out of respect for Major Hoffman, a decision had been made to keep the numbers down. It would just be the three of them, along with John's fiancée, Mara, and the diener—John's assistant who helped with the positioning of the body and was in charge of lights and photography. Jay Thomas hadn't minded when Elise told him not to come.

"I'll just stay in my room and type up my notes," he'd said, relief in his voice at not having to witness another autopsy.

Their covered shoes made a shushing sound as they shuffled across the polished cement floor. Taking their places around the zipped and sealed body bag, they dropped their face shields.

The room always had the same mood, and that was one of respect and calm. Odd to say, but Elise thought of it as soothing. She even associated the sound of the exhaust fans and the smell of formalin with peace.

John started with the time, dictating into a microphone. That was followed by the stats of name and age and height and weight. The red dressing gown was carefully removed and put in an evidence bag. Photos were taken, and an external exam was made. Birthmarks and tattoos were documented. After that, John noted and measured abrasions and contusions and lacerations, most superficial.

Hoffman's hands had been bagged at the scene. John carefully cut the bags away and took fingernail samples, the bags themselves not discarded but logged as evidence, which Mara labeled as John worked. Hair samples were collected, along with skin scrapings. Fingerprints and blood cards would remain on file at the morgue.

The diener positioned a rubber body block under Hoffman's neck to allow for easier access to the chest cavity, leaving the head tipped back, the neck gash agape.

"He practically severed her spine," Elise said.

Lamont nodded. "That would take a lot of strength."

"How much?" Elise asked. "Are we talking about a big man?" David was not a big man.

"Not necessarily," Lamont said. "I've seen scrawny guys do some serious damage when they're full of adrenaline. Think about the instances of women being able to lift cars."

"What about the murder weapon?" Elise asked.

John motioned for the assistant to take a photo of the gaping wound. "Going by the clean edges and depth of the cut, I'd say this was done in one motion with an extremely sharp blade. Maybe a hunting knife."

A half hour into the autopsy, John ran the rape kit, standard in murder cases. He handed a swabbed slide to Mara. "Check that, darlin'."

Mara carried the slide to a microscope at the counter in the corner of the room. "Sperm present," she announced over her shoulder. "Fresh as the day they were launched."

That got everyone's attention. Sperm usually disintegrated after one or two days. If the sperm ended up being David's, it would be enough to arrest him even though it wouldn't unequivocally put him at Hoffman's house at the time of the murder.

"We'll get samples to Atlanta for a DNA test," John said.

"Any indication of sexual assault?" Elise asked.

After a visual exam, John shook his head. "No bruising, no contusions. Can't say one hundred percent, but it appears the sex was consensual."

Which might also implicate David.

"That goes along with my theory," Lamont said with satisfaction. "She knew her assailant."

"The sex could have happened before the perpetrator arrived at her house," Elise pointed out. "There might not be any connection between the murder and the sexual act."

Lamont gave her a long look of exasperation, shaking his head. "That's stretching the time frame in which semen will remain viable."

"It still falls within the parameters. It's a stretch, but even May eleventh falls within the parameters."

"We're here to find evidence, not launch a defense," Lamont said.

"Defense?" John asked. "Who are you defending?"

Elise gave him an almost imperceptible shake of her head. "I'll fill you in later."

"I'll fill him in right now," Lamont said.

Elise fixed him with a hard stare. *Don't say a word.*

Without hesitation, Lamont said, "Our main suspect is David Gould."

Mara let out a gasp. John's hands froze over the body, and he looked up at Lamont. "David Gould is going to be my best man."

Lamont shrugged inside his yellow gown. "Sorry about that. He's our prime suspect."

Mara joined them over the body. "What about innocent until proven guilty?"

"I'm all for that, but right now Gould is looking damn guilty." Lamont waved a gloved hand at the body. "So can we just continue?"

"He didn't do it," Mara said with defiance and conviction.

"Do you think David is guilty?" John asked Elise through his face shield. She could see the disbelief on his face. "It can't be David. It's not David."

She had no words of assurance to offer. "I don't know," she whispered. "I honestly don't know."

"Let's keep moving," Lamont said. "The autopsy? Will you continue? You can sob over Gould later."

"None of this leaves this room." Elise wasn't worried about Mara and John, but the diener was practically salivating behind his mask. What was his name? James? Jimmy? She gave him a stern look. "If this news hits the streets, I'll know where it came from."

He blinked. "You don't need to threaten me," he said, clearly offended. "I have ethics. I signed confidentiality papers."

Elise nodded. "Okay. I know. I'm sorry. Just wanted to make sure everybody was on the same page."

The exam continued, but the tone of the room had changed. Elise felt bad about that, and she felt she was as much or more to blame for the change as Lamont. The feeling of peace was gone, replaced with unease and resentment.

Hoffman's mouth was examined, the condition of her gums and teeth noted, and her tongue and throat were swabbed, the sample slipped into a tube with a fixative solution. As John passed the solution to Mara for labeling, he kept his eyes on Hoffman's face. "That's strange," he said, almost to himself. He leaned in closer. "Bring me a light, Jimmy."

Jimmy.

High-powered flashlight in one hand, forceps in the other, John probed Major Hoffman's oral cavity.

Murder was strange enough, but many murderers left calling cards. The Savannah Killer left his on the body, but the mouth and rectum were favorite places for others.

Like someone handling nitroglycerin, John worked carefully to extract something from Hoffman's throat, finally depositing a blood-soaked ball about the size of a grape on the stainless steel tray Mara provided.

The object looked like a wad of papier-mâché.

Elise felt a surge of hope.

All five people gathered round as John gently coaxed the bloody piece of pulp open.

"Water."

A bottle of sterile water appeared. Mara uncapped it, breaking the seal and handing it to John.

He poured it gently over the material.

Like a flower, the thing on the tray began to slowly unfold.

A rectangle of newspaper, the edges torn, not cut with the precision of scissors.

"I'd hoped for a note." Elise didn't try to hide her disappointment.

John continued to examine the material with forceps. "The newsprint has run so badly I can't make anything out."

Lamont straightened away from the evidence. "It's a crossword puzzle."

He was right. "It'll have to go to the Georgia Bureau of Investigation," Elise said. "They have an expert who might be able to decipher the text."

"Put that under a magnifying glass, will you?" John handed the tray to Mara. "See if you can make anything out."

A few minutes later, Mara said, "The date. That's all I can see."

A date would seem insignificant to most people. "What is it?" Elise asked with growing dread.

"May twelfth."

Elise looked at Lamont's smug face, easily reading his thoughts. *The anniversary of David's son's death.*

"I want a full copy of your report." With a sound of satisfaction, Lamont snapped off his latex gloves and dropped them in the biohazard bin near the door. "I also want to see the autopsy report on Flora Martinez."

"Martinez?" John frowned behind his face shield and shot Elise a puzzled glance.

Tell you later.

"I also want you to compare both reports," Lamont said. The yellow gown joined the gloves.

John stood over the body. He'd be there another hour, removing organs and weighing them. "Are those your orders?" he asked Elise.

"I'm federal," Lamont said. "You answer to me."

"I work for the city," John said.

Elise reached behind her back to untie her gown. "It's okay."

John shrugged. "Will do."

"Tell the lab to call with the results as soon as they get them," Lamont said. "And put a rush on everything."

Thirty minutes later, Elise's phone rang as she was getting into her car.

David.

She answered, careful to keep her voice neutral, hoping he wasn't calling to ask about the autopsy.

"Coretta's funeral has been scheduled," he told her, naming the date and time. "You wanna ride together?"

"Sure," she said with temporary relief. "I'll pick you up."

CHAPTER 32

Turned out Major Hoffman did have relatives; they showed up for the funeral. In a small white wooden church located west of Martin Luther King Boulevard, officers filled the pews. Pretty much the entire police department was there, at least all of the officers who weren't on duty, along with some, like Elise, who were. David, Avery, and Jay Thomas sat on one side of Elise; John Casper and Mara on the other. Lamont sat in the aisle across and behind them, keeping his eye on his prime suspect. At the last minute, Jackson Sweet had chosen to stay home, brought down by a wave of dizziness, while at the same time deciding it would be best if he kept a low profile. His forte.

The front pews were filled with elderly family members and an aunt who'd made the funeral arrangements. The closed casket, set front and center, was white and covered with wildflowers. In the center of those flowers was a photo of Major Hoffman.

A female minister gave the eulogy, and a soloist sang. Relatives, old and needing assistance getting to and from the podium, spoke about Major Hoffman's childhood on Sapelo Island. They talked about what a joyful and God-fearing child their Cora had been. They told stories about her mischief and her generosity.

This was a person Elise had never known. This was a person she wished she'd known.

At one particularly poignant part of a story, when sniffles were heard moving through the church, David shifted and Elise glanced at him. His face was ashen. He'd said he hadn't loved Coretta and that the relationship had been a mistake, but maybe he was crying for the secret Coretta.

Elise felt for his hand and gripped it, hoping the gesture would give him a bit of comfort. He turned his head and looked at her, his eyes like stars, lashes wet.

This was not the face of a killer. No matter how guilty the evidence made him appear, the murderer couldn't be David. He wouldn't have killed Coretta.

Not consciously, came the reminder. *Not with awareness.*

For a weird fraction of a second, she thought, *So what?* So what if he'd done it? This was David.

Her reaction horrified her. She instantly rejected her thoughts, kicked them away, and buried them deep, but that moment of deviancy had brought with it a deeper understanding of the criminal mind and of the women who followed their men into murder. It took only a small tweak, a small misfiring of synapses to be okay with aberrant behavior.

The pallbearers were uniformed officers. Walking slowly down the aisle, they carried the casket high, as if it were no burden. Outside, they slid it onto the bed of a shiny black carriage pulled by a white draft horse. The procession of mourners moved on foot behind the carriage, singing sad songs of hardship as they went. On the street, people stopped and bowed their heads.

The burial took place in Laurel Grove Cemetery. Elise heard that one of the family members wanted to take Coretta's body to Daufuskie or Sapelo Island, where a few of Hoffman's relatives still lived. The aunt from Atlanta won, claiming Coretta would have wanted to be buried in the city she'd loved.

In the cemetery, birds sang and traffic roared past. In the distance, children laughed while another prayer was said, and grave diggers waited in the shade.

"I'm gonna find whoever did this," David said under his breath as he and Elise watched the casket being lowered into the ground.

They'd arrived at the awkward part of a funeral. Where everything was done, but there was no real ending. No credits rolled, nobody said it was time to leave, and nobody said it was over. People wondered if every song had been sung and every prayer prayed. At last a few began to drift and fan out in a slow dance. The rest followed.

Elise's phone vibrated, indicating a call. She checked the screen: *Georgia Bureau of Investigation Crime Lab.*

She answered while moving away for privacy.

"We have DNA results on that rush order," the girl calling from Atlanta told her. "Most of the print matches belonged to David Gould. The rest belonged to Coretta Hoffman. I'm faxing the results to your office right now." The sound of shuffling paper. "We also got a DNA match on the semen." A pause. "Also David Gould's."

It was eighty degrees out, but Elise felt a chill run through her. She'd mentally prepared herself for this, but in the back of her mind she'd clung to the hope that they wouldn't find David's DNA.

A heartbeat later, the rationalizations began. Of course his DNA was found inside Coretta. They'd been lovers. Of course his prints were everywhere.

Numbly, Elise signed off. Seconds later, across an expanse of cemetery, she saw Lamont answering his phone. With the device to his ear, he scanned the dispersing crowd, stopping when he spotted David.

The FBI agent was getting an identical call from the Georgia Bureau of Investigation.

Sometimes life-changing decisions were made, not with long hours of deliberation, but without thought, in a split second.

Elise made one of those decisions now.

She pulled out her phone and sent a text message to David, who stood near Coretta's grave. *Run.*

CHAPTER 33

David read the text from Elise.

Run.

He looked up to see Lamont striding toward him, jaw rigid, face intense.

David ran.

People everywhere.

He dodged a fragile old woman with a cane, cut to the left, past a guy who smelled like cigars, then right around a table tomb, leaping over graves and headstones until he reached a flat, open area where he could really haul ass.

The cemetery was long and narrow, covering a shitload of acres, with flat dirt roads that wound through live oaks, past statuary and mausoleums.

The landscape was a blur because one thing David could do was run—even in a suit and tie.

As he moved, as his arms and legs pumped, he put the pieces together. Elise and Lamont had both received phone calls, probably from the crime lab, probably finding DNA that incriminated him.

He couldn't go to jail. He had work to do, murders to solve.

Behind him, way behind him, Lamont shouted for him to stop. "You're under arrest!"

David kept going.

The terrain changed, and blue water sparkled in the distance. He knew this area. He'd been here before.

Slide down the hillside into a shallow valley, heart pumping, breathing harsh. What kind of shape was Lamont in? Bad, hopefully.

Lamont must have called for backup, because David heard sirens, the sound normally welcoming, normally the sound of help. They weren't coming to help him now.

He paused to get his bearings.

From behind the top of a hill, Lamont's head appeared. The bastard could run faster than David would have guessed. But his face was red, and he was sweating profusely. "You're under arrest." The gun in his hand was aimed at David.

David dove behind an altar tomb, scrambled to his feet, and kept going, pouring it on.

He heard a series of pops. Tufts of grass exploded around his legs, dirt flying as bullets peppered the ground. He felt a sting in his shoulder.

This was the part of the story where David knew he should stop, knew he should raise his arms and clasp his hands behind his head and give up. But Lamont now had a real reason to lock him up and throw away the key, and David seriously began to doubt the choice he'd made to run.

Too late now.

With a hand pressed to his shoulder, he kept moving, the sound of sirens increasing while Lamont began to lag.

David veered back to the dirt road where he could run flat out. A couple of minutes later, he rounded a bend and spotted what he'd been looking for. A mausoleum. The mausoleum where he'd almost died.

It was a popular spot with kids, probably more popular now that the story had gotten out about the events that had taken place there. The lock was broken.

Thank you, vandals.

Diving inside, David pulled the heavy marble door shut behind him. The sound of the closing tomb was like nothing he'd ever heard before. Like the sound of finality. The sound of death. And the darkness inside was absolute.

He dug out his phone and hit the flashlight app, scanning the space. There was the altar in the center; there were the vaults lining one wall where cremains were stored. A nasty blanket lay in the corner with some half-burned candles, along with empty beer cans and broken glass.

And what he was looking for.

An opening that led to the fragile and dangerous underground tunnels where, years ago, the bodies of yellow fever victims had been transported to the cemetery for burial.

David slipped through the opening, climbing over rubble that had either fallen or been removed by kids in order to gain access.

The tunnels were arched and lined with brick, much of which had crumbled away. Tangled roots had broken through walls and the tabby floor in their search for water, and as David moved, they grabbed at his feet.

The smell. He remembered it. Like mildew and stagnant water and a long-dead past.

David wasn't light-headed, and no blood dripped from his fingers, which gave him hope that the bullet from Lamont's gun had merely grazed him. With the flashlight app illuminating his escape route, he moved as quickly as he could, given the terrain, sometimes running, sometimes stopping to dig through bricks and dirt. Each time he came to a barrier, he feared the collapsed area might be too extensive for him to break through to the other side, but each time he made it.

He wasn't sure if Lamont would figure out his escape route, but just in case, David wanted to put as much distance between himself and his old partner as possible. Every junction and every new tunnel added to the maze and increased his chances of ditching Lamont—if the guy was even after him anymore.

At one point David stopped and unlocked his phone, read Elise's last message, and laughed quietly to himself.

Run.

He replied: *Delete that. And this.*

Elise: *Where are you?*

David: *It's better if you don't know. I'll contact you later.*

Elise: *OK.*

David: *Delete all of this.* A reminder.

Her reply: *Be careful.*

David: *Gotta go.* He dropped the phone to the ground, stomped on it so it couldn't be tracked, pulled out his key-chain light, then continued down the tunnel.

"You tipped him off, didn't you?"

Two hours after David had eluded the police, Lamont confronted Elise in her office on the third floor of the Savannah PD.

"You discharged your weapon on one of my officers," Elise said.

Hell-bent on intimidation, Lamont towered over her. His face was red, his hair and shirt soaked with sweat. "He's not your officer."

"David Gould is on temporary suspension. He's still an officer with the Savannah PD."

"That's not how I see it."

"Did you hit him?"

"If I did, it was just a graze, because he didn't slow down."

"No blood?"

"I didn't stop to look."

He hated her. That was obvious. He hated them all, and he was no longer trying to hide it. "Because I was chasing a *murder suspect*." He uncapped a bottled water, chugged it, and wiped the back of his hand across his mouth. "You know what? I hope to hell I did hit him. I hope to hell he's bleeding like a stuck pig right now."

Funny how she'd thought he was kind of nice-looking when they first met. Now . . . "I want to remind you that the mayor made me interim chief of police."

"That's not a big surprise. He had to appoint someone until he can find a replacement. You're just a placeholder—somebody to satisfy the press while this situation continues to unfold."

She crossed her arms over her chest, one hip resting against her desk. Casual, relaxed pose. "As interim chief, I'm telling you to leave," she stated quietly.

"What?"

"You heard me. Leave. Get out of here."

"You don't have the authority to dismiss me."

"No, but I have the authority to kick you out of my office. So get your stuff and get out of here."

Instead, he got in her face. She didn't flinch or recoil.

"I'm gonna bring you down," he said. "I'm gonna bring your whole department down. And this place is going to see a housecleaning like it's never seen before." He tossed the empty bottle in the trash can and began packing his laptop. "Crazy voodoo woman. Everybody who knew Gould at Quantico laughs about it. How he's working down here in this backward town with the crazy daughter of a witch doctor."

She wanted to find out how much of a believer he was. "Maybe I'll cast a spell on you." She wanted to see if she could make him squirm. "Maybe a broken-mind spell."

He paled.

She smiled. "Yeah, we're crazy here."

Of course she wouldn't cast a spell. She didn't do that kind of thing, not anymore, but she liked his reaction. And she liked the feeling of power her threat carried with it. It felt good to let go of the restrictions of her station. Maybe that was where her conflict with her job came from. The rules she had to follow, whether she agreed with them or not. Well, she was done with rules. Today in the cemetery, when she'd sent David the warning text—that marked a turning point in her career. From now on she'd be true to herself. And if Lamont succeeded in cleaning house the way he threatened, so be it. It might be time to move on. Past time. Socrates said the secret of change was to focus all of your energy, not on fighting the old, but on building the new.

Lamont picked up his briefcase and strode off.

Elise smiled to herself and thought, *Don't let the door hit you in the ass on the way out.*

Someone clapped. Looking over, she was surprised to see Jay Thomas sitting in a chair in the corner of the room. Forgotten again.

This must be how it was with those reality shows where the participants forgot about the camera. Jay Thomas had become a part of the room, a part of the furniture. She wondered how many times she'd said something she shouldn't have said in front of him.

CHAPTER 34

David took back what he'd said about not being light-headed. Could be the air quality in the tunnels, which wasn't good.

Yeah, tell yourself that.

Every step stirred up the dust of a million dead rats and a thousand yellow fever victims. Add to that the fact that pretty much all the entrances were sealed off, either by collapse or a solid safety barrier, and it didn't allow for much oxygen.

He paused, leaned against the wall, then deliberately slid to the tunnel floor. He shut off the fading key-chain light to save the battery and sat there, his head resting against brick, arms dangling over bent knees.

In the dark he felt the sleeve of his jacket and was slightly alarmed to find it saturated with blood. He stumbled to his feet and moved on.

Elise's phone rang as she drove down Drayton in the direction of home. She checked the screen, hoping it was David. No, but close. David's mother.

Pulling in a deep breath, Elise hit the "Answer" button on her steering wheel. "Hello, Mrs. Gould."

"Elise, what's going on?"

Elise's stomach dropped at the panic in the woman's voice. Did the terror that was motherhood ever stop? She had this unrealistic idea that once Audrey was grown, she wouldn't worry about her as much. But it seemed the fear and worry never went away—because your child is always your child no matter her age.

"I just saw the news," the older woman said. "There's a manhunt on for my son."

Elise had met David's mother one Christmas when she'd come to visit. She was a lovely woman, but nervous and high-strung. "David's okay," Elise said with a level voice.

"Where is he? Can I talk to him?"

"No, but he's safe."

"How do you know?" Mrs. Gould pulled in a tremulous breath. "I swear, whenever I think things are looking up for him, something happens." This more to herself than to Elise. "The news said he's a murder suspect. That's insane. David catches murderers. He doesn't commit murders."

"It's a misunderstanding. I can't go into the details, but I'm hoping we get this straightened out soon."

They talked more. Elise tried to reassure her, but it was hard when you had no reassurance to give.

"You'll let me know as soon as you hear anything, won't you?"

"Yes, I promise."

Elise ended the call.

CHAPTER 35

Strata Luna sat up in bed. "There it is again." A strange sound, coming from the bowels of her house.

"Rats," Jackson Sweet said, stroking her thigh. "They swim the river and enter through the tunnels."

"I'm gonna have a look." She pushed herself from the bed and slipped into a black gown that covered her from throat to feet. She would have had Javier check on the noise, but she'd sent him away so she and Jackson could have the house to themselves.

A month ago she wouldn't have believed she'd ever allow Jackson Sweet into her bed again, but now they were having sex in the middle of the day like two teenagers.

She was gettin' soft. She didn't like that. Jackson did that to her. He'd done that to her in the past. Made her weak; made her lose her resolve. Gave her a baby that was crazy. Got her acting like any other lovesick woman. And she wasn't any other woman.

"Stay," she told him when she saw he planned to join her in her search for the noise. He was as helpless as a kitten. How he'd managed to walk to her house she wasn't sure. A mojo, most likely. But his condition hadn't kept him from coming inside her while she sat astride him. "Stay in bed, weak man."

He laughed, but the sound was breathy and spoke of illness.

After finding out about his cancer, she'd tried another round of roots, different roots, but nothing seemed to be helping her conjurer

man, and she was about to sacrifice an animal, even though she
didn't like killing of any kind. She'd had enough of killing. But for
Jackson Sweet, she'd kill.

"What time is it?" he asked, looking around the room for a
clock. "I have to meet Audrey to walk her home from school."

"You're too sick to walk a girl home. What she need that for?"

"Protection."

Now it was Strata Luna's turn to laugh. "Darlin', you couldn't
protect a spider."

"Maybe I could if you'd quit draining my strength."

"I'm going to the tunnels." She felt a flash of pain at the memory of what had happened down there, and how her own flesh and
blood had betrayed her.

"Don't think about her," Jackson said, aware of her thoughts.

They'd always been that way, from the first time her eyes fell
upon him and he'd made her warm between her thighs, back when
he was young and strong and everybody feared him. Then he went
away, and Strata Luna never stopped thinking about him, sometimes with hatred, sometimes with despair.

Now here he was, in her bed, tamed like a sick animal was
tamed, his hair long and gray, his arms unable to hold her the way
they once had. But what remained was that aura of power and inner
strength, and his eyes, when he looked at her, were every color, and
every color made black.

Strata Luna would never admit to having love for him. Never.
Because Jackson Sweet didn't live for anybody but himself. Of that
Strata Luna was certain. He'd not only turned his back on Elise;
he'd given Strata Luna a baby he'd never seen. So now she was careful. She would let him into her bed, but not into her heart. She'd
learned her lesson there.

He watched her with a silence that ran as deep as his soul, then whispered, "Marie."

Hearing that name on his lips made her both sad and happy. Nobody but a few cats and dogs knew Strata Luna's real name was Marie Luna. Her dead daughter, the daughter a police officer killed to save David Gould, had been her namesake.

Strata Luna used to call her girl "sweet Marie," a little inside joke since the child had been fathered by Jackson Sweet. Strata Luna might have told him if he'd stuck around, but there hadn't been much reason after he'd packed his bags and never looked back.

He'd stopped by and told her he planned to disappear, said men were after him and that his very bones, the bones of a conjurer, were worth a fortune. He'd told her a body would be found and buried on St. Helena Island, and people would say it was the body of Jackson Sweet.

"My woman—she's pregnant with my child, and the men who are after me would use her to get to me. So I gotta go. And I gotta die. Once I'm dead, the child will be safe," he'd said.

His woman.

His child. That child being Elise.

Strata Luna was *the other woman*. His diversion.

In that moment, she'd realized she was just the darker and false reflection of his real life, but she wasn't his real life. And she didn't have his heart. They'd sought each other out when the moon was full bright and drugs were singing in their young bodies, their souls needing a bit of graveyard dirt on them to satisfy the craving for a life and destiny they'd been too new to fully understand. They were more like sleek black cats born to the same litter under the same broken porch under the same meteor shower.

He'd come to her, not out of love, but because he'd seen himself in her eyes.

She'd kept his secret, along with her own. Maybe out of spite, maybe 'cause who needed a man, anyway? But his desertion had planted a root of bitterness deep in her bones. And she wasn't the only one he'd damaged. Elise Sandburg had suffered too. She and Elise had been twisted by the same wind. How strange and pathetic for a man to cause such suffering just by his very absence. Didn't seem right.

Yet despite her resolve, Strata Luna had felt herself softening of late, even before Jackson came knockin'. She figured it was because of Elise. Funny, being friends with a detective—but Elise was different. Elise was Jackson Sweet's kid. Which had made Elise and her Marie half sisters.

Think of that. Just think of that.

If he'd stayed, would things have been different? Would Marie Luna still be alive? Or would he have looked at their daughter, known her evil, and understood that the child couldn't be allowed to draw another breath?

These were the thoughts that went through Strata Luna's head whenever she lay beside the old man with cancer, a man she still ached for even though she didn't want to.

She refused to linger, even though he urged her to return to his side. "I'll be back," she said, gliding from the bedroom and into the hallway to take the wide, sweeping staircase to the first floor.

Strata Luna's mansion had once been a morgue. It was huge and sprawling and too much house for one person, yet at the same time it was everything she needed, because more than anything she needed to lock out the world, and she needed a place to feel safe.

She'd thought of leaving a few times, but Delilah, her younger daughter, had died here. Sometimes, on still nights, Strata Luna sat next to the fountain and reached for the reflection of the moon and stars just like her beautiful, darling girl had done the night she drowned. And she would feel a sense of peace. No, she would never leave this place.

The sound she'd heard earlier wasn't as strong now, almost like a cat scratching, and for a moment she thought Javier could check in the morning. Jackson Sweet was probably right. It was some rabid rat, come up from the Savannah River.

But the sound persisted.

She followed another set of steps, these narrow and dark, down to the wine cellar, to the wooden door with the curved top and three two-by-fours so no unwelcome visitors could enter her house through the tunnels.

"Who's there?" she demanded.

"Me."

Human. Male. Not a rat. "Who is me?"

"David. David Gould."

Now she recognized the voice. Yankee, with a hint of smooth Savannah drawl.

She slid the boards from the brackets and tossed them aside. Then she turned the dead bolt and pulled open the door.

David fell into the cellar, rolled to his back, and blinked at the dim lights. "Fancy meeting you here."

If he hadn't spoken, she might not have believed it was him. His hair and face were covered with a layer of dirt, his white shirt was unbuttoned, sleeve torn, his stomach bare, dress pants caked with mud and filth, a tie wrapped around one bicep.

"Is that blood?" she asked.

He tried to look at his arm, gave up, and let his head drop back to the floor, wincing as it hit. "Sorry to be such a pain in the ass. I've been shot. I'm pretty sure there's a BOLO out, and my face is probably plastered on all the news stations, so if you want to call the cops, I wouldn't blame you."

"I don't have a television."

He let out a weak chuckle as he rolled to a sitting position. "Of course you don't."

"Come on upstairs. You can get cleaned up, and then I'll look at your arm." She held out her hand.

He eyed it doubtfully. "You'll get dirty."

"Honey, I'm already dirty."

He laughed again. The fact that he still had a sense of humor was a good sign.

He grabbed her hand, and she pulled him to his feet. Once upright, he staggered backward and hit the wall.

"Stay there."

While he leaned against the wall with his eyes closed, she locked and barricaded the door.

"Put your arm over my shoulder." She guided him into position, grasping his hand while wrapping her free arm around his waist. "How's that?" she asked.

"Cozy."

CHAPTER 36

The morning after David's escape, Lamont caught up with Elise in the police department parking lot. He'd obviously been waiting for her to arrive—a behavior more in keeping with Jay Thomas's MO.

"I've got a search warrant for Gould's apartment and car," Lamont said with relish. "If the building manager won't let me in, I'll break down the door."

Elise was sure Lamont would love a display of force. "That won't be necessary. I have a key," she said.

"Knew it."

"You really don't." She turned around to head back to her car. "I'll drive."

"No need. Avery's coming with me."

"I'll drive," Elise repeated, firmly this time. No way was she turning Lamont loose in David's apartment with no one to keep an eye on him. She'd seen him with Avery, and Avery was too easily intimidated.

Moving back across the parking lot, she noticed Jay Thomas's car wasn't in its usual place. He typically beat her to the police station no matter how early she arrived. Funny how she so often didn't notice him when he was around, but she noticed when he was gone. What would his story angle be now, with David on the run?

It hadn't happened yet, but she'd agreed, at the mayor's insistence, to allow Lamont to speak at a press conference scheduled for later in the day. She fully expected the agent to share the DNA results, along with more details of David's escape. Right now David's face was plastered all over the local news and would surely be hitting the national media anytime. Once again, Savannah had managed to capture the attention of the rest of the country, and not for being the safest place to live.

While cameras were rolling, Mayor Chesterfield planned to introduce Elise as the new interim chief. "We must present a united front," he'd told her over the phone. But what she dreaded most was fielding questions about David.

On the way to Mary of the Angels, Lamont grudgingly rode in the passenger seat of Elise's car. Ten minutes later, they arrived at David's apartment building. "I can't believe Gould lives in this hole," Lamont said as they took the marble stairs to the third floor; he'd refused to get in the cage elevator. "It's a sign of his mental deterioration."

"It's not the happiest of places, but it's grown on me." Even as she defended David, Elise found herself agreeing with Lamont on a certain level. She was pretty sure her partner's choice of housing had originally been a punishment. The dark sorrow of Mary of the Angels had appealed to him when his soul was hurting.

On the third floor, Elise slipped the key into the ancient lock and pushed open the door.

Isobel hid under the bed while Elise and Lamont searched the space. At one point, Elise took a break to clean the litter box and put out fresh food and water.

"Nothing but this," Lamont said with disappointment two hours later. He held up an evidence bag containing the brown prescription bottle of sleeping pills.

Not exactly true. It seemed David had saved all of his worked crossword puzzles. May 12 was missing, a finding Elise wasn't yet sure she should mention—she was afraid Lamont would read too much into it. David carried his unfinished crossword puzzles with him until he finished them, so it wasn't necessarily unusual for a recent puzzle to be missing.

"Let's check out his car," Lamont said, holding up a spare set of keys he'd taken from a hook next to the door. "I spotted it in the parking lot."

Going through David's vehicle was like processing an archeological dig as they sifted through the layers of years. In the console between the seats Elise found a newspaper.

With gloved hands, she pulled it out, stood back, and unfolded it.

Her small sound of dismay caught Lamont's ear, and he abandoned his search of the driver's side to look at her over the roof of the car—and to especially look at what she held.

The May 12 paper, with the crossword puzzle removed. Not cut with scissors, but torn.

Everything she thought she knew about David Gould shifted and collapsed, and yet she refused to believe murder was anything he'd done with conscious thought. And now he was in hiding. Not only in hiding—he might have left the city, all because of her. All because she hadn't been able to see what was right in front of her.

While Elise's mind reeled, Lamont circled the car, evidence bag in hand. She wanted to drop and pound her fists against the ground. Instead, without a word, she passed the paper to him.

He gave it a quick scan, smiling when he spotted the date. He pulled out his phone and took a series of photos. The clearest one would be sent to John Casper and the Georgia Bureau of Investigation to see if it matched the piece found in Major Hoffman's throat. Elise had little doubt as to what they'd find.

Lamont attached the image file to an e-mail and hit "Send." "Should have confirmation within hours," Lamont said. "Now we just need to find Gould."

"That might not be so easy."

His eyebrows lifted in mock disbelief. "Come on, Elise. How stupid do you think I am? Somebody tipped Gould off yesterday, and I know damn well it was you. I'm willing to let that go if you help me get him for good this time. You'll be hearing from him if you haven't already. When you do, we'll be ready."

CHAPTER 37

I don't have anything much against rootwork," David said, "but does it have to include things like cat piss and some nasty-smelling weed?"

It was late morning, the day after Strata Luna had answered David's knock, and he was comfortably settled in one of her bedrooms, the bed itself so soft he almost got trapped in it a couple of times.

The previous night he'd managed a shower. Afterward, Strata Luna applied some kind of healing crap to his arm. She claimed the bullet had grazed him; he preferred to say it ripped a furrow. But he'd live, and now, after a breakfast served up by Javier, David felt almost human.

"They don't smell bad to me," Strata Luna said as she redressed his wound. "Something that's gonna help you heal shouldn't be derided like that."

"I haven't caught a whiff of anything that doesn't make me queasy."

"You ungrateful child." Finished with his arm, she straightened away from the bed. "Jackson and I worked this up last night, and you should be damn glad to have it."

"I know, I know." Contrite now.

No reprimand from her about what he'd done. No talk of his running from the cops, and no encouragement to turn himself in.

He liked that about Strata Luna. She didn't judge. "Do you get the *Savannah Morning News*?" he asked. "Since you don't have a television, I'm guessing you don't read the paper."

"You're making me old and irritated. If you weren't so good-looking, I'd toss you out."

He knew better, but she had a reputation as a hard-ass to maintain, a reputation that was quickly slipping. He'd seen the way she acted around Sweet.

"I'll have Javier see if today's issue is outside. The delivery boy's afraid to come close to the house. Sometimes he doesn't get the paper over the gate, and people steal it."

"I work the crossword puzzle every morning," David said. "You should give it a try. It's as good as a cup of coffee to get the brain going."

"My brain is always going."

Strata Luna glided away. Javier brought the *Savannah Morning News*, handed it to David, and left the room.

David gave the paper a crisp snap. Damn, if his own face wasn't staring back at him from the front page. Without reading the article, he flipped to the puzzle, folding it just so. Five answers in, his hand stilled and his gaze tracked down as he read one clue after the other.

Son of a—

David threw the paper aside, tossed back the covers, and lunged out of bed. After a wave of dizziness passed, he grabbed his keys from the bedside table and, barefoot, hurried downstairs, wearing nothing but the striped pajama bottoms Strata Luna had produced from somewhere, and the gauze taped to his arm.

He found Javier in the kitchen chopping vegetables, a white towel slung over one shoulder. He looked like he should be in a fashion spread. "Can you do something for me?" David asked.

"Strata Luna said to get you whatever you want."

On the surface, Javier was polite, but David sensed resentment. And why not? Javier had been Strata Luna's boy toy ever since the last one was killed. But now, with Jackson Sweet on the scene, Javier probably wasn't spending much time, if any, in Strata Luna's bed.

"I need you to go to my apartment and pick up something," David said. "You'll have to use the tunnels because the cops will be watching. Here." David offered him the set of keys.

Javier didn't take them. "I don't like the tunnels."

"It'll be okay. I'll draw you a map."

"I won't go through the tunnels," Javier said firmly.

"Fair enough. But whatever you do, don't take Strata Luna's car to get to my apartment. People will recognize it. Drive your own vehicle, ride a bike, whatever. When you get there, just walk in the front door. If cops are watching the building, and they will be, they'll think you're a tenant."

Javier took the keys. "You sure about that?"

"No."

An hour later, Javier knocked on the guest room door. Stepping inside, he placed a bag—along with David's clothes, washed and pressed—on the bed. "You were right. Nobody gave me a second look."

Once Javier left the room, David opened the bag and sifted through the contents. Within minutes, his suspicions were confirmed.

The newspaper pieces are a match.

Standing in the task force station of Savannah PD, Elise stared at the text from Lamont.

"Everything okay?"

She looked up to see Avery watching her closely and with concern. Behind him, officers sat at computers and manned tip lines.

Elise had known the match was coming, but even now her mind tried to reject the results and instead raced ahead, going down one path after the other in an attempt to find a different answer.

"Fine," she said, trying to pull herself together, unwilling to share the news with Avery until she'd fully absorbed it herself. "I . . . um, just remembered something." She turned and left the room.

In the crowded hallway, her phone vibrated with another text. Expecting a follow-up from Lamont, she checked the screen.

Not Lamont. Strata Luna.

She swiped the screen and realized the message was from David and he was using Strata Luna's phone.

I have to see you. Right away.

She swallowed hard, and her hand shook as she typed her reply: *Where are you?*

Strata Luna's.

Be there in fifteen minutes.

With resolve and a weighted heart, Elise headed to her office where she checked and holstered her weapon, tucked a set of handcuffs into the waistband of her slacks, and covered everything with a jacket even though the day was hot.

She wouldn't tell Lamont about the text message. Not yet. She wanted to see David alone. Not that she expected to learn anything new, but she didn't want Lamont rushing in with a SWAT team and assault rifles.

CHAPTER 38

You shouldn't have texted," Elise told David once Javier led her deep into the heart of the mansion. "Lamont is watching me." She wasn't sure why, but she felt the need to subtly warn him about what was about to transpire. Not so he could get away, but to hint that he'd initiated the steps that would lead to his capture and arrest. Her visit was about easing him in slowly. Or maybe it was about easing herself in slowly.

They were alone in a room Elise had never seen, located at the back of Strata Luna's home. It had pink walls and heavy gold curtains that blocked the light and supplied privacy. Above their heads was a ceiling painted with cherubs on a pale blue background. David couldn't have looked more out of place as he got up from an ornate chair, a bundle of folded newspapers in his hand.

"You're the one who told me to run," he said. Wearing black slacks and an untucked and mended white dress shirt, he was pale and needed to shave, but otherwise didn't look in grave physical danger.

"An impulse."

"I'm sensing it's an impulse you regret."

He was picking up on her discomfort and distress. "It's an impulse I regret because now you're in more trouble than you were before." A logical explanation for her agitation. "Lamont said he fired at you."

David lifted his arm slightly, and now she noticed what looked like a band of gauze under the fabric. "Graze."

She nodded, relieved, all the while aware of an emotional distance between them that was new and foreign.

Getting to the point, he said, "I've got something I want you to take a look at." He lifted the papers.

"Crossword puzzles? Really, David. Not now." Leave it to him to make light of a serious situation. He wouldn't be making light if he understood what was coming.

He gave her one of the folded newspapers. "Today's," he explained. "Look at the answers. It's about Coretta's murder."

She glanced over the completed squares, but didn't see any strong connection. A desperate man will grasp at anything. "I could see how you might misconstrue this." She attempted to return the paper—a gesture he ignored.

"That's what I thought at first. Just a coincidence, right? But look at these." David's voice was typically laid back even in the most stressful of circumstances. Now he was talking fast, clearly excited as he spread the puzzles on a table in the center of the room, arranging them by date of issue.

She stepped closer and recognized his handwriting and the bold black ink he preferred. The very puzzles that had been in his apartment just that morning. "How did you get these?"

"That's not important. I want you to look at the clues. These earlier puzzles?" He tapped a paper. "They reference a string of murders in Pennsylvania that took place over a period of a year. Last one occurred five months ago, before the Layla Jean Devro murder here in Savannah." He looked up at her with expectation.

"I'm following this to a degree," she said cautiously. "I can see the puzzle designer is fascinated by serial killers. A lot of people are."

"That's not all. After the killings here, the tone of the puzzles began to change. The answers began to reference details of the Savannah Killer murders. Some were things the media and public didn't know, like the exact word left on one of the bodies."

Elise leaned closer as he pointed to several other puzzles.

"David, this is like a horoscope. You can always find a way to apply it to your own situation."

He ignored her skepticism. "Look at them from a distance. Stand back and look at them."

She did. She gave it two minutes, then shook her head.

"You don't see a pattern?"

"No."

He made a frustrated sound. "We keep talking about how the murders have no patterns, but we all know serial killers like to re-create. That's part of their psychosis. Here's the pattern." He shoved a paper toward her.

"I don't see anything."

"You aren't looking." Frustration.

She shook her head.

He grabbed a Sharpie. Leaning over the table, he began outlining the answers, stopped, and looked at her. "How about now?"

"If you really stretch it . . . an Egyptian soul glyph, I suppose. But it also seems like a typical crossword pattern."

He shook his head. "No. Look at them. All of them. This one, this one, this one."

She tried to keep the doubt from her face while she thought about the newspaper they'd found in his car. The newspaper that matched the puzzle shoved down Coretta's throat. Was Lamont right? Had David lost his mind? Was he unaware of his role in this?

"One of these things by itself might be me projecting," he said, "but this is too much to be a coincidence. This cannot be a coincidence."

"Okay, let's say it's not. It still means nothing. I'm going to go out on a limb here, but I'm guessing if you profiled ten crossword puzzle makers, you'd find that almost all of them have some form of obsessive-compulsive disorder. From the clues, we already know our puzzle maker is obsessed with current events. This pattern you're seeing is just an outlet for that obsession."

David tossed down the Sharpie. "Damn it, Elise."

She'd delayed the real purpose of her visit for too long. "I have something I need to tell you." She looked up at a cherub, then back at David. When she finally spoke, her words were clear and concise. "Your apartment and car were searched." She watched him for a reaction.

He shrugged. "I figured that would happen."

"We found something." Pause. "In your car."

No sign of guilt, but that didn't surprise her, especially if he had no memory of what he'd done. "I don't like the look on your face," he said.

"Major Hoffman's autopsy turned up something interesting," she said. "A crossword puzzle torn from the newspaper."

"Okay . . . ?" The word was a careful question.

"It was determined that it was the puzzle from May twelfth."

"And?"

"The day your son died."

"I know that. Believe me, I know that. What about the car, Elise? Get to the point."

"They found the May twelfth paper in your car. With the puzzle removed. Torn out."

He stared at her, not with guilt, but shock.

He might be a cop, yet Elise understood his need to hear it all. She had to lay it out. "An examination of both pieces of evidence determined that the paper in Major Hoffman's throat exactly matched the paper in your car."

Still no strong response. Instead, he said, "So, you finally drank the Kool-Aid."

"Lamont was right," she said. "I'm afraid the anniversary of Christian's death set you off. That, combined with Hoffman's treatment of you on the twelfth."

"You think I killed Major Hoffman." His voice was wooden, removed.

"Yes," she said quietly. "That's why you shouldn't have texted me."

She reached behind her back and pulled out the set of handcuffs.

"You're arresting me? Are you kidding? You're the one who told me to run."

"I thought you were innocent."

"But not now."

"Not now."

"Jesus H." David dropped into a chair and passed a hand over his eyes, then looked up at Elise, puzzlement and confusion on his face.

There were documented cases of killers who'd killed without knowing it, without memory of the event. He knew that better than anyone . . . and she could see he was wondering, doubting himself.

She wanted to reassure him. Tell him she would be there for him, help him get through this. Then she thought of his mother. Someone, maybe David, would have to break the news to her.

"Stand up, turn around, and put your hands on your head." She followed with the Miranda warning: "You have the right to remain silent; anything you say can and will be used against you in a court of law."

As she continued, David turned. He knew the drill. After one handcuff was in place, he lowered his arms so she could attach the next one. The movement broke open his wound, and a small area on the sleeve of his white shirt bloomed red. "We'll have someone look at that," Elise said.

"You have to pursue the crossword puzzle lead," David told her. "Get in touch with the *New York Times*. Call syndicates like Unified. Get a court order. Get the name of the designer. You have to get the name of the designer. And Isobel. Feed Isobel."

Without replying, Elise pulled out her phone and called for a team of officers to escort David downtown.

CHAPTER 39

At her desk the following morning, Elise put in a call to Jay Thomas Paul. She hadn't been to see David since his arrest, but she'd watched the video interview conducted by Lamont. Her partner had appeared defeated, but he hadn't confessed to killing Hoffman.

"You work for the *New York Times*," Elise said once Jay Thomas answered his cell. "I need the publisher's phone number." She planned on going straight to the top. Payroll wouldn't have the authority to share the information she was after.

"I don't have that."

"Don't you work for the *New York Times*?"

"Yeah, but I don't talk to the publisher. I met her one time at an event. Do you know how many employees they have? She wouldn't even recognize my name."

"Call whoever you report to and get it."

"That won't be easy."

"Do you actually know anybody at the *New York Times*?" His elusive response struck her as odd. "I'm beginning to wonder if you really work there at all."

As hoped, her words lit a fire under him. "Okay, okay. I'll see what I can do."

She hadn't promised she'd try to track down the puzzle designer, but she also knew she wouldn't be able to put it from her mind until she dug a little deeper. She spent most of her time chasing false leads. What was another one?

While waiting to hear back from Jay Thomas, she called the *New York Times*' main line and was routed to the personnel department. A woman with a young voice answered. Elise introduced herself and zeroed in on her new suspicion: "Do you have a Jay Thomas Paul on staff there? A reporter?"

Her question was followed by a series of clicking keys. "Yes. Jay Thomas Paul, lifestyle reporter." More key clicks. "Looks like he's on extended vacation."

"What does that mean?"

"He's taking some personal time. Employees do that now and then."

"So he isn't on assignment?"

"Not that I can see."

"Okay, thank you." It was a long shot, but she tried anyway: "I'd like the number of the publisher."

"I'm sorry. I'm not authorized to give out that information."

A knock at the open door of Elise's office. She looked up, spotted Jay Thomas, and motioned for him to come in.

"Got it," he whispered, tearing a sheet from the tablet he always carried. On the scrap of paper was the name and number of the publisher of the *New York Times*.

Elise thanked the woman on the other end of the line, hung up, and leaned back in her office chair. "I just had an interesting conversation," she told Jay Thomas. "With the personnel director at the *New York Times*."

He blanched.

"The lovely person who answered the phone said you weren't on assignment—that you were taking personal leave."

"Yeah." He looked down at the floor, then back up at her. "That's true."

"Then what the hell are you doing here?"

"It's not as weird as you might think. I read about you and Detective Gould in the paper, and I got the idea for the story. I pitched it to my supervisor, but he turned it down. To me, it was a no-brainer. I decided to take some time off and write it on my own. On spec. Reporters do that."

"So you're here on your own dime?"

"Yeah."

"Why did you lie?"

"I didn't think you'd be willing to let me shadow you if you knew this wasn't an assigned project."

"What about the contract?"

"It was something I had drawn up. It's legal and binding."

He'd probably come down thinking he'd end up experiencing a John Berendt–style *Midnight in the Garden of Good and Evil* adventure. It wasn't the first time a reporter had moved to Savannah looking for fame. But instead of fame, Jay Thomas was living in a nasty dive, probably existing on ramen noodles and cheap beer.

"I'll leave," he said. "I'll pack up my things and get out of here."

Once again she felt sorry for him. "No. That's okay."

"I don't have to go?" He looked baffled and astounded and as grateful as a puppy.

"It doesn't really change anything," Elise said. Except his story might never be published anywhere.

Eager to make himself useful and show his gratitude, he asked, "Do you need anything? Food? Coffee?"

"Coffee would be nice."

He smiled and took off down the hall.

. . .

Elise called the number Jay Thomas had given her. The publisher's assistant answered the phone. The words "chief of police" opened doors, and within a minute of placing the call, she was speaking with the publisher herself.

"A large part of the appeal of the puzzle is the mystery about the designer," the woman, Yvonne Harper, said. "I don't know who it is. Nobody here knows who it is. And even if I did know, I wouldn't share that information. The puzzle can be credited with single-handedly rejuvenating hardcopy newspaper sales across the country. Our subscriptions have tripled in the last year. People want to hold the paper in their hands. When you're standing in line waiting for a latte, strangers discuss the daily puzzle. People are engaging in real conversations."

"I'm not disputing or negating the phenomenon," Elise said. "My partner and I work the puzzle every day. But you have to understand when I tell you my homicide team might have made a connection between the puzzles and the murders taking place here in Savannah."

"My guess is that the designer reads the paper. He—everybody here refers to the designer as a he, but it could be female—is inter-ested in serial killers. A lot of people are. If you work the puzzles, you know they're topical. The murders in Savannah have made national news, especially the recent death of your chief of police. Listen, I'd like to help you, and I'm sorry for the losses your city is suffering, but I think you're reaching here. And my hands are tied. Without a court order, I won't release what little information I have."

"Then you'll be seeing an order from the FBI." Lamont might finally earn his keep.

A thoughtful pause. "Okay. But I should tell you that the column is syndicated. It doesn't even originate here."

"What company?"

"We use only two syndication companies. Unified and Broad Reach."

"Do you have contacts there?"

She rattled off names and phone numbers. "You didn't hear that from me."

Once Elise hung up, she tracked down Lamont and gave him the numbers, telling him to show her what he could do.

Twenty-four hours later, Lamont knocked on Elise's office door and handed her a single sheet of printer paper. "There you go," he said. "For all the good it will do you. Money is being sent to an offshore account in Denmark with no trail. I suspect the use of a third-party intermediary. That's pretty common." He crossed his arms over his chest, his white shirt going tight in the biceps. The guy obviously worked out, and even that seemed creepy; she wasn't sure why. Probably because to her mind Lamont had simply reached the tipping point where he didn't need to do much of anything to evoke revulsion.

"While your partner is in jail, you're chasing some crazy theory about a crossword puzzle designer. Brilliant."

She refused to be baited. "How do we trace this intermediary?"

"Can't be done. Maybe a branch of government like the CIA would have the resources, but they're too busy and smart to get involved in hormonal nonsense like this."

At first she thought his remarks were just your average bullying, but she was beginning to suspect he was trying to get her to lose her cool, and she wouldn't even be surprised if he was recording their encounters.

"Thanks for the information," she said, swiveling away from him to face her desk.

He let out a sound of disgust as his footsteps echoed down the hall and away from her.

Elise put in a call to the Georgia Bureau of Investigation, giving the operator her badge number. "I'm looking for someone who specializes in investigating offshore accounts."

The young female on the other end of the line said, "I'm sorry, but at this time we don't have anyone who deals with those matters. You might want to contact your local branch of the FBI."

"Didn't you have a young kid there at one time . . . His name was something like Sam . . . Samuel . . . He tracked down a computer hacker."

"Simon. He's still with us."

"Could you put me through to him?"

Although interested, Simon doubted he'd be able to come up with any answers. "That's not really my thing," he said. "But I can give it a try."

While they talked, she scanned the paper Lamont had handed her. "Give me your GBI e-mail address and I'll send it."

"I'm not promising anything."

"Just do what you can."

She hung up, typed in his address, and hit "Send."

CHAPTER 40

Twenty-four hours after Elise figured out his deception, Jay Thomas was lying on the bed in his motel room, depressed and watching television in an effort to fill the lonely evening. The movie was boring, and he couldn't concentrate. When his cell phone indicated a text message, he welcomed the distraction.

He hoped it was Elise, which was ridiculous, because why would she text him at night? But he fantasized about her reaching out to him, texting to invite him to meet her for a drink. Just friends. Or coworkers, partners, chewing the fat about the case. Or maybe more. More would be okay too. And it would add to his story. Any of those things would add to his story.

Instead, the message was from Chuck, the salesman Jay had met at the Chameleon.

I'm back in town. Want to get together?

Jay Thomas felt a rush of excitement. He shut off the television, tossed down the remote, and typed his reply.

Yes. Smiley face. *Where?*

I have a room at Traveler's Haven on Pennsylvania Avenue. Room 234.

Want me to bring anything?

Yourself.

Jay's heart beat faster. They'd swapped numbers the last time, but Jay was accustomed to one-night stands, so he hadn't been surprised when Chuck hadn't called him back and hadn't responded to texts. But that didn't mean Jay hadn't hoped to see him again.

Now he wanted to run to his car and drive over the speed limit to get to the hotel. Instead, he took a shower, scrubbed himself down, and briskly toweled off, finishing with deodorant. Clean clothes, glasses back on his face, deep breath.

At the last moment, he happened to think of a few things he wanted to bring along, things that could make the night more pleasurable.

Chuck answered Jay's knock with a welcoming smile. They embraced.

"How long will you be in town?" Jay asked, setting aside the paper bag he was carrying.

"A week."

"I was surprised to get your text because . . . well, you didn't respond to my earlier ones." Jay hoped that didn't sound like a complaint.

"I'm sorry. I've got a lot going on in my life."

"I understand."

Jay thought they might make love right away, but Chuck wanted to talk. He ordered pizza and beer, and they sat on the bed eating and catching up. It was nice.

"How are things going with the police department job?" Chuck asked. "Getting along with the detectives any better?"

Jay was so grateful to have someone interested in him and interested in his job and interested in how he spent his days that he went into detail about the murders.

And Chuck listened. *He listened!*

Jay had a buzz going, so that might explain his imprudent behavior. Even though he knew it was unwise, he pulled out his phone and showed Chuck photos he'd taken at crime scenes, photos Elise and David didn't know about.

Chuck took a swallow of beer and asked, "Have you ever thought about killing somebody?"

"What? No!"

"Come on. Be honest. Sometime, somewhere, there has to have been somebody you thought of killing."

Jay stared at him, horrified. "Have you?"

"Yes."

"Who?"

"My ex-wife."

Jay wasn't expecting that. He wasn't expecting a lot of what was happening right now. "You used to be married?"

"Yeah."

Jay didn't like the direction the conversation was going, but he played along. "So, how would you kill her? Would you do it yourself, or hire somebody?"

"I'd strangle her. Because I'd want the pleasure of watching her life drain away."

People were never what they seemed. Never. For some reason, Jay had kinda wanted Chuck to remain this average person who golfed in his spare time. This new Chuck threw off his game plan.

"I have a thing about women," Chuck said, as if needing to explain why he was so bloodthirsty. "I think it's because I have to hide who I really am, and it makes me mad. I get so pissed about it. So when I hear this stuff about the Savannah Killer . . . I get it. I understand."

"You're scaring me."

"Sorry." Chuck put the pizza box aside and reached for Jay, pulling him close and looking contrite. But how could Jay forget what he'd just revealed?

"You're so sweet, so innocent," Chuck said. "I'd never hurt you." He kissed him, then pulled away to look into Jay's eyes. "I'm really glad I could share this with you. I've been keeping it bottled up for a long time."

Jay relaxed. A little.

Chuck pushed him back on the bed and began unbuttoning his shirt. "You smell so good."

"It's motel soap."

Chuck laughed. "See. Innocent. Have you been doing the crossword puzzle?"

"Yes."

"Did you notice one of them had my name in it?"

Jay shifted so Chuck could pull his shirt from his shoulders and toss it aside. Then he went to work on Jay's pants. "I did. Shortly after we met. I thought that was a weird coincidence."

"I loved it. I took it as a sign, as more than a coincidence."

Pants and underwear joined the shirt on the floor, until Jay was naked and Chuck was still fully dressed.

"Would you want to tie me up?" Jay asked. "I brought rope." Why had he said that? Especially after Chuck's confession?

His friend laughed in delight. "You want me to tie you up after I've been talking about murder?"

And then Jay understood that the rope would be the ultimate expression of trust after what Chuck had shared. "You can do whatever you want to me."

"Jay, Jay, Jay." A shake of his head. "Don't you know you can't trust anybody?"

"That's not true. How about me? Do *you* trust *me*?"

Chuck straddled Jay and began working his way down his body, leaving a trail of kisses as he went. "I do, but only to a point. I'm not going to tell you my last name, and I'm not going to give you my bank account number."

"So you'll share your innermost thoughts, but you won't tell me your last name?"

"Brown. Charlie Brown."

Jay laughed. "No way." Then he whispered: "The rope is in the paper bag."

Chuck paused and looked up at Jay. "You're delightful." The bed shifted as he pushed himself away and walked to the bag Jay had left on the low dresser. "Ah, you really came prepared, I see," Chuck said. "You have other toys in here as well."

He dug around and found the knife. "What's this for?"

"The rope."

"Or maybe your protection?"

"No."

Chuck cut four pieces, closed the knife, and stuck it in his pocket. Then he crawled back onto the bed, fashioning loops around Jay's wrists and attaching the other ends to the headboard. He did the same with Jay's feet, until the reporter was spread-eagled and helpless.

"You really are way too naive," Chuck told him.

"I just wanted you to know how much I trust you."

Chuck pulled the knife from his pocket and opened it. He looked at the blade, then dragged it gently across Jay's chest, near a nipple. "I could cut you wide open," he whispered, leaning close, his breath brushing Jay's cheek. "Wide open."

Jay's heart thudded. "Okay, I changed my mind. You're freaking me out." At the same time, he was thinking that *this* was the *oomph* his piece on Elise and David needed. If he lived.

"Isn't that what you wanted? To be freaked out by a strange man?"

Chuck pressed the blade into Jay's stomach. Not deep, but enough to hurt, enough to pierce the skin and draw blood. Then he moved the blade down lower until Jay felt the cold steel against his penis. "Maybe I'll take a souvenir," Chuck said.

Jay let out a whimper of fear.

"Or maybe I'll just kill you."

Jay inhaled, ready to scream. Chuck's hand clamped down over Jay's mouth, silencing him.

CHAPTER 41

Dressed in the conservative pajamas that looked like they belonged in a sixties sitcom, Elise sat cross-legged on her bed, a lamp casting a shadow over the photos spread in front of her. It was late. The house was quiet, and Audrey was asleep down the hall with Major Hoffman's dog, Trixie, curled up beside her.

One by one, Elise picked up the photos, examining them closely and looking for anything she might have missed. Most police departments had gone digital, but she still liked having the eight-by-tens to examine.

Many times she'd been engaged in an event, something fun, maybe a gathering where photos were taken. And afterward, looking at the photos, she'd wondered if she'd been there at all because the pictures told a much bigger story than the one she recalled.

Same with crime-scene images.

She shuffled through the shots, taking a few notes as she went, stopping when she came to an eight-by-ten of a handprint on Hoffman's thigh. She stared at it a moment, got out of bed, went through the briefcase she'd left on a chair near the television, and dug out the file on the mayor's daughter. She riffled through the photos to find the one she was looking for. A handprint bruise. Carrying it back to the bed, she placed the image next to the one taken of Hoffman.

As she compared the photos, Elise sank back down on the mattress, tucking a leg under her and reaching for the phone to call John Casper.

"Yeah." His voice was thick and groggy.

Elise checked the clock on the dresser. Just after midnight. "John, I'm sorry. I didn't realize it was so late."

He pulled in a deep breath, the kind that went along with trying to wake up. "That's okay." She imagined him rubbing his face. "What's going on?"

"I'm comparing crime-scene photos of the Hoffman and Chesterfield cases, and both victims have a similar hand bruise."

"I thought it was decided that the two cases have nothing to do with each other."

"It was, but these photos . . ."

"All the DNA collected will go into the database, so if there's a match, we'll know about it regardless."

"But that's just DNA."

"Right. I'm not following."

"I'd like you to compare the images. Tell me what you think."

"I can tell you right now. It won't matter. Bruising is in no way specific, unlike a bite mark. Even if the images looked identical, it would mean nothing. Well, unless you had more evidence. A lot more evidence."

Elise sighed. "I'm grasping."

"Go to bed. Get some sleep. Let's talk in the morning."

"Good night. Sorry to wake you."

"No problem."

She disconnected.

John Casper dropped his iPhone on the mattress, closed his eyes, and tried to fall back to sleep.

Wasn't going to happen.

He finally tossed the covers aside, slipped into a pair of jeans, grabbed his phone and keys, and headed for the morgue. During high traffic, it could take more than a half hour to get there. Tonight he made it in ten minutes.

He parked in the lot, punched in the code for the back door, and stepped inside, hitting switches. Fluorescent lights buzzed and sequenced on, starting at the door and moving down the hallway into the deeper recesses of the building.

In a single drawer of their massive filing system, John dug out the images Elise had referenced on the phone. And, just as he'd thought, they were nothing that would be admissible in court. Yes, the prints were in the same location, but there the similarity ended.

He sat there awhile, thinking about making coffee, when he had another idea. Using his passkey, he gained access to the evidence room.

The length of time they kept evidence varied, but recent homicides could still be found on the shelves. He located the boxes he was looking for and carried them, one at a time, back to the lab.

Elise's smartphone rang. She groped blindly across the mattress, located the ringing device, picked it up, and produced a sluggish hello.

"Casper here."

Elise looked at the clock: 1:28 a.m.

"I couldn't get back to sleep after you called, so I hit the morgue and compared the images you were talking about. Like I thought, they aren't anything. But"—his voice rose—"I decided to compare some of the evidence."

Elise pushed herself to a sitting position. "Yes?" She was wide-awake now.

For once, John got straight to the point. "I examined black fibers found at both scenes and found a match."

"My God. Are you sure? How close is the match?"

"I'm no expert, but I'm guessing one hundred percent. This is a lot better than a handprint."

"You know what this means, don't you?"

"It's highly likely that whoever killed Hoffman also killed the Chesterfield girl."

More important, it meant David either committed both murders or he was innocent.

"Get those samples to our fiber expert in Atlanta," Elise said. "Hopefully he can tell us where they came from. With any luck it won't be something mass-produced."

CHAPTER 42

Savannah had a reputation for being weird. In fact, the city embraced it, just like it embraced ghost tours and all the *Midnight in the Garden of Good and Evil* rah-rah. It was great for the economy. But Bud had lived in the city five years, and so far he hadn't seen anything any weirder than stuff he'd witnessed in Atlanta before his retirement.

A little after 3:00 a.m., Bud stepped from his row house on Alice Street to take out his black Lab, Sadie. She was getting old, and her bladder was weak, so their middle-of-the-night walks up and down the block were a common event.

Bud heard the noise before he saw anything. It came from maybe two blocks away, the intensity increasing by the second.

Screaming. Hysterical screaming.

"Come on, Sadie."

He pulled the dog back toward his house. She balked and squatted in the grass while the sound increased. Bud didn't make it far before he spotted someone running down the middle of the street, arms flailing, head back, screaming and babbling incoherently.

Bud tugged at the leash again. Instead of following, Sadie began to bark, deep and threatening, even though Sadie wouldn't hurt a fly.

The person in the street heard her and changed course, heading straight for them. Now Bud could see that the man was naked as a plucked chicken. Probably high on meth or something. He thought all of this while Sadie lunged, her barks becoming more frantic as the guy zeroed in on them.

Bud tugged Sadie, harder this time. She reluctantly gave up some ground, but not without a fight as Bud continued to bring her around to his way of thinking—which was to get the hell out of there.

If she'd been some little dog, Bud would have scooped her up and run into the house and called the cops. But she was big and overweight, and there was no way he could lift her, not with his bad back.

Lights appeared in some of the neighboring houses, and a few doors opened. Hopefully somebody else would call the cops. Hopefully the guy didn't have a weapon.

The naked man barreled down on Bud and gripped him by the arms. The force of the rapidly moving body caused Bud to stagger, then catch himself while the dog continued to bark.

"Help me!" the man said.

Under the lamplight, Bud saw that the man had curly hair and was maybe in his early forties. To add to the oddness of the scene, Bud noted that he had writing on him. On his face, his arms, his stomach.

"Help me," the man repeated.

Along with the writing, the man's face was bleeding, and he had cuts across his stomach. He threw his arms around Bud and hung on.

Bud didn't touch him. He just stood there with the leash in one hand, the other hovering over the man's shoulder, unable to decide whether he should give him a reassuring pat or push him away. At least he could be pretty sure his new friend didn't have a weapon.

The man sobbed and babbled incoherently, clearly terrified.

Sadie's barking was drowned out by the sound of sirens. *Thank God.* Now that help was on the way, Bud gave the man a gingerly pat. The guy flinched, but didn't let go.

Two cop cars arrived, one after the other. Sirens were cut, doors slammed, flashlight beams moved across the sidewalk to illuminate the man's face.

Decipio.

The same word, written over and over.

Bud felt a chill travel up the back of his neck. The prostitute killer wrote words on the girls he killed. Bud had heard about it on the news. And if he remembered correctly, the killer used a black marker. But the other victims had been young women in their twenties, two of them hookers, which was why Bud hadn't been worried and why he was on the sidewalk in front of his house at 3:00 a.m.

"What seems to be the problem here?" a big barrel of a man asked, his flashlight blinding.

"Lovers' quarrel?" another cop added with amusement. Apparently cops thought naked people were funny.

The naked man was still hanging on. *The cops think we're lovers.* Bud tried to extricate himself, but his new friend wouldn't let go. "I've never seen this guy before in my life," Bud shouted over the sobs. "He just came running down the street."

"Hey." The cop put a hand on the hysterical man's back. Another cop appeared with a blanket and spread it over his shoulders. "Why you wandering around with no clothes on?"

The man loosened his grip on Bud. He straightened and grabbed at the edges of the blanket, tugging the fabric around him. "Somebody tried to kill me," he said breathlessly, his voice shaking.

"Let's get a better look at you. Why don't you step back."

The man staggered and straightened, squinting at the flashlight beam. After a long second, the cop addressed his partner. "You seeing this?"

"Yep."

"Who are you?" the cop asked.

"I work for the *New York Times*. I'm a reporter."

"And I work for the *Wall Street Journal*," the smaller cop said. Both cops laughed.

Annoyed by their behavior, Bud asked, "What's your name, son?"

"Jay Thomas Paul."

"Why don't you tell us everything that happened," the cop who seemed to be in charge said. "Were you at a party?"

"You need to call Detective Elise Sandburg," Jay Thomas Paul told him. "She'll vouch for me."

The cop shifted on his feet while continuing to eyeball Jay Thomas Paul. "How do you know Detective Sandburg?"

"I'm a reporter. I work for the *New York Times*," he repeated. "I've been shadowing her and Detective Gould for an article. You need to call her. Let me talk to her. I need to talk to her."

"You." The cop pointed at Bud. "Stay where you are."

Bud wanted nothing more than to go home, go to bed, and forget this ever happened.

The cop looked over his shoulder at his partner. "These are probably the rantings of a lunatic, but we'd better get Detective Sandburg on the line."

The other officer pulled out his phone and made the call.

CHAPTER 43

I got a naked guy here. Says he knows you."

An hour and a half after John Casper's fiber discovery, Elise scooted up in bed with the receiver pressed firmly to her ear. Sleep was beginning to seem like something reserved for other people.

"Can you repeat that?" Elise asked. She must have heard incorrectly.

"Give me the phone," someone near the calling officer said. "Give me the phone!"

A shuffling noise, then another voice began babbling incoherently.

"Who is this?" Elise demanded.

"Jay."

"Who?"

"Jay Thomas. The guy with three names. Listen, Detective. I was almost killed tonight. This guy tied me up and had a knife, but when he fell asleep, I managed to get away."

"Are you okay?" Elise asked with concern. He might annoy her, but she'd hate to see anything happen to him.

"I have some cuts, but I don't think any of them are deep. But that's not important. I have to tell you something, Detective . . . He wrote on me."

Elise's blood ran cold. "Wrote on you?"

"Yeah. In black ink."

She released a breath. "Where are you?"

"On a corner near Pulaski Square." That was followed by the names of the intersecting streets.

"Be right there." She disconnected, shed her pajamas, tugged on a T-shirt and a pair of jeans, grabbed her badge and gun, and headed down the hall to Audrey's room.

She shook her daughter's arm. "Honey, I have to leave."

Sleepy, Audrey blinked and shaded her eyes against the light pouring in from the hallway. "Is it a body?"

"Not this time." What a thing for your child to have to ask.

"What then?"

"Something to do with Jay Thomas Paul. I'll lock the door and set the alarm." Elise never thought she'd say it, but David had been right about having Sweet living with them. She didn't worry as much about leaving Audrey alone.

"Is Jay Thomas okay?" Audrey asked.

"He's fine. I just talked to him. Go to sleep. I'll be back in time to take you to school."

"M-kay."

Audrey turned away and pulled the covers over her shoulder. The sleep of the young.

Downstairs, Elise knocked lightly on Sweet's open door.

His voice, when it came out of the darkness, was alert.

"I'm leaving the house," she said.

He switched on the lamp. "Another body?" A popular question, it seemed. Covers were tossed aside as he reached for a pair of ratty jeans. He'd recovered from the negative effects of chemotherapy, but another round was just a few days away.

"You need to stay here. With Audrey."

His hand dropped the pants. "Oh. Right." He didn't yet get this responsibility thing, but he was catching on. Despite her resentment of him—resentment that might or might not fade—she'd become oddly used to his presence in her house.

At the back door, she set the alarm and locked up as she exited.

Savannah was never quiet, not even at 3:00 a.m. Deliveries were being made, and parties were taking place. Add to that the weirdly comforting sound of the street sweeper. Just the idea that entire streets could be swept and cleaned while people slept seemed a magical thing. And waking up to a shiny new world always left her with a sense of peace.

Silly of her.

As if the street sweepers could wash away death.

When Elise arrived at the scene, officers were wrapping up their interview with an older gentleman holding a black Lab on a leash.

"Jay Thomas Paul is in the patrol car," said the officer in charge, a man who looked and acted like a bouncer.

"Officer Dunn, right?" They'd had some dealings in the past. Decent guy, if a little abrasive. Typical cop.

"Over there," he told her, pointing.

Elise slid into the backseat of the patrol car, and her breath caught when she saw the ink and blood on Jay Thomas's face. The word written on every spare inch of skin was *decipio*. Latin? Another enigmatic clue? Or just some sicko messing with Jay Thomas's head?

"Do you need medical attention?" she asked.

"He cut me, but not deep. I think it can wait."

Relief. "What happened, Jay?" she asked softly.

Haltingly, he told her about a man he'd met in a bar a couple of weeks earlier. "He called me tonight. Asked me to come to his room."

"Hotel room?"

"Yeah, I can tell you where it is."

"How about the man's name?"

"Chuck. That's all I know. Well, he said his name was Charlie Brown, but I'm pretty sure that was a joke. I don't even know if Chuck is his real name." He paused in embarrassment. "He tied me up. I—I asked him to. I thought it would be exciting, but once I was strapped to the bed, he began cutting me."

"How did you manage to get away?"

"He was drunk, really drunk, and he passed out. I was able to work the rope loose from one hand, then undo the rest. Once I was free, I ran. I didn't even stop to grab my clothes or phone or anything. I just ran."

"You did the right thing."

He nodded and wiped at his nose with the back of his hand.

"I'm going to have someone take you in so the crime-scene team can process you," Elise said. "They're going to need to get samples."

"Do you think this might be him? The Savannah Killer?"

"I don't know, but we have to make sure we don't miss anything."

"He was always asking about you and the case." He let out a groan and put a hand to his forehead. "Probably pumping me for information." His mouth trembled. "I'm so sorry."

"This word . . . *decipio*. Are you familiar with it?"

"It's Latin. It means trapped or deceived. Beguiled. Guess he had that right."

She pulled out her phone and called the head of the local crime-scene team, a man named Abe Chilton. "I've got an assault victim who needs to be processed right away," Elise told him.

"Sexual assault? Rape kit? Have her go to the hospital. You don't need me for that."

"This is a little more involved. The victim is male, and it's possible the assailant was the Savannah Killer. We're going to need skin and nail samples. You'll have to treat his body as if it's been involved in a homicide."

"Be right down."

Elise exited the backseat. The encounter, the writing on Jay's face, could have been a sick mind having some twisted fun. It was no secret that the Savannah Killer left words on his victims.

This time Elise called Lamont. He answered with a gruff and groggy voice three rings later. She related the fiber discovery, filled him in on Jay Thomas, and gave him the location of the hotel where the journalist had been victimized. "Meet me in the parking lot."

"Are you getting a warrant?" Lamont asked.

Judge Abernathy didn't appreciate the seriousness of off-hour calls, and Elise was afraid they might already be too late. The man who'd assaulted Jay Thomas might have run. "We've got enough justification to go in warrantless, but I'll contact the judge anyway." *Worth a try.*

"Good call."

His agreement surprised her. Who'd given him happy pills?

"Meet us in the side lot, and we'll go in together."

"Be there in fifteen minutes."

At the three-story hotel in a run-down area of town, Elise pulled out her badge and introduced herself to the big blond woman behind the desk. "We had a report of a possible assault taking place in room 234, and we need to speak to the guest. Can you give me his name?"

The woman bit her lip while Elise silently profiled her. Single mom with a couple of kids, struggling to make ends meet while holding down two jobs. She would have been within her rights to refuse to share the name. Instead, she hunched down over the computer screen while clicking keys. "Charles Almena."

"How many ways in and out of the building?" Lamont asked.

"There's a back and side door"—she pointed—"and the door you came in."

Elise thanked her. With little conversation, the team fanned out. One officer remained in the lobby, and two others headed down long hallways to guard the exits while Elise, Lamont, and Dunn took the stairs to the second floor.

At room 234, Lamont reached over Elise's head and knocked heavily on the door. "Police. Open up."

So much for keeping a low profile.

"I believe in going in bold," he said upon seeing Elise's irritation.

They heard the sound of movement from inside, and Elise displayed her badge in front of the peephole. "Homicide."

The door opened, and a hastily dressed, bleary-eyed man stood there, shirt unbuttoned, in wrinkled khaki dress slacks. "What's this all about?"

"Are you Charles Almena?"

"Yes."

It hit her that he was Lamont's profile in the flesh, from the top of his head to his toes. Age, race, height, and weight. Even clothing.

Dunn spoke into his radio. "We have the suspect engaged. Repeat, suspect is engaged."

"Suspect?" Almena looked from Elise to Lamont. "You've got the wrong room."

"Do you know a Jay Thomas Paul?" Elise asked.

A door down the hall opened, and a frightened woman peeked out.

"Everything's fine here," Dunn assured her.

The woman's face vanished and the door closed.

"Mr. Paul has filed a report against you," Lamont said.

"For what?"

"Assault with a deadly weapon and unlawful restraint."

"That's ridiculous."

Elise's phone rang: *Judge Rita Abernathy.*

"I've e-mailed a warrant," the judge said.

"Thank you." Elise disconnected. "Got the search warrant."

The other officers appeared.

"Read him his rights," Elise said.

Almena let out a roar of rage, pushed past them, and made it a few yards before he was tackled, his arms pulled behind him, cuffs slapped on his wrists.

"Add resisting arrest to that list," Lamont said.

Two of the officers helped Charles Almena to his feet, then pushed him toward the elevator. "Let's go."

Elise would have preferred to let the crime-scene team collect evidence, but they wouldn't be there until morning, and even sealing the room was no guarantee it would go undisturbed. A housekeeper could come along with a master key and destroy everything, so Elise retrieved her kit from the trunk of her car, and she and Lamont got to work.

"Look at this." Lamont held up a piece of rope that had been left on the bed. "This could be a match for the burns on the bodies of Devro, Murphy, and Chesterfield." He tucked the rope into an evidence bag. "You noticed the guy fit my profile, right?"

"I'd think that would disappoint you," Elise told him, "because if Charles Almena is our killer, it means David Gould is innocent."

"This could just be a nut job who's following the killings and decided to scare your buddy, Jay Thomas. That guy is bully bait."

With gloved hands, Elise lifted a black marker and dropped it in a labeled evidence bag. "Washable," she said. "The press didn't have that information."

"Yeah, but Jay Thomas did. So they're having this affair or whatever you want to call it, and Almena is pumping J.T. for information on the case. Then he acts out the very stuff Jay Thomas has told him. I'm betting it will all be made apparent in the interview."

"Which I'll conduct."

Lamont frowned. "Or, hey, how about that father of yours. Why don't you have him do it? Isn't that why he was brought in to consult?"

"By Major Hoffman. And since she's dead . . ."

"I think you should abide by her decision, just out of respect. Let your dad put on those special glasses he wears."

He was baiting her. "How did you know about the glasses?"

"I hear things."

She let it go. No way was she getting into it with him at a crime scene.

An hour into the evidence collection, Elise attempted to engage Lamont in actual conversation. "What happened between you and David? Why does he dislike you so much?"

"I'm surprised he hasn't told you."

"He has. A little, but I don't know the whole story."

Lamont paused as he dug through a paper bag. "His wife . . . She was beautiful. The kind of woman who stopped men dead in the street. I think she even did some modeling. They were mismatched, that's for sure. But I couldn't blame Gould. He wasn't that smart about women. Kind of inexperienced, really, and oblivious to her misery. Because she *was* miserable—even though they had this perfect suburban life in this newly minted neighborhood."

How strange it was to think the person Lamont was talking about was the person Elise knew. Or didn't know.

"I'd stop by their house and she'd be crying. I don't know. Maybe she had postpartum depression, or maybe she'd just gotten herself into a situation she couldn't get out of. But anyway, yeah. We started seeing each other. When Gould was out of town for weeks at a time, I practically lived at his house. And he thanked me for it. Thanked me for watching out for his wife."

Not an unusual tale.

"I felt bad." He gingerly held up a sex toy before tucking it into an evidence bag. "I really did. Gould and I roomed together at Quantico. We'd partnered on a lot of cases. I finally told Beth we had to stop. When she asked why, I tried to let her down easy, so I told her I didn't want to get involved with someone who had a kid." He shook his head. "You don't think somebody is going to do something like that. I mean, how could I have ever guessed? And Gould? I have damn good reason to think he's capable of these killings. You didn't know him back then, but he went nuts. Nuttier than now. When he found out what happened, when he found out I was the one who'd said that to her about the kid, he showed up at my door planning to kill me. And he might have succeeded if I hadn't been having my weekly poker party, all cops. Somebody hit him with a stun gun, and he went down. We all agreed to keep it quiet, but now I wonder about the wisdom of that decision."

Lamont might have been putting his own spin on the story, but everything he said made sense. She believed him. "I think we've covered what we can," she said. "We'll seal the door and let the crime-scene team finish up."

Lamont handed her an evidence bag. "It wasn't my fault," he said. "Nobody sane kills her own kid so her boyfriend won't leave her. Who does that?"

David's wife.

CHAPTER 44

I'm sending you some crime-scene photos, plus photos from last night's assault on Jay Thomas Paul, the reporter I was telling you about." Eyes on her computer screen, Elise dragged several images to her e-mail and hit "Send."

"Got 'em," said the voice on the other end of the line. Felix Drummond was one of the best handwriting analysts in the country, and typically even law enforcement had to wait months for a report.

"I appreciate your working me in," Elise said.

"I'm all for helping to catch the bad guy if I can. I'll call you with the results."

"Thanks."

She placed the receiver in the cradle and was about to call Jay Thomas to see how he was doing, when her cell phone rang. She checked the screen, and didn't recognize the number. Without identifying herself, she answered with an abrupt and distracted hello.

"Hey, darlin'."

Not a voice she recognized. "I think you've got the wrong number."

"I'm hurt. This is your old high school buddy, Tyrell King. I'm still waiting on that date."

"Tyrell, I'm a little busy right now."

"Yeah, I've been watching the news. Some crazy shit goin' down."

Maybe he was calling for a reason. A *real* reason. "Do you have any information for me?"

"As a matter of fact, I do."

Alert now, she said, "I want you to come in so we'll be able to take your statement if it comes down to that."

"I'm just gonna tell you over the phone."

Better not to push him. "I'm listening," she said, grabbing pen and paper.

Tyrell's voice dropped and became serious. "I might have seen the guy you're looking for."

So far the only report released to the media stated merely that they were "following a strong lead." Nobody knew anything about the arrest of Charles Almena.

"Shoulda called before, but I didn't want to get involved," Tyrell said. "I thought it would blow over."

"Murders don't blow over."

"I know, but I thought you'd either catch him or he'd go somewhere else. Leave Savannah."

"Give me a description."

"A white guy. Aren't they all white? These crazy fuckers?"

"Usually."

"Have you ever known a brother to murder people just for the fun of it? 'Cause I ain't never heard of one."

"What else can you tell me about him?"

"Early thirties. Medium brown hair. Tan skin. Really tan, like maybe he golfed or something. Polo shirt kinda guy. Clean and shiny."

He could have been describing Charles Almena. "If we put a lineup together, would you be willing to come in?"

"Sugar, you know I can't do that. Tyrell King can't be seen hanging around the police station. I called you because I want to keep my name out of this. I don't want anybody knowing I said anything."

"Tyrell, this is important. I need your help."

"I live under the radar."

"You ride around in a limo with a driver. How's that under the radar?"

He laughed. "You're sassy."

That was a first. Nobody had ever called her sassy. "Tell you what. You can come in a side door. I'll be waiting to escort you to the interrogation room where we'll conduct the lineup."

"If I say yes, will you go out with me?"

"You're charming, but no."

"Got a man?"

"No, I don't have a man."

"Then a woman?"

"No. I'm a cop. You're a"—she used his own description—"businessman."

"That's no excuse. I know you're friends with Strata Luna."

"That's different."

"Is it?"

"Strata Luna and I have a history."

"We go back even farther. To high school."

She steered the conversation to the murders. "We have someone in custody, but right now we don't have enough evidence to hold him much longer," she said. "If he's the killer, your ID would keep him locked up until we get evidence back from our analysts. Come on. Be a hero." She didn't add that his ID would be another step toward getting David out of jail.

"Okay, but I'm just doin' this for you."

"Don't do it for me. Do it for yourself. For the girls. For my daughter and your daughter, if you have one."

"You're a persuasive woman," he said. "I like that."

"It's my job," she reminded him.

They made arrangements for him to come in that evening, after dark, with the hope that few people would spot him and his reputation as a badass would remain intact.

As promised, Elise met Tyrell at the side door. He entered the building, wearing a baggy black jacket, dark sunglasses, and a ball cap pulled down low. A male officer did a quick body search, patting Tyrell down before pronouncing him clean.

The interrogation room located on the lower level of the historical brick building was cramped, and the viewing area with one-way glass seemed a luxury in the tight space. Agent Lamont was waiting for them.

"You didn't tell me anybody else would be here," Tyrell said, irritated.

Afraid he might back out, Elise tried to reassure him. "We need more than one witness, and Agent Lamont is working the case with me."

Tyrell let out a snort.

Elise wasn't sure if it was the presence of an FBI agent that bothered him, or the fact that it would be harder to flirt with her with someone else in the room.

Lamont spoke into his phone. "Bring 'em in."

As they watched through the one-way glass, a door opened and several men filed into the brightly lit room, then turned, their hands clasped low in front of them, expressions blank.

All white men.

All between the ages of thirty and fifty.

One of them was David.

They'd cleaned him up, made him shave, given him fresh clothes so he'd look the way he might have looked on the night Layla Jean Devro died.

Angry, Elise turned to Lamont. "We did not discuss this." Not to mention that it went against protocol to have more than one suspect in a lineup.

"Seemed like a good idea to include him."

Not the time to argue; she'd deal with Lamont later. "Any of these men look familiar?" Elise asked Tyrell. "Do any of them look like the man you saw on the night of Layla Jean Devro's murder? Do any of them look like the man who picked her up just hours before her death?"

Tyrell nodded. "Number two."

"You sure?" Lamont asked. "It would have been dark."

"I'm sure. I got a good look at his face under the streetlamp. That's him. That's the guy I saw."

Charles Almena.

And more important, not David.

CHAPTER 45

The morning after the lineup, David's belongings were handed to him in a Ziploc bag. Billfold, keys, some change. In the lobby of the Chatham County jail, Elise stood up when she spotted him.

"I'll give you a ride home," she said.

"No." He could see she was worried. She wanted to make amends, probably apologize for not believing him, believing *in* him, but it was too soon. He couldn't talk to her. "I'll take a cab."

She pressed her lips together and gave him a small nod.

He didn't watch her go.

Before leaving the building, David used the pay phone to call his mother.

"Oh my God, David. I was just looking into purchasing plane tickets to Savannah."

"Everything's fine," he assured her. "I've been released, and I'm ready to head home."

They talked awhile, and when the conversation ended, he called his sister. More reassurance and relief. "Gotta go," he said, spotting a cab through the glass entry doors. "Love you."

At home, he took a shower to wash off the antiseptic stench of jail. Then he sat down on the sofa, Isobel jumping on his lap. A half hour later his landline rang.

Elise.

He considered not answering, but at the same time he figured she'd just show up at his door if he continued to avoid her.

"I want you to come back to work," she said once he picked up.

Not what he'd expected. "I don't know how I feel about that." The cases weren't completely wrapped up, and there was, as yet, no explanation for the newspaper found in David's car, even though most everyone agreed it had been planted there.

"Lamont will be leaving now that we have Almena in custody."

"I'll have to give it some thought." Isobel rubbed her head against his chest and purred louder than he'd ever heard her purr. "Is that all?" he asked.

"No. David, I'm sorry."

He was pretty sure those were the words she would have spoken earlier if he'd allowed her to give him a ride home. Her apology didn't change anything.

"You did what you had to do," he said. But her betrayal hurt. At the same time, he'd almost believed his own guilt. "I thought I might have killed Coretta," he admitted. "But even so, I would have expected you to know better, to convince me I hadn't done it." With a distracted hand, he continued to pet the cat. "I've always had your back, Elise."

She didn't reply, and he tried to picture her in his mind. Was she at work? In her car? At home?

Through the receiver came the sound of a sob that she managed to cut off, but not before he heard it. "I know," she whispered.

But David wasn't about payback or twisting the knife deeper. "You should come over tonight," he told her. Truth was, Elise was the most important person in his life, and he'd always believe in her more than she would believe in him. Just the way it was. "We can watch a movie."

Another long pause, then, "I'll be there."

He smiled at the relief in her voice. Seconds later he came to a decision. "I heard Lamont was using my desk. Do me a favor and smudge some sage before I return tomorrow."

CHAPTER 46

Jeffrey Nightingale considered it maintenance. The evenings spent watching sappy movies on his laptop while exactly mimicking actors' gestures and expressions could never be considered a waste of time. It was the only way he could emulate the people out there in the world who weren't like him. *Emulate.* Because he didn't want to actually be like them. Hell no.

He'd spent years honing his craft, and like some of the greatest actors, he rarely broke character, even in his own head. He *became* the person he was playing. He lived it, night and day, until he took on a new skin.

Now, with his back against the headboard of the bed, he sat in the dark room and stared at the screen, waiting for scenes where he could really pour it on. The compassion, the empathy, the pain and sorrow, then the tears. He didn't know how the tears happened for him, but they didn't come from sorrow. He was sure of that. All it took was concentration, and there they were, rolling down his cheeks.

He'd enjoyed his days in Savannah, and he'd particularly enjoyed outsmarting David Gould once again. And now David was back to work at the Savannah PD, which meant their paths might cross at some point in the future. Nightingale hoped so.

He might have been hooked on death, but he also got off on fooling people, on setting false traps for them and seeing them squirm—while he remained in complete control.

It had been fun, but now it was time to move on. He'd gotten a little carried away, and he'd killed too many people. Like the mayor's daughter. Like the chief of police. The murder of Hoffman had been stupid and careless, but he'd thought it entertaining and thought it would have been amusing if Gould had been found guilty.

Using the salesman had been genius, and leaving important evidence behind—so easy. Writing on his own body—not so easy. Yes, he'd had to fuck the guy. Truth was, it hadn't been unpleasant. But the planting of the newspaper in Gould's car and the puzzle in Hoffman's mouth—quite possibly his best play to date.

When the movie ended, he opened another window on his laptop, rechecking his latest puzzle a final time. He laughed out loud when he read the answers.

His good-bye to Gould.

Would the detectives get it? Probably not. They hadn't picked up on anything yet, even though he'd left so many clues. There had been a few times when he'd thought they were getting close, only to have them move in another direction, away from him.

The puzzle pattern itself was genius—visually appealing, the answers creating a design that echoed the placement of the bodies.

He never sent the puzzles directly from his laptop. Instead, he used an online drop site that alerted the syndication service of an uploaded file. It wouldn't be impossible to trace the source, but it would be difficult.

His finger hovered over the keyboard. He smiled to himself, then hit "Send."

.   .   .

The next day he packed. After a late checkout, he tossed his suitcase in the backseat and drove away from the motel he'd called home since his arrival in Savannah. Not a great place, but quiet, and nobody bothered him or tried to strike up a conversation.

In his car, he noted that he was low on gas, and he decided to fill up on the way out of town. For now he headed toward the Historic District, intent on taking one last drive around the squares. Savannah *was* a beautiful city. Even though the sight of the live oaks with their Spanish moss did nothing for him, he understood why people went on about the place. If anything could evoke some kind of emotional response, it would be Savannah.

But for Nightingale, the only thing that awoke the emotional wasteland of his soul was killing. The only time he felt alive was when he was taking a life. How funny was that? He'd pondered it long and hard, but it was a puzzle he'd never solve.

That was okay.

He pulled up to the curb, got out, and stuck a few coins in the meter.

This wouldn't take long.

He walked down the brick sidewalk. Beyond the wrought-iron fence was Colonial Park Cemetery. Beyond that, the Savannah Police Department.

The girl at the front desk smiled at him. He nodded and smiled back.

He took the stairs. Up three flights and down the hall to the closed door.

He rapped lightly against the milky glass, then reached for the knob and stepped inside. "Hope I'm not interrupting anything."

Sitting at their desks, Detectives Gould and Sandburg swiveled to look at him.

"Hey, Jay Thomas," Gould said.

CHAPTER 47

I came to say good-bye."

"You're taking off?" Elise asked.

"Yeah." He patted his messenger bag. "I have enough for a good story. I'll let you know if it ever runs."

Elise got to her feet and approached him. She held out her hand, and he shook it.

There had been a few times when he'd come close to liking her. Maybe it was her background, the root-doctor legacy, and the cemetery; she'd been a little more interesting than a lot of the idiots he ran into. And then there was Gould, reinstated, who was at that moment leaning back in his chair, his hands behind his head, the sleeves of his white dress shirt rolled up a couple of turns. A fine specimen.

"Don't be a stranger," Gould said.

Very few things made Nightingale laugh, really laugh, but that line cracked him up.

Don't be a stranger.

He wasn't surprised that he'd been able to trick two homicide detectives. When you were shut off, blank, it was easy to fool people, because you had no emotional response to trip you up. There was no chance that some unwelcome and fleeting reaction would flash across your face.

He'd fooled his own mother for years. The only reason she'd found out about him was because she caught him in the act of killing a neighbor child. A girl in his class. That was his first, and he'd just wanted to see what it felt like. Weird thing? His mother never told anybody, but she'd been afraid of him after that. She never yelled at him anymore, and she always fixed his favorite food. And she took his secret to her grave.

Nightingale fumbled in his bag and pulled out a folded newspaper. "I brought today's puzzle. Have you done it yet?" he asked, handing it to Gould.

"Nope. Thanks."

Elise's cell phone rang. She checked the screen, then answered, frowning in concentration. "Okay, honey. I'll be there in ten minutes." Disconnecting, she explained. "Audrey needs a ride home from school. Something about a science project and having too much to carry."

Nightingale had met the kid a couple of times, once at the police station and once at Elise's house. She was like any other teenager. Disrespectful, narcissistic, and gullible. But mothers loved their brats. "I can pick her up," he said. "It's not much out of my way, and I'd like to tell her good-bye too."

"You sure?" Elise asked, while at the same time looking relieved. "Jackson Sweet can't help because he's at the hospital getting another round of chemo."

Nightingale smiled the kind of warm smile he'd practiced so many times in front of the mirror, a smile that was meant to look genuine and heartfelt and reassuring and innocent. All of those things. "No problem."

Elise sent a text to Audrey, letting her know Jay Thomas Paul would pick her up. Then Elise told Nightingale the address, even though he already knew it. At one point he'd considered killing

Audrey, but the times he'd swung past the high school to try to pick her up, Jackson Sweet had been there. And Jackson Sweet was somebody Nightingale didn't want to mess with.

But now the old man was out of the picture. It was really something how things worked out.

With care, Nightingale chose the last words he planned to speak to Elise Sandburg: "What a relief to know Audrey is safe."

And now he would deliver what the detective feared the most.

CHAPTER 48

Twenty minutes after Jay Thomas Paul left, Elise leaned a hip against her desk and set her coffee cup aside. "I should feel relieved," she said. The killer that had held the city in a grip of terror was in jail. And today was a day for taking it easy, for catching their breath, even as they dove back into cases they'd put aside during the murder investigations.

"It's hard to shut down after the adrenaline rush of the past weeks." His feet crossed on his desk, David pulled a pen from behind his ear and filled in a line of squares in the crossword puzzle resting on his thigh.

"That's probably it." Elise settled into her chair and slid a stack of case files toward her. Back to the grind.

"I'm glad you didn't move into Hoffman's office," David said without looking up from the paper.

"I don't want the position, and the mayor is interviewing new people right now." She opened the top file: a cold case, one of many. As she shuffled through the papers, something changed. The air in the room suddenly felt hollow, like a storm was coming, still and silent.

The sun hadn't stopped shining. No stars fell from the sky. But suddenly the unease she'd felt all day morphed into a fear of unknown origin. And she knew, in her heart of hearts, that something was wrong. Yet the warning bell didn't come from a place within her, and it didn't come from a place beyond the brick walls of the police station. It came from nearby.

From David.

With a jerky movement, she looked up from the paper-clipped photo of a smiling girl. Her gaze tracked slowly to David, where he sat frozen, unmoving, staring at the crossword on his leg. Not an unusual thing, and not so different from a minute ago, yet at the same time everything had changed.

Everything.

It was odd to feel such a powerful emotion, an emotion that was completely true and valid, and yet to have no knowledge of its cause. But in that moment Elise felt her world tilt.

"David?" Her voice trembled while the peculiar and unnamed fear continued to blossom.

Without taking his eyes from the paper, he lifted a finger in the air, telling her to wait. And odder, he continued with the puzzle, rapidly filling in squares, reading some of the clues aloud for her input. They were easy; they must have been easy, because she figured them out even as her heart pounded and the back of her neck felt as if a cool breeze were blowing across it, though no windows were open and no fans stirred the air.

Clues like:

Michelangelo's what? *David.*

M*A*S*H actor. *Gould.*

Opposite of always. *Never.*

"I don't understand," she said.

Please stop the clock. Please turn it back five minutes. Better yet, rationalize this moment. Scoff at this moment. Look at me and smile. David and his obsession with the crossword puzzle, trying to say it was aimed at him. Silly, silly stuff.

His feet dropped to the floor. He leaned forward, placed the paper on his desk, and began drawing circles around words. Elise told herself to get up, to step close to see what he was doing, but she couldn't move. She was afraid to find out.

David tossed down his pen and turned the folded paper around. His name was outlined in black ink. And there were other words outlined as well. Put them together and they said: *You'll never catch me, David Gould.*

Elise's phone rang. She picked it up automatically. "Detective Sandburg."

"This is Stella Edwards from the *New York Times* personnel office. You contacted me several days ago asking about one of our employees."

"I appreciate the call, but Jay Thomas Paul left town today, so my request is no longer a priority."

"That's odd, because after doing some digging, I discovered Jay Thomas Paul died several years ago."

The darkness gripping Elise intensified. "I thought you said he was on leave."

"The records were incorrect. It's very possible someone tampered with them since it appears we don't even have an accurate photo on file. An expert is looking into it right now."

"Thank you," Elise said woodenly.

She finally and truly understood the fear that had dogged her for so long. Fear of losing Audrey.

She didn't remember hanging up, but she must have, because there was the phone back in the cradle.

It was David's turn to question and wonder what was going on.

"You were right," Elise said. From the very beginning, back when Lamont came up with his profile and David shot it down.

David swung her around so she was facing him, his hands on the arms of her chair. "What are you talking about?"

He didn't know. He knew they had the wrong guy, but he didn't know the rest. "Jay Thomas Paul is the killer," she said.

Seconds passed. "I don't get it. Tyrell King supplied us with a positive ID," David said. "The rope and the knife used on Jay Thomas matched the Savannah Killer murders." Still trying to figure it all out.

"For some reason King lied," Elise said. "But he wasn't the only liar." He wasn't the biggest liar.

She watched as the full meaning of her words sank in. She could track David's thought process, from the bafflement and disbelief at learning the true identity of the person who'd committed such horrendous crimes—a person who'd worked beside them—to the real story here.

The story of Elise and Audrey.

And when he got it, she saw the recoil, saw the reminder of his own loss, along with the anger. And the sympathy. That might have been the hardest to process, because the depth of his sympathy meant he was already thinking the worst.

Too many times she'd told a mother her child was dead. Too many times she'd watched the recipient of that news dissolve before her eyes. They usually collapsed. And then came the loud sobs of denial as arms were lifted to the sky.

Inside, Elise did all of those things. Inside, she was a mother crumbling into a million terrified pieces.

David pushed himself upright and took a few faltering steps away from her.

"You've already written her obituary," Elise said.

He spun back around, his face registering sudden awareness of his own behavior, followed by the correcting, the masking. "I'm sorry."

"You can't fall apart right now. I need you. Audrey needs you."

He passed a trembling hand across his forehead. "Okay, first thing. Call Audrey. Then call the school."

Shaking, Elise pulled out her phone and made the call. It went straight to voice mail. Not unusual. If Audrey was still in the school building, her phone would have been silenced or put in airplane mode. She left a voice mail, warning Audrey about Jay Thomas and telling her not to get in the car with him.

Next to her, David placed a call to Avery, quickly filling him in and instructing him to organize a team to move once David gave the order. "And somebody bring in Tyrell King for questioning. Find out why that son of a bitch lied about Charles Almena."

Elise opened their supply locker and pulled out two bulletproof vests and two boxes of shells, one for her Glock and one for David's Smith & Wesson. In less than a minute they were heading for the emergency stairs.

CHAPTER 49

Audrey waited at her school's south entrance where Jay Thomas Paul was supposed to pick her up. Beside her on the ground was a large piece of folded cardboard, and in her arms were the two boxes of supplies for the terrarium she had to put together over the weekend.

She'd met Jay Thomas a couple of times, once at the police department and once when he'd stopped by their house for a photo shoot for the article he was writing about her mom and David. He'd made her feel shy and awkward. She'd thought he was cute, which was really creepy since he was probably as old as her dad.

She didn't know what his car looked like, so she was glad to see him striding up the wide sidewalk toward her, a friendly smile on his face. Jeans, his vest with all the pockets, and a light blue T-shirt.

Maybe it was his curly hair. She really liked guys with curly hair.

"Hey, Audrey! How's it going?"

"Thanks for picking me up."

"No big deal. This yours?" He indicated the giant piece of cardboard she'd cut from a refrigerator box.

She made a face. "Sorry."

"Don't worry about it. I'm just glad I got a chance to see you before I head out." He took the boxes from Audrey. "I'll get these; you get the cardboard."

"You're leaving?"

"Yep. I'll sure miss Savannah."

"Think you'll ever visit again?" she asked as they fell into step and moved toward a big gray car.

"Hard to say."

"Mom liked having you around." Kind of a lie, but not a complete lie. What she'd actually said was something about getting used to him always lurking behind her.

Jay Thomas hit the "Trunk Release" button on the key fob and paused to look at her. "That's really nice of you to say."

She shrugged, feeling a fresh rush of bashfulness now that he was standing so close.

He dropped the boxes inside the trunk. The cardboard wouldn't fit, so Audrey shoved things around, trying to make room and accidentally knocking over a paper bag. The contents spilled.

Silver duct tape, rope, and a knife.

She stared.

"Just call me a Boy Scout," Jay Thomas said with a "ho-ho-ho, silly me" tone. "Duct tape fixes everything, right? Have you seen those billfolds made of duct tape? They're pretty cool."

Audrey's shoulders relaxed. "I tried to make one myself, but it was a disaster. It stuck to everything."

Jay Thomas laughed and shut the trunk. "Hop in."

Moving in unison, they circled opposite sides of the car, opened the doors, and got in, Jay Thomas behind the wheel and Audrey in the passenger seat, her floral print skirt fanning out over her legs.

There was so much room.

"Hook your seat belt," he said as he turned the key and started the car.

She hooked her seat belt.

He put the car in gear, and they chugged away from the curb.

Audrey kept thinking about the duct tape.

That was crazy. Jay Thomas was a nice guy. And her mother had sent him to pick her up. Her mother knew all about bad guys.

"What's your project?" Jay Thomas asked.

"Terrariums and sealed ecosystems."

"I love that kind of thing."

"It was either that or steam engines."

"I think you made the right choice."

He took a wrong turn, followed by another wrong turn.

"Do you know how to get to my house from here?" Audrey asked.

"I thought I'd take a more scenic route since I'm leaving town soon."

Except he really wasn't taking a scenic route. "I should get right home."

"It'll only take a little bit longer."

Her mother had lectured her on the importance of listening to your gut.

Even when everything seems okay on the surface, Elise told her, *pay attention if deep down you feel that something isn't right. And if something isn't right, exit. Remove yourself from the situation. If you're wrong, no big deal. Being embarrassed is better than being dead.*

Audrey could have tested him by asking him to pull over. She could have tested him by telling him she was sick and she needed to get out and throw up. But her instinct also told her not to give him any warning.

He slowed the car for a turn.

With her left hand she pushed the release on her seat belt. With her right, she opened the door and dove out. The car was moving faster than she thought, and she hit the ground hard, her bare legs sliding across the pavement.

Jay Thomas slammed on the brakes and threw the car in reverse. The vehicle flew backward, stopping with the open passenger door even with her.

"What are you doing?"

The look on his face. Gone was the friendly, warm person who'd walked up the sidewalk. The friendly guy who'd taken her photo at their house. In his place was someone she wasn't even sure she'd have recognized—his face looked so different.

Like nothing.

No expression at all. Just emptiness.

She scrambled to her feet. "I'm gonna walk."

On the floor of the car was her backpack. In the backpack was her phone. Her keys.

"Get in the car, Audrey. I promised your mother I'd see you safely home."

"I can see myself safely home."

She turned and ran, ignoring the pain in her scraped legs, ignoring the dripping blood. Her black boots slammed against the pavement, her arms pumped, and her hair flew behind her.

She heard a car approaching. She glanced to her side, caught a glimpse of gray bumper. In the opposite direction was an alley. She plunged down it. The car went straight.

She kept running.

Her head was full of her beating heart and her heavy breathing, leaving no room for anything else. In the distance, at the end of the alley, the gray car appeared.

She screamed and turned. Abandoning the alley, she cut through a yard, pausing long enough to knock loudly on a door. When no one answered, she tested the handle, then kept running.

Most of the homes in the Historic District had private back-yards with high fences and courtyards. There was no easy way to get from point A to point B. As she wove through yards and alleys, she kept moving in the direction of home.

As she ran, she tried to make sense of what was happening.

That face. Jay Thomas Paul's face. That was not the face of a normal person.

But they'd caught the killer, the man who'd murdered Major Hoffman and those other girls.

She was three blocks from home.

Arms and legs pumping, chest and lungs on fire, she didn't slow down. At the same time, she kept having stupid thoughts. Like how her science project stuff was still in his car. And how she needed to get it back so she could work on it this weekend.

Then her yellow Victorian house came into sight.

Seeing it gave her a burst of power, and she felt as though her body could hardly keep up with her flying feet. She looked over her shoulder long enough to see the gray car coming down the road.

She bolted to the front door and pressed the thumb latch. Nothing. She rattled it. Locked.

The car pulled to a stop.

She ran through the yard to the back of the house, across the patio that Avery, David, John, and Mara had all helped make. To the back door.

Locked.

She let out a sob, then quickly scanned the houses on both sides—owned by couples who worked during the day. No help from them. She pounded on the door, then remembered that her grandfather was at the hospital getting chemo.

From inside, Trixie let out an excited bark.

Audrey raced to the garage. Inside, she felt above the walk-through door for the key she used when she forgot hers or when she snuck out at night.

Her fingers made contact. The key dropped to the floor. In the darkness of the garage, she searched blindly, finding it.

Run.

To the house, slip the key in the lock. Hands shaking.

A sound, followed by a blur and the force and weight of a body slamming into her. A turn of the key and the door flew open. She crashed to the kitchen floor, Jay Thomas Paul on top of her.

Before he could get a secure hold, she scrambled to her feet and ran.

CHAPTER 50

Elise's cell phone rang as she and David raced to the parking lot and her car.

The call came from Elise's home phone. She hit "Answer."

"Mom." The word was a whisper.

Key fob in her hand, Elise pressed the "Unlock" button. "Audrey! Are you all right?"

David motioned for her to take the passenger side. She circled and dove in. Doors slammed. Behind the wheel, David grabbed the key from her and stuck it in the ignition.

"Jay Thomas is in the house," Audrey said. "And, Mom, he's not who you think he is. I ran away from him, and he followed me inside."

Engine running, David reversed, then shot from the lot, the car bottoming out as they rounded a corner. "Where are you now?" Elise asked, bracing for the next turn, surprised Audrey was able to sound so calm.

"In my bedroom with the door locked."

"Stay there. We're coming. Don't hang up."

Elise heard a crash and the phone went dead.

CHAPTER 51

The nurse handed Jackson Sweet his home care kit. It contained little more than repeat follow-up instructions and a handful of pink sponges on sticks. "We'll see you next week," she said with a cheerful smile. "Just three more treatments and you'll be done."

They were always so damn happy here.

His one and only goal was to get back to Elise's as quickly as possible and dive into bed, a bucket beside him on the floor. Based on his last treatment, he knew he didn't have long before the nausea hit, and they'd already warned him that this time would be worse.

A young girl in a striped apron wheeled him out of the hospital. The sun was blinding, and he shielded his face, flinching like a vampire, the very brightness of the day and the blueness of the sky an insult to his poor health. He should have gone out bravely, just crawled into the woods and died. Instead, he'd let Elise and Audrey talk him into pumping himself full of poison.

Not that he had anything against poison. But this poison, even if it cured him, didn't have the power to make him any less of a bastard. It wouldn't erase the things he'd done in his life. It wouldn't repair his relationship with Elise. It wouldn't absolve him of anything. Even as he had these thoughts, he still tried to make excuses for himself. He'd been young, and young men were stupid, full of fire and selfishness.

In the cab, he gave the driver Elise's address, leaned back in the seat, and closed his eyes, trying to ignore the movement of the vehicle.

He must have dozed off, because it didn't seem a minute had passed when the driver asked, "This it up here? The yellow Victorian?"

"Yep." Sweet reached for his billfold in order to pay with money Elise had given him—because he couldn't even afford his own cab. He had no idea how he was going to cover his treatments. He was kinda hoping he'd be dead before he had to worry about it.

He paused, his billfold still in his pocket as he watched a car exit the alley behind Elise's house. The driver looked in his direction, and Sweet recognized the curly-haired reporter who was writing a story on Elise and David.

Sweet didn't like him. That didn't mean all that much by itself, since there were few people Sweet could tolerate, but this was more than just basic dislike. He was pondering his reaction to Jay Thomas when his phone—a phone also supplied by Elise—rang.

He hated the damn thing, and it took some fumbling before he was able to answer.

"Where are you? Home?" Elise, talking rapidly.

"Just pulled up," he told her.

"Listen to me. Jay Thomas Paul is after Audrey. And Jay Thomas Paul is the Savannah Killer."

Full alert, all drowsiness gone. "Where's Audrey now?"

"She called me from her bedroom. Jay Thomas is *in the house.*"

Sweet had a decision to make. He could go inside, hoping to find Audrey alive and well, or he could follow the car that was fading into the distance. If Audrey was in the house, she might already be dead. But if she was in the car . . .

"I just spotted the reporter driving down your alley," Sweet said.

"Was he alone?"

"I'll let you know." He disconnected. "Follow the gray car," he told the cab driver, "but keep your distance."

Minutes into the chase, Sweet realized Jay Thomas had spotted them. Kind of obvious when a bright yellow cab was mimicking his every turn. Jay Thomas increased his speed.

"Don't lose him," Sweet instructed, trying to keep his voice cool.

The cab screeched to a stop at a red light, but not before Jay Thomas Paul blasted through the intersection.

"Run it!" Sweet shouted.

The driver stayed where he was. "Get out!" he shouted. "Out of my cab! You don't even have to pay—just go!"

"Sure. Okay."

Sweet slipped out the left side of the vehicle, slamming the door behind him. Then, in a movement that belied just how damn sick he was beginning to feel, he ripped open the driver's door and grabbed the man by the throat. "Now *you* get out."

At first the cabbie appeared more angry than afraid, but as he stared, Sweet saw true fear wash over him.

"My God," he managed to strangle out. "You're Jackson Sweet."

"And you're going to let me borrow your cab."

The man unlatched his seat belt while Sweet loosened his grip—not relinquishing it fully until the driver stood in front of him.

"Don't curse me," the man said, backing away, hands in the air as if being threatened with a gun. Behind them, cars honked. Sweet looked up to see a green light.

He jumped in the vehicle and pushed the accelerator to the floor. Never the best of drivers, he swerved, tires squealing, almost hitting a guy on a bike and a mother pushing a stroller. In the far distance sirens wailed—maybe for him, maybe for Audrey.

A couple of blocks later he spotted a gray car stuck in traffic just as a warning wave of nausea washed over him.

CHAPTER 52

Jeffrey Nightingale, aka Jay Thomas Paul, spotted the cab in his rearview mirror, and damn if Jackson Sweet wasn't behind the wheel.

Nightingale laid on his horn, transmitting his emergency to the people in front of him. Cars moved out of his way, and he broke through the traffic jam and turned right, taking Highway 17 to the Talmadge Bridge, crossing the Savannah River. When he hit land again, he opened the car up, his mind racing. One old man. Just one old man. He could handle one old man.

Three miles, and he looked in the mirror to see the cab on his bumper.

He spotted a road of broken concrete winding between two sprawling fields of swamp and grassland. In the distance was a complex that looked like an old factory. He turned and aimed for it. The cab followed.

The distance between the car and the padlocked gate surrounding the complex shrank, but Nightingale didn't slow. Instead, he pressed harder on the accelerator. The engine roared, propelling the car through the barrier. A direct hit, followed by the sound of metal scraping metal.

But Nightingale had only a moment to celebrate as the car rapidly lost speed and finally sputtered to a stop. At first he thought he'd damaged the engine in the crash through the gate, but looking down, he saw that the gas gauge was on empty.

Bailing out, he hit the "Trunk Release." A sprint to the back of the vehicle and he jerked the girl to her feet.

"Run!" he commanded.

Her mouth was covered in duct tape, her hands tied in front of her with his favorite rope, but when he dug his fingers into her arm and pulled her along, she followed.

The terrain was flat. In the distance, Sweet saw two people—a man and a girl—moving across a parking lot of weeds and broken concrete that belonged to what had once been a paper mill. Sweet pulled out his phone and pushed the number Elise had preset for him. She answered.

"I'm about four miles from the Talmadge Memorial Bridge, off Highway 17. We took a left at a decaying strip joint called Place of Dreams. Jay Thomas abandoned his car and is on foot. Heading toward the old paper mill. He's got Audrey with him."

"She's alive?" It was impossible to miss the tremor in Elise's voice.

"Yes." Another wave of nausea hit him.

CHAPTER 53

E lise wasn't sure how much time passed before she felt David tugging at her cell phone. Only then did she realize she was staring at the screen.

They were standing in Audrey's room after making a sweep of the house. There were obvious signs of struggle, but no blood. *No blood.*

"Jay Thomas has Audrey," Elise said. She repeated what Sweet had told her.

David produced his phone and called Avery at the task force center, calmly and efficiently relaying commands and ordering a BOLO. "This has to be a stealth operation," David said into the phone as he and Elise moved quickly through the house and down the stairs. "We can't have cops going in there, guns blazing. Right now the only objective is to make sure he doesn't kill Audrey. If we lose Jay Thomas in the process, we lose him."

Jackson Sweet didn't have a gun; he didn't have any kind of weapon. And he was no kid. Fifty-eight wasn't nursing home age, but he felt a hundred, and he'd seen himself in the mirror lately. Right now he looked seventy.

Years ago he'd brought killers to their knees just by being in the same room. And when he'd regarded them with unblinking eyes through the blue shades he'd given to Elise, the killers broke. They always broke.

He was still Jackson Sweet.

Somewhere in this pathetic weak body that had turned on him—this casing, this shell of bones and skin—Jackson Sweet still lived and breathed.

He drove past marshland and ground so saturated it would suck the boots off your feet. At the gate, he didn't slow down. It was all about surprise. He hurtled toward the people running for the mill. Passing them, he turned and braked, skidding to a complete stop yards away.

He pulled the keys from the ignition, pushed open the door, and stepped out.

Audrey's mouth was covered in duct tape, her hands bound with rope. The man who called himself Jay Thomas Paul gripped her by the hair, holding a handgun to her temple while using her as a shield.

Sweet could see the terror in his granddaughter's eyes, and for the first time in his life he experienced true fear for someone else.

Most men on a chase would have had a weapon, and the lack of one was something Sweet deeply regretted. But taking a gun to chemotherapy was frowned upon, even in Savannah.

"Let the girl go." The words were quiet, not much above conversational, but they carried. "Let her go. Take the car. Get the hell out of here."

Jay Thomas laughed. "Go away, old man. Go away or I'll kill you."

"You're done. They know who you are. It's all over. I'm offering you an escape."

"It's never over." Jay Thomas shifted the weapon from Audrey's head to Sweet's.

"Let the girl go." A fresh wave of nausea washed over Sweet, but he fought it. His leg trembled with weakness while he called upon his inner strength to get him through the next few minutes. Just a few minutes. That was all he needed.

Fear was the key, and belief was born out of fear. To test Jay Thomas's fear and belief, Sweet chanted something he'd learned years ago:

"If I hang by a single thread
In a place no one shall see
When the time comes for you to sleep
A sleep of death will be."

White men weren't conjurers. White men couldn't bend people to their will. But when an old Gullah man chose Sweet to follow in his footsteps, Sweet had taken up the mantle. He should have refused. Look how it had screwed up his life. And Elise's.

And yet she'd become a cop. Like Sweet. And she had whatever he had. He'd felt it in her. Audrey too.

Not magic. Hell no. It wasn't anything supernatural, even though he let people think so. What he had was a *connection*, an ability to tap into something he didn't understand. And from practice, he knew the person on the receiving end needed to believe.

Elise had been right about him all along. He had no real power. The power was in the belief. Question was, did the man in front of him believe?

Sweet was close enough to see the color of Jay Thomas's eyes. Green and gold. "Let the girl go." Sweet held out his hand, car keys in his open palm. "I take Audrey; you take the keys. Simple as that."

Without breaking eye contact, without blinking, Sweet began to chant a confusion spell:

"Cobwebs in your brain
Fear I do sow

Allow your thoughts to scatter
Let the girl go."

The reward, when it came, was everything Sweet could have hoped for—that split second when Jay Thomas redirected his attention to the keys in Sweet's hand, when the chant distracted him, confused him.

Belief.

Sweet lunged, taking Jay Thomas by surprise and knocking him to the ground. Leaping back to his feet, Sweet stomped the killer's wrist, jarring the weapon free—he quickly swept it up and aimed it at Jay Thomas while Audrey ran to her grandfather's side.

Keeping the weapon trained on Jay Thomas, Sweet pulled the tape from Audrey's mouth, and she let out a gasping sob.

Sirens sounded in the distance, and Sweet detected what might have been the approach of a far-off helicopter. Or maybe the hum came from inside his head—because with no warning, the picture tilted. Sweet tried to catch himself, stumbled, then pitched forward, slamming into the ground.

Audrey screamed as a foot kicked Sweet in the stomach.

He curled into a ball and shouted, "Run, Audrey!"

Sweet opened his eyes in time to see her black boots turn and leave his field of focus, the sound of her feet pounding over the cracked pavement as she raced toward the abandoned mill. "Hide!" he shouted.

Jay Thomas kicked him again. Sweet gasped in pain as the gun was wrenched from his hand and the sound of sirens increased.

Elise's cell phone buzzed, indicating a text message. Heart hammering, she checked the screen: *Jay Thomas.*

Hands on the wheel, David glanced over at her, then back at the road.

"He sent a video," Elise said.

"Wait! Don't—"

She understood his command. He was afraid she'd see something no mother should see. She hit the "Play" icon.

A second passed before her brain made sense of the scene: Jackson Sweet on the ground, his face bloody and pale. After a moment, Jay Thomas turned the camera on himself and said, "Call off the cops or I'll kill your father."

In the background, she heard a pain-filled laugh. Sweet. "You just made her day."

Beside her, David put in a call to Avery. "I ordered stealth. Tell everybody to back off. Immediately!"

Elise hit the "Return Call" button, and Jay Thomas answered. "No police," he said. "Get rid of them right now."

"Done. It's done."

"Good. And Elise? Your dad doesn't look so hot."

"Where's Audrey?"

"No roadblocks, you hear?" Jay Thomas told her. "No helicopters. I'm bringing your father with me. If I see a roadblock or a helicopter, he's getting shot in the head."

"Where's Audrey? Where's my daughter?"

"It's your dad you need to worry about." He hung up.

Jeffrey Nightingale kept the gun trained on Jackson Sweet's head. "Get up."

Sweet curled to his knees, then slowly pushed himself upright. "Walk."

Sweet began moving, achingly, shakily, his feet shuffling through the dirt. He staggered, and for a moment Nightingale thought he might go down again. "Hurry, old man."

The words had barely left Nightingale's mouth when Jackson Sweet pivoted and came flying through the air, tackling Nightingale, both of them hitting the ground with a loud *whoomph*. Sweet was strong for a sick man, but not strong enough. A minute into the struggle, the gun went off and everything stopped. Nightingale broke away in time to see Sweet's eyes roll back in his head. The killer stumbled to his feet, and with detachment he observed the man on the ground.

One down, one to go.

CHAPTER 54

David and Elise were first on the scene.

David pulled to a hard stop and slammed the car into park. Dressed in black bulletproof vests, they dove out, weapons drawn.

The cab was gone, but Jay Thomas's car sat beyond the mangled gate, its doors open.

"Could be a trap," David said as they approached the vehicle, guns braced.

More cops were coming, following without sirens. Along with reinforcements, unmarked cars were moving to designated areas along the escape routes most likely to be taken by Jay Thomas.

"Blood." Elise nodded toward a dark stain on the cement. "A lot of it."

David pointed. "Shell casing."

A wave of weakness washed over Elise. Jay Thomas had her father with him, and there'd been no mention of Audrey. She lowered her weapon, its weight suddenly too much.

This was it. The thing she most feared, the thing that had snapped at her heels for years. Maybe she *did* have some kind of power, because she'd felt this day coming for a long, long time.

She tracked the path of blood—one wide strip that led to the trunk of Jay Thomas's car.

"No . . ." The word was long and quivering. Her knees buckled, and she hit the ground.

She felt a hand on her shoulder, knew it was David. Didn't matter.

"Don't jump to conclusions," he said.

She dragged her gaze from the blood to David. She wanted to grab his words of hope, hug them to her, but she saw his face—saw her own pain and shock there.

His hand dropped away. "I'll look."

She might have said something; she wasn't sure. Breathing, living, were suddenly too much work, but she managed to shove herself to her feet. Upright, she moved stiffly in the direction of the car.

"Locked." Peering through the windows, David did a visual sweep of the interior, then circled to the back of the vehicle. Positioning himself so the bullet would miss the trunk cavity, he fired at the lock, kicked it hard two times, then raised the lid.

A body, curled among boxes and a flat of cardboard.

Gray hair.

Gray hair.

Elise let out a sob and pressed her hand to her mouth while David pocketed his weapon and leaned into the trunk.

"He's still alive."

Elise pulled out her phone and called dispatch. "We're going to need an ambulance at the paper mill. Gunshot wound. And tell them no sirens."

After disconnecting, she asked, "Is he conscious?"

"No."

Which meant he wouldn't be able to tell them anything about Audrey.

"I'm guessing Jay Thomas never intended to let him live," David said. "He just wanted us to think your father was with him. He shot him and hid the body."

"Audrey?" Elise knew the answer. She was a cop. She'd worked homicide for years. Audrey was either with Jay Thomas or she was dead.

"He would have told us he was holding her hostage if she was still alive," Elise said. "She was a better bargaining tool." The words they were both thinking. "He would have sent us a video of Audrey, not Jackson Sweet."

David didn't speak. He didn't need to. His thoughts were written on his face. Audrey was dead.

For the second time in a matter of minutes, Elise's world stopped, and the life she'd known that morning no longer existed. There was nothing to feel, nothing to keep her going.

Yes, a killer was on the loose.

And yes, he'd most likely murdered Elise's daughter.

But in that moment, Elise died inside. She didn't have enough emotion left in her to want to catch him and bring him to justice. Trying to catch him was why her daughter was gone. Gone, not dead, because she couldn't say dead, not even in her mind.

"I'll find him and I'll kill him," David said.

"I don't even care."

She collapsed and rolled to her back to look up at the sky. "I don't even care."

From off in the distance came engine and tire sounds of approaching vehicles. Probably the ambulance. Probably police cars.

She didn't care.

She rolled to her side, curled into a ball, and began to sob.

"Mom?"

She heard, but the import of that one word didn't connect with her grief-stricken brain, not until the word was repeated.

Elise turned enough to look beyond an expanse of cement. Black boots. Bare, skinned legs. A floral skirt. Just like the floral skirt Audrey had worn to school that morning.

Elise was unaware of getting to her feet, but suddenly she was flying across the cracked cement to sweep Audrey into her arms, hugging her, pressing her face into her hair, breathing in the scent of her, both of them crying. Finally, Elise leaned back to get a good look at her daughter, smoothing her dark hair over and over, removing the rope from her wrists. "I thought you were dead."

"Me too. I mean, I thought he was going to kill me." Her gaze shifted. "How's Grandpa? Is he . . . ?"

Elise turned to see medics lifting her father onto a stretcher while a third medic prepared an IV.

David joined mother and daughter, embracing Audrey, appearing unable to speak. Over Audrey's head, he caught Elise's eye, reached for her, and squeezed her hand.

CHAPTER 55

Elise pulled a female officer aside. "Please escort my daughter back to town."

"Of course."

"No. Mom."

Elise would have liked nothing better than to return to Savannah with Audrey. Take her home, close and lock the door, and stay there, waiting for a call from David to report that Jay Thomas had been caught. Jay Thomas. Not his real name, she knew that now, but Jay Thomas was the name in her head.

She held Audrey firmly by both hands. "I have to see this through."

"Elise. Go back with her," David said. "I'll take care of it. You've been through too much already."

"I can go through a lot more."

David watched her, understood, and nodded.

"Take her to the police station," Elise told the officer. "She can wait in my office."

"He tricked you both for a long time," Audrey argued. "He'll trick you again."

Elise's phone rang. It was Avery.

Elise gave her daughter a gentle push. "Go on, honey."

A final look of pleading, and Audrey turned and walked away with the officer.

On the phone, Avery said, "We've got roadblocks set up at Talmadge Bridge and Highway 17. Officers stationed on side roads. We've got a helicopter in the air and another coming from Atlanta."

"Have you contacted the crime-scene team?"

"They should be there in an hour."

"How about the media?" Elise asked as she and David ran for her car. "I want his face plastered on every television screen, every Facebook page, every Twitter feed."

"We're in the process of putting a package together to send to local and national news outlets. Should have it ready in five minutes."

"Keep me posted." Elise disconnected and relayed the message to David as a line of police cars exited the plant and dispersed onto the highway. Their own car came to a hard stop at the end of the cracked cement road. "Right or left?" David asked.

"He wouldn't have headed back to Savannah," Elise said.

"Unless he thought he might have better luck blending in there. He's driving a yellow cab, which is going to be hard to miss outside the city. He has a pretty good lead on us. He could have easily gotten into town before the roadblock was set up."

"We have to decide." They couldn't afford a mistake. Yes, a manhunt had been launched, but she was afraid the killer would escape once again. Those chances would be reduced if she and David were in on the capture and takedown.

"I'm trusting you to make the decision," she said.

"Both choices feel wrong." Foot on the brake, car idling, time ticking away.

"If both feel wrong, what remains?" Elise asked.

Hands on the steering wheel, David looked at her. Then, without a word, he slammed the gearshift into reverse, executed a three-point turn, and drove back down the broken cement road in the direction of the plant.

"What are you doing? The cab is gone," Elise said. They'd both seen police cars making a cursory sweep of the grounds before leaving to pursue Jay Thomas. "He's not here."

David pulled up behind a crumbling retaining wall that surrounded the plant and cut the engine. "Maybe." He removed the keys from the ignition and checked his .40 caliber Smith & Wesson. "Maybe not."

Elise allowed her brain to consider what he was saying. "You're guessing he never left."

"He's not going to have a prayer in a yellow cab." David opened the car door and slipped out.

Elise followed while at the same time doubting David's choice. "So he'll ditch it as soon as he can," she argued. "He might have ditched it already."

"A solid possibility."

"And he's a chameleon. He'll charm the county cops working roadblocks. It only takes one error."

"You told me to decide."

She was regretting that.

"Take the car." David tossed her the keys. "I agree that at the very least they're going to need one of us to make a positive ID."

The idea that Jay Thomas was still on the grounds had merit, but what David was suggesting wasn't the typical behavior of a criminal, especially a murderer.

She pocketed the keys and pulled her weapon.

Half crouching, they moved as silently as possible over the broken scrabble that used to be a parking lot. With each step, Elise's doubt increased. Playing cops. That was what it felt like. While the distance between them and Jay Thomas increased by the second.

On top of which, daylight would be gone in a few hours, and once darkness hit, their chances of catching Jay Thomas would greatly decrease.

"David." She shouldn't have turned him loose. "This is wrong."

"Give me fifteen minutes." He kept his voice low.

In deference to speed, they split up while keeping each other within visual range.

The old paper mill was like a small city, covering acres, with towering stainless steel tanks and miles of piping. Remaining at ground level, they cut through the heart of the structure to access loading docks located on both sides of a wide cement walkway, where flatbeds once delivered timber to be pulped. David took one side, Elise the other.

Elise reached the end of the cavernous room and looked to see David motioning for her, pointing. Ten steps, and she was looking down into the bay . . . at a yellow cab.

From the vulnerability of her location, she gripped her gun tighter, her gaze panning up as she took in the staggered walkways of steel four stories high. She was lifting her arm to motion for David to take cover when a gunshot exploded in the hollow space.

Elise flew backward, hitting the ground while the echo from the blast unrolled in waves. Another of her misconceptions. She wouldn't have expected Jay Thomas to be such a good shot.

CHAPTER 56

David heard the gunshot, saw his partner go down, and began firing in the direction of the shooter as he ran for Elise. At the same time, she dug in her heels and side-crawled toward the nearest wall, taking cover.

He joined her.

"I'm okay." She gasped, touched the area on her vest where the bullet had lodged.

Remaining on the ground, Elise pulled out her phone and called Avery. "Jay Thomas Paul is still in the factory. Repeat, Jay Thomas Paul is inside the old paper mill. Shots fired. Requesting backup." A pause for reply, then Elise went on to describe the layout of the building and where they were located. She listened a moment, responded, and disconnected. "They ran his photo through facial recognition software," she told David. "His real name is Jeffrey Nightingale."

Assured that his partner was okay, David reloaded and said, "Stay here. Keep him focused on you, and I'll try to take him by surprise." Without waiting for Elise to protest or order him to stand down, he took off, crouch-running for a set of metal stairs in the far corner of the plant.

He took the steps three at a time, hit the second floor, then spotted another set that took him to the third, followed by the fourth level, each walkway narrower than the previous.

Jay Thomas—or rather Jeffrey Nightingale—might have honed his craft when it came to cold-blooded murder, but those were crimes of persuasion, and the victims usually went with him willingly.

The chase was David's turf.

David spotted Nightingale crouched on the third level behind a metal barrier. From below, Elise shouted, telling Nightingale to give up. She followed with several random shots.

His footfalls covered by the echoes of gunfire, David moved quickly until he was positioned directly above Nightingale.

He made a perfect target, and David couldn't deny that part of him wanted to pull the trigger. He didn't. Instead, he pocketed his weapon, climbed on the wide iron railing, and dropped ten feet, propelling Nightingale to the metal floor, knocking the gun from his hand, the killer's body breaking David's fall.

The man's strength took David by surprise. They rolled. Nightingale reached for David's throat. David grabbed him by both shoulders and smacked his head against the floor. Stunned, Nightingale let go. David scrambled to his feet, pulled his gun, and kicked Nightingale's out of the way.

Lying on his back, Nightingale looked up at him, a smile blossoming on his face. "David, David."

It occurred to David that Nightingale was enjoying this—as much as someone like him could enjoy anything.

"You think you know me," Nightingale said. "But you don't."

"Oh, I know you." David kept his gun trained on the man on the walkway. "I know more about you than you do. There's the surface, easy stuff. That you're a sick son of a bitch. And your first kill was probably someone you knew pretty well. A neighbor. A friend. A family member. How'm I doing?"

"Not bad, but you could do better."

"Sometimes I think you really wanted to be Jay Thomas Paul. Not always, but sometimes I think that person you were pretending to be bled through. Just a little. Is that right too? Because I don't believe anybody is one hundred percent evil. I've never known a killer who didn't have a line he wouldn't cross. Sometimes it's a line that makes no sense to the rest of us, but it's a line."

"You're projecting. A good agent doesn't project."

"What do you get out of it?" David asked. "The killing? What does it feel like to be you?"

"You shouldn't knock it until you've tried it. I'm sure you've killed people in the line of duty. That's different. To kill an innocent— that's where the high comes from." He gave David a look of consideration. "What about your wife? Did you ever ask your wife how it felt to kill your son? If you're so curious about it? No? You didn't? You had a case study right there in your hands, and you didn't pursue it? I can tell you how it feels. She drowned him, right? I'll bet she took him into the bathroom and gently helped him take off his clothes while she filled the tub. Maybe she even put some toys in there, like a rubber ducky. And maybe she even talked sweetly to him, all soft and intimate. And maybe he wrapped his little arms around her neck and she buried her face in his hair and inhaled the baby scent of him. And maybe she stroked his head and told him everything was going to be okay. What happened next, David? Want to tell me?"

The scene had played out in David's mind a million times. It would play out a million times more. Nightingale was right. The ritual of the bath. And the toys. He was right about that too.

Nightingale wanted to die. He was goading David because he wanted David to kill him.

But David wanted him to live. He'd be sentenced to death, but they could learn a lot from the killer before he took his final breath. The longer he was kept alive, the better.

"Okay, I'll tell you," Nightingale said. "She put him in the water, and he began to play with the toys. And then she grabbed him by the arms, told him good night, and held him under. He struggled, but he was just a child, no match for her strength. She might have even sung him a lullaby as the life left his eyes. What do you think?"

"David, he's baiting you!" Elise shouted from below.

"And you—" Nightingale glanced in Elise's direction, his voice louder now, carrying and echoing in the cavernous space. "I know all about you, about the things you won't discuss, not even with David. About what happened with Tremain. About what he did to you."

"You don't know anything," Elise said.

"Oh, but I do. Because I read between the lines, and I understand him. He tied you down and raped you in every way possible. He tore you up and banged into you until you passed out. Am I right?"

"Shut up," David said.

"Don't shoot him, David. That's what he wants."

Nightingale smiled a cold smile. "I'll bet you have nightmares about it," he shouted to Elise. "Remember how you attacked me that first day at the police station? Post-traumatic stress. You're both really messed-up people. David, married to a baby killer, and you, sodomized by an old acquaintance."

David's gun hand was shaking.

"You still haven't figured it out, have you?" Nightingale asked. "If you'd worked the crossword puzzles from the beginning, you'd know. We go way back, you and I, and our long friendship was documented in clues and answers. I'm sorry you missed out on those."

The echoes of the familiar that had haunted David from the beginning of the Savannah Killer case were overwhelming now.

"I have to admit you did a little better on this investigation than Puget Sound," Nightingale said.

Maybe David had, in some unconscious way, known the answer all along. The night at Elise's where he'd felt the air shift. The days when deep in his gut he knew something was off about *everything*, but on a practical level he recognized that what he was feeling didn't match the facts in front of him. And now David finally understood that the man at his feet was the very man who, in a twisted and indirect way, was responsible for everything that had gone wrong in David's life.

"That's right," Nightingale said once he saw the pieces drop firmly into place. His next words were measured and proud. "I'm the Puget Sound Killer. And not just the Sound Killer. There were other killings. A lot more."

From below, Elise attempted another warning. "He's lying."

Without taking his eyes off Nightingale, David said, "No, he's not." And yet the man's damning revelation wasn't enough to make David snap.

"And what about Audrey? Sweet, sweet Audrey?" Nightingale asked, realizing he hadn't yet pushed the right button. "Did she tell you what I did to her? No? I'll bet she didn't have time because she was whisked away so quickly. I *will* tell you that if she was a virgin this morning, which I doubt, she isn't one any longer."

David wanted nothing more than to put a bullet through Nightingale's skull. Instead, he holstered his gun and charged.

"David!" Elise shouted as she raced up the metal stairs.

Fists pummeled and the men rolled. Nightingale, straddling David, slamming his head repeatedly into the metal floor. Dazed, David gripped Nightingale by the throat and squeezed.

"Don't kill him!"

David wasn't listening.

Nightingale's arms flailed in an involuntary effort to survive. His hands pounded at David in desperation. Elise saw a flash of metal, saw David's gun in Nightingale's hand, saw that hand rise, saw the weapon turn toward David's head.

On the second landing, Elise paused, aimed, and fired.

CHAPTER 57

Elise felt Nightingale's neck for a pulse, straightened, pulled out her phone, placed the call, and hit "Speaker." When Avery answered, she said, "Nightingale is dead."

"How dead?"

The question might have seemed odd, but after what had happened with Atticus Tremain . . .

Elise contemplated the body at her feet. "Pretty dead."

"Anybody in need of medical assistance on-site?" Avery asked.

She looked at David, who was lying on his back, his face spattered with Nightingale's blood. *No*, he mouthed.

"We can wait until we get to town," Elise said. "How's Audrey?"

"She's with Strata Luna. Audrey called her when she arrived at the police station, and the two of them went to the hospital. I'll tell her you're fine."

"Jackson Sweet?"

"Last I heard, he was going into surgery." Avery's voice dropped. "Glad you guys are okay."

"Thanks. Me too." Elise disconnected, pocketed her phone, then held out her hand to David. He grabbed it, and she pulled him to his feet, both of them grimacing in pain.

"Chest?" he asked.

"Yeah." It was the first time she'd taken a hit wearing a bullet-proof vest. It was every bit as unpleasant as people said.

"Have that looked at when we get back."

Together, they moved down the steps, slowly this time. From a distance came the sound of sirens.

"Well, this is anticlimactic," David said.

"Sure you're okay?" Elise asked.

"I will be. Once I'm back in my apartment with a beer in my hand and a cat on my lap."

"Here." She draped his arm over her shoulder, and he leaned heavily into her—a testament to just how not okay he was.

"You're always saving me," he said in amazement and gratitude, and maybe a little jealousy since he was the one who most likely preferred to do the saving.

Elise watched as police cars filled the lot, lights flashing, tires squealing, clouds of dust drifting toward them. "It's a dirty job, but somebody's gotta do it."

CHAPTER 58

Asurgeon dressed in yellow scrubs, a blue mask around his neck, stepped through the double doors. "Are you Jackson Sweet's family?"

"Yes." A unanimous lie and truth, spoken by Elise, David, Audrey, and Strata Luna.

"He's in recovery right now."

"Is he going to be okay?" Audrey asked.

"It's too early to tell, but he's tough. The bullet missed his vital organs, but with the cancer and chemo . . . His immune system is compromised right now, and we're concerned about infection. He'll be in intensive care for at least twenty-four hours, but you can visit him for a few minutes."

Strata Luna surprised them all by bursting into tears.

Elise and Audrey patted her on the back in an awkward attempt at comfort, even though Strata Luna didn't seem like a woman who would welcome such a thing. She pulled a damp handkerchief from her black sleeve and looked up at the ceiling. "The man just comes back to me, and now this. Does everybody I love have to die?"

Elise wondered if Strata Luna realized she'd spoken the L-word. "He's not dead," came her gentle reminder.

Strata Luna pulled herself together, tucked the handkerchief back in her sleeve, and stood up straight. "You're right." She looked at Elise. "We'll put some rootwork together, the likes of which this place has never seen."

Far be it from Elise to dash her hope. And if Sweet did recover, Strata Luna could always claim that she, and not the doctor standing patiently nearby, had saved him.

In intensive care, the four of them gathered around Sweet's bed.

Heavily sedated, an IV in his arm and tubes in his chest, oxygen in his nose, he still managed to exude something. That Jackson Sweet presence.

He immediately spotted Audrey. "You okay?" he croaked.

"Fine," Audrey said. It was true. Just minutes ago Elise had pulled Audrey aside to ask if the awful things Nightingale had revealed were true.

"He never touched me," Audrey said. "Not like that." More of Nightingale's lies. Thank God.

"You probably saved Audrey's life," David told Sweet.

"At least that's something." Sweet drew a shallow breath before continuing. "Jay Thomas?"

"Dead," Elise told him.

"Who?" One word was enough. *Who killed him?*

"I did," she said, thinking about the conversation they'd had the day he collapsed in her alley.

"Good." Important questions answered, his focus shifted to Strata Luna. Even though she'd pulled herself together, he read her. "Don't cry, woman," he said. "Don't ever cry for me. I don't deserve anyone's tears."

"If I wanna cry, I'll damn well cry."

Sweet smiled, and his eyes drifted closed. In alarm, they all looked at the vitals screen, then relaxed.

"Time's up," the nurse announced.

Before leaving, Elise touched the back of Sweet's hand, lightly,
so as not to disturb him.

CHAPTER 59

What do you think this is all about?" Elise asked as she pulled the car into an empty parking spot in front of city hall.

David unlatched his seat belt. "Some kind of award? A plaque we can hang on the wall?"

Three days had passed since Nightingale's death, and it was looking like David had been right from the very beginning. The FBI was involved in processing the information, and matches were rolling in. Nightingale was on track to being one of the biggest serial killers the country had ever seen. Odd thing was, he really *had* been writing a story on Elise and David. The article, along with hundreds of photos, had been found on his laptop. The guy knew how to play a role.

The salesman, Charles Almena, had been released. Tyrell King, Elise's old high school buddy, was in jail for falsely identifying the killer. Seemed he'd succumbed to coercion and bribery. Nightingale had been in the surveillance car with David the evening Elise met with Tyrell. The killer had simply gathered the information he needed, along with a license plate number.

And the public . . . rather than applaud the capture of a notorious serial killer, the entire nation was mourning the loss of its daily puzzle. The syndication company had announced plans to find a replacement, but Elise was pretty sure it would never be the same.

She and David exited the car and strode up the wide walk into
city hall. After leaving their weapons at the checkpoint, they took
the elevator to the third floor and the mayor's office.

"Take a seat." Mayor Chesterfield indicated two empty chairs.
Directly behind him, in Elise's line of vision, were photos of his
daughter that hadn't been there before.

Once Elise and David were settled, the mayor adjusted his
tie, cleared his throat, and folded his hands on his desk. All signs
pointed to nervous.

Elise and David shot each other a look of puzzlement.

"I want to thank you for risking your lives," Mayor Chesterfield
said. "And the city of Savannah appreciates the sacrifices you've
made." He stopped, blinked too slowly, then looked at them one at
a time. "There's no easy way to say this, so I'll just come right out
with it. We're letting you both go."

Jesus, Mary, and Joseph. Not what Elise had expected.

"We caught Nightingale," David pointed out.

"I know," the mayor said with an accompanying nod. "City
council and I debated long and hard about this. It's not a decision we take lightly, but in the end it was unanimous. We're letting you go. At this moment your police department computers are
being collected, along with all files. You'll no longer have access to
your office. When you leave here, you're to go directly to Savannah
PD and turn in your gun and badge. While there, you'll find your
belongings in boxes waiting for you."

Elise leaned back in her chair, trying to appear unfazed. "What
you mean to say is we're fired."

"Not fired. Let go. We prefer let go. We're not just turning you
out with nothing. We put together a compensation package. Six
months' full pay with health benefits that will last another month."

"Why are you doing this?" Elise asked. He wasn't thinking straight. He'd lost a child. "I'm deeply sorry for the loss of your daughter," she told him, "and I'm sorry we couldn't have caught the killer earlier."

"It's not just that. All of this has gone on too long," Mayor Chesterfield said. "Friendship with a woman who owns a house of ill repute. The constant press about you and your father, along with the never-ending hoodoo talk. The final straw for us was this case and the way you handled it. It was unprofessional. You brought in Gould when he'd been sidelined. The killer himself was with you from day one. Not to mention the affair between Gould and Major Hoffman. I think the city of Savannah has a pretty high tolerance level, but we've simply reached our tipping point."

"Who's replacing us?" David asked.

"We found somebody, don't worry."

"Who?" David repeated.

"Agent Vic Lamont has agreed to leave the FBI and take over homicide."

David let out a loud snort. "That's some messed-up shit."

"That's exactly the kind of thing I'm talking about. That attitude. In discussing this dismissal, we looked up your record. You've been here less than three years, and you've been on probation numerous times. Any other police department would have kicked you out after the second infraction."

Elise had to get out of there. And get David out of there. "Anything else?" she asked.

"That covers it. You'll be receiving paperwork from us, and if we have any follow-up on the Nightingale case, we'll be expecting your full cooperation. Beyond that, you're done."

They left.

She'd be able to do normal things, Elise thought as she and David walked down the sidewalk to the car. "Just think. Mornings sitting on the back patio drinking coffee."

"And movies. We can go to movies."

"A concert."

"What about that trip to an island somewhere?" David asked. "What about that beach we're always talking about? You know, this could very well be one of the best days of my life."

They paused, looked at each other, and burst out laughing.

CHAPTER 60

Standing in Savannah's Chatham Square, Elise watched in horror as the bridal bouquet flew toward her. She ducked, and the girl behind her caught it.

David strolled across the grass and handed Elise a glass of champagne. He was dressed in a black tuxedo while she wore a strapless blue gown. She'd been hesitant to wear such a revealing outfit, because the low back revealed her tattoo, but as Mara said, she'd earned it.

"I saw that," David said, sipping his drink.

"No need to waste a good flower tossing."

John Casper joined them. "What are you two going to do once you get back from this vacation you're taking?"

"We should open our own private detective business," David said. "Gould and Sandburg Investigations. Or Sandburg and Gould. I could go either way."

Their own agency was something David had joked about in the past, but doing it for real? Elise wasn't sure how she felt about that.

"We already have a great team," David added. "John here can consult, along with your dad. We have the contacts we need, and think of it—no rules."

"I wouldn't get in too big of a hurry to go off on your own," John told them. "I predict Savannah PD will soon be begging you to come back."

Elise's phone rang. Anybody who would possibly call her was here at the wedding. Audrey, her father, Strata Luna, Mara, and the two men standing next to her. She checked the screen: *Mayor Samantha T. Becker.*

She knew that name.

"Excuse me." She walked away and answered the phone. The mayor introduced herself, then got straight to the point. "Like the rest of the country, I've been riveted by the news. I also heard about your recent loss of employment, and I wonder if you and Detective Gould would consider flying to Chicago to consult on a case."

Chicago. Elise had never been to Chicago.

"We'll pay you by the day," the mayor said. "Lodging and travel expenses included, plus we'll provide a stipend." She mentioned figures that were more than generous.

"I'll have to discuss it with my partner," Elise said.

"Understandable, but we'd like to have your answer by this evening."

Elise must have had an odd expression on her face, because as she disconnected, David crossed the grass to see if everything was okay.

"That was the mayor of Chicago," she told him. "She heard about us on the news and also heard we lost our jobs. She wants to fly us up to consult on a murder investigation."

"When?"

She looked across the square and spotted her father and Strata Luna sitting on a bench in the shade, while Audrey and Avery stood on the brick path talking to them. A few days earlier, Elise, Audrey, and Strata Luna had concocted some nasty-smelling mojo that Jackson Sweet carried with him today—a pouch tied around his neck, hidden in his jacket. Elise swore she'd caught a few whiffs of it during the ceremony.

He was recovering from the gunshot wound, but it was too early to know about the cancer treatment. "Soon," she said to David in answer to his question. "She wants us to come soon."

He took a sip of champagne. "Your father can take care of Audrey, and Audrey can take care of your father."

"What about the beach?"

"Chicago is on Lake Michigan." He looked at her over the edge of his glass. "And lakes have beaches, right?"

A soft breeze blew their way, carrying with it the scent of a thousand stories. Elise smiled and said, "I'll let the mayor know we're coming."

ABOUT THE AUTHOR

Anne Frasier is the *New York Times* and *USA Today* bestselling author of twenty-five books and numerous short stories that have spanned the genres of suspense, mystery, thriller, romantic suspense, paranormal, and memoir. Her titles have been printed in both hardcover and paperback and translated into twenty languages. Her career began in 1998 with *Amazon Lily*, a cult sensation and winner of numerous awards. Her first memoir, *The Orchard*, was a 2011 *O, The Oprah Magazine* Fall Pick, number two on the Indie Next List, and a Librarians' Best Books of 2011. She divides her time between the city of St. Paul, Minnesota, and her writing studio in rural Wisconsin.